*almost perfect*

Also by Brian Katcher

*Playing with Matches*

# almost perfect

## BRIAN KATCHER

DELACORTE PRESS

Copyright © 2009 by Brian Katcher

All rights reserved. Published in the United States by Delacorte Press, an imprint of
Random House Children's Books, a division of Random House, Inc., New York.

Delacorte Press is a registered trademark and the colophon is a trademark
of Random House, Inc.

Visit us on the Web! www.randomhouse.com/teens

Educators and librarians, for a variety of teaching tools, visit us at
www.randomhouse.com/teachers

*Library of Congress Cataloging-in-Publication Data*
Katcher, Brian.
  Almost perfect / Brian Katcher—1st ed.
    p. cm.
Summary: With his mother working long hours and in pain from a romantic break-up,
eighteen-year-old Logan feels alone and unloved until a zany new student arrives at his
small-town Missouri high school, keeping a big secret.
  ISBN 978-0-385-73664-0 (trade)—ISBN 978-0-385-90620-3 (lib. bdg.)—
  ISBN 978-0-375-89379-7 (e-book)
  [1. Dating (Social customs)—Fiction.   2. High schools—Fiction.   3. Schools—
Fiction.   4. Friendship—Fiction.   5. Identity—Fiction.   6. Transgender people—
Fiction.   7. Single-parent families—Fiction.   8. Missouri—Fiction.] I. Title.
  PZ7.K1565Alm 2009
  [Fic]—dc22      2008037659

The text of this book is set in 11.5-point Caslon 540.

Book design by Cathy Bobak

Printed in the United States of America
10 9 8 7 6 5 4 3 2 1
First Edition

*To my sister, Katie.*
*See, there's a sister in this one. Happy?*

*Everyone* has that one line they swear they'll never cross, the one thing they say they'll never do. Not something serious like *I'll never kill anyone* or *I'll never invade Russia in the winter.* Usually, it's something less earth-shattering.

*I'll never cheat on her.*

*I'll never work at a job I hate.*

*I'll never give up my dreams.*

We draw the line. Maybe we even believe it. That's why it's so hard when we break that promise we make to ourselves.

Sage Hendricks was my line.

# chapter one

I'M NOT SURE what I loved most about being on the track team. Maybe it was the crippling shin splints. Or constantly feeling like I'd just smoked three packs of cigarettes. Maybe it was the empty stands at every meet, or the way the results got buried in the local sports section.

The football field was by far the best feature of Boyer, Missouri. My hometown, which barely boasted two thousand people, pumped nearly every tax dollar they could into maintaining the facility. The city of Boyer was little more than a half-dozen trailer parks, an electronics factory, and five churches, but the football field was always pristine. The maintenance staff mowed the grass twice a week and watered it every day in the summer. The bleachers gleamed, the locker rooms sparkled, and the scoreboard towered like some great pagan idol. The crumbling structure of Boyer High School stood across the parking lot, almost as an afterthought.

Us track poseurs were permitted to run the perimeter of the sacred field, but only when the football heroes had no use for it. During the fall we had to run laps in the parking lot while the Boyer Bears practiced. One time we were run off by the marching band, which gives you an idea of where we stood in the school food chain.

It was mid-November. My friend Jack Seversen and I had managed to squeeze in some after-school running, trying to stay in shape for the winter. The cold wind chilled my sweat-soaked body, making me shiver and swelter at the same time. Exhausted and thirsty, I walked a final lap to avoid muscle cramps, then limped toward the watercooler.

"You suck, Logan!" shouted Jack, jogging up behind me. Even though he'd run as much as I had, he was still vibrating with raw energy. Thin as a whip and gangly, Jack reminded me of a broken fan belt, wildly flailing in no particular direction. Track wasn't a sport for him; it was merely an excuse to move.

"Hey, check it out." He jabbed his bony, spastic hand toward the football field. The Boyer cheerleaders were wrapping up their practice. I'd heard that in bigger towns, only the pretty, graceful girls made the squads. In Boyer, with a student body of about two hundred, the only membership requirement was a majority of intact limbs and the ability to bend at the waist.

Jack and I reached the water table. I chugged a couple of cups, while my friend, in spite of the low temperature, dumped his over his head. He shook like a wet dog. Eventually, he managed to focus on me. Even then, his protruding brown eyes spun in their orbits like a weather vane in March. Jack had that intense mania common in serial killers and car salesmen.

"You should go talk to Tanya. She likes you."

Without meaning to, I glanced over at the squad. I could just make out Tanya's form as she did jumping jacks with the others.

"It's a wonder she doesn't knock herself out," I muttered. In elementary school (in Boyer, you knew all your classmates since kindergarten), Tanya had been the fat girl. Then, in eighth grade, most of her body mass had migrated into her chest. She wasn't exactly bikini material, but she did have a couple of good points.

"C'mon, Logan. Don't tell me you wouldn't like to press your face into her chest and make motorboat noises."

I stifled a laugh. "Piss off, Jack."

I walked over to the bleachers and grabbed my bag from next to my old bike. Jack followed me, almost uncomfortably closely, and then suddenly grabbed my shoulder.

"Dude, it's time to get back in the game."

I yanked away. "Drop it, okay?"

He didn't drop it. "You're a senior, Logan. In May, we leave this place forever. Don't spend your last semester moping about your ex-girlfriend."

I stormed into the gymnasium, a blocky building that we shared with the middle school next door. I made sure I was alone in the locker room. Then I drove my fist into a metal door. The sound echoed through the empty room. Pain radiated through my wrist and shoulder.

Jack thought he was being helpful. He thought Brenda

had just been another girl. For the past month, he'd been trying to fix me up. To him, all I needed to do was make out with some random chick and I'd forget about how Brenda had dumped me.

To be quite honest, she never actually dumped me. It was her decision to sleep with another guy that had put the strain on our three-year relationship.

I quickly stripped down and hopped in the shower. As the stall steamed up, I thought about Brenda. The homecoming dance in early October. I'd sold my baseball card collection just to pay for her corsage and had to drive to nearby Columbia to rent my tuxedo.

I paused, midlather, remembering that night. My tux hadn't fit exactly right; my arms were too long and my chest too broad. With my advanced hairline and jutting forehead, I'd thought I resembled a shaved ape. Even with my mom's help, I looked like some Mafia don's bodyguard; a muscle-bound lummox, washed and dressed for a night out with sophisticated people.

Brenda had told me I looked suave, like a James Bond supervillain. She'd said I had the face of an angel and the body of a god. I found out later she didn't always tell the truth.

Brenda had been dolled up like someone you'd see on a movie poster. Her long black hair had been styled at the local salon. She'd worn blush on her high cheekbones and had left her glasses at home, even though that meant she was almost blind. Her dark blue dress had exposed her smooth shoulders. As I strapped the corsage onto her delicate wrist, I'd felt a sting of electricity shoot through my arm, down my legs, and out the heels of my rented shoes. Of the dozens and dozens of guys in Boyer, Brenda had chosen me. If I'd won a million dollars in the lottery the next day, I'd have called the money the *other* good thing that happened that week.

After the dance, I'd driven her in my mom's car to the empty field out by the water tower. I don't think I'd ever been that nervous. I wanted everything to be perfect. I had a blanket in the trunk and her favorite songs in the CD player. I had driven all the way out to Moberly to buy condoms.

We'd kissed for about two minutes. Then Brenda had asked me to drive her home. I could still remember the little speech she gave me as we pulled into her driveway at eleven p.m.

*Logan, I'm just not ready for that. Could we wait a little longer? Please? Think about how special it will be.*

As I turned off the shower and wrapped a towel tightly around my waist, I wondered how special it had been for Brenda. I just wished I could have been there.

## chapter two

"MOM! I'M HOME!" That was totally unnecessary for me to say. When you live in a single-wide trailer, it's pretty obvious when someone comes in.

As far as mobile homes go, it wasn't too bad. We had nearly an acre of land, which I kept neatly mown. Whoever had owned the lot before us had built a nice outbuilding. I kept my weight bench out there, along with my mower, weed eater, and snow shovel. During the summer and winter, I'd pull in about a hundred bucks a week cutting grass or shoveling driveways.

I found Mom in our living room/dining room/kitchen. She had already put on her waitress uniform, ready to work the night shift at Ron's Grill, Boyer's only nonchain restaurant. As long as I could remember, my mother's nicest clothes consisted of sturdy shoes, black pants, and a top with her first name stitched on it.

Mom smiled when she saw me.

"Hey, honey, how was school?"

I shrugged. "Dinner shift again? That's, like, the tenth night in a row."

She frowned, and I felt a little guilty for bringing it up. When she worked evenings, I'd only see her for about half an hour.

"I'm sorry, Logan. They've been shorthanded since Dori quit, and . . ." She left the rest unspoken. *We could really use the money.*

I couldn't remember a time when we couldn't have used more money. I'd been four years old when Dad peeled out of our gravel driveway, headed for the green pastures of New Mexico or Utah or somewhere. All I knew was that we'd never seen hide nor mullet of Dad again. Mom was left with me and my older sister, Laura, to take care of.

Mom searched for her keys. "Do you have any jobs tonight?"

I plucked the keys from the bowl by the front (and only) door and handed them to her. "It's a little late in the year for mowing. Pray for a long winter." The snowplows didn't scrape the dirt roads that ran around Boyer, and a heavy snow could trap people in their homes. During especially bad storms I could make a killing shoveling driveways, provided I was willing to work fourteen-hour Saturdays. Maybe that's what had given me my powerful chest.

Mom smiled. With most guys my age, an after-school job meant gas money, maybe a date now and then. I knew better. I spent some money on clothes and school supplies.

The rest I turned over to Mom. It had bothered her at first, but *we could really use the money.*

Mom picked up her jacket. "Can I fix you some dinner before I go?"

I pecked her cheek. "You're already running late. Bring me back some hot wings." It was an empty gesture anyway. Mom used to leave me a meal every night, but eventually stopped. I think she got tired of fixing me a casserole only to find me eating cold SpaghettiOs right out of the can.

She grabbed her purse. "Don't stay up too late. And no girls in the house." She was through the door before I could answer.

Mom didn't intentionally try to rub it in; she knew Brenda was history. But like Jack, she just thought I was nursing a broken heart. I'd dated Brenda since our freshman year, after all. I needed a few weeks before I was ready to find someone else.

That's what everyone thought. Everyone but me.

I plopped onto the couch, too exhausted to get up and turn on the TV (the set was so old it predated remote controls). I stared at the imitation-wood-paneled walls. It was about five-thirty. I'd go to bed in six hours. And I couldn't think of a damn thing to do in the meantime.

I didn't have a car, so I couldn't go hang out at Mr. Pizza or cruise what passed for the main drag in Boyer. I couldn't drive out to Columbia, the only sizable city within a hundred miles. And I didn't want to sit in a garage and huff paint like so many other people in this town.

I wished Laura still lived at home. She was a lot of fun, even if she did hog the bathroom. We'd talk, go for walks, and eat fast food together. But the year before, she got a scholarship to the University of Missouri in Columbia. It hadn't really bothered me when she left. I missed her, but I still had Brenda. I thought I'd always have Brenda.

And now I had jack shit.

Massaging the hand I'd punched the locker with, I thought back to the past Fourth of July. Brenda and I had gone to "downtown" Boyer to watch the annual Independence Day parade: the mayor and aldermen in some not-quite-classic cars, the Boyer marching band endlessly bellowing "Louie Louie," two tractors, and an unshaven clown. Afterward, I'd invited Brenda to the trailer for lunch.

Mom had barbecued some chicken (the one time I'd tried to be manly and run the grill, I ended up using my entire supply of driveway sand to douse the flames). Laura was still living at home then. She'd tried to engage Brenda in conversation.

My girlfriend had sat on a plastic lawn chair, listening to my extroverted sister but not saying much. She was almost painfully shy, especially around loud, friendly people like Laura or Jack. When my sister had gone inside for a drink, I asked Brenda if she wanted to go for a walk.

We didn't say anything as we walked down the dusty gravel road in front of our lot. She was wearing the Boyer High T-shirt I'd given her. Her slender, pale arms stood out starkly against the dark blue of the school colors. Though hardly a breeze stirred the air that day, her long black hair always seemed to blow into her face.

I smiled as we paused in front of Scott Henderson's

cornfield. That was where we'd made out for the first time. The first time either of us had made out with anyone.

I was about to ask Brenda if she'd like to revisit that old memory when she suddenly turned and hugged me, burying her face in my shoulder. I stood there, enjoying the moment. She didn't usually care for public displays of affection. When she pulled away, I noticed the glint of tears in her eyes.

"Brenda? What's wrong?"

Brenda snorted, then wiped her eyes and gave me a real smile. "Nothing, Logan. Just, um, girly stuff. I'm okay."

Hand in hand, we walked back to the trailer. I'd smiled inside, thinking that Brenda had teared up because she was just so overjoyed to have a boyfriend like me.

I couldn't have been more wrong.

## chapter three

THE NEXT MORNING, I sat on a bench in the school commons, watching my few dozen classmates file in. The walls were lined with class photos, beginning with the twelve students of the Class of 1939. If you took the time, you could find graduating pictures of your teachers, your older siblings, and your parents. In fact, the Class of 1986 picture was the only place I could look at a photo of my father.

The second of three buses pulled up to the school and began spitting out students. I knew them all, even the eighth graders who, due to space limitations in the neighboring middle school, had classes in our building. I'd see all of them every day. The same people. In twenty years, their kids would be coming here.

I used to think I'd avoid that. Last spring, I'd been so damn smug. I was going to leave Boyer, go to college. I was going to get a good job and never come back to this shit hole. And I was going to do it all with Brenda. We were going to go to MU together.

Now she was gone. Did I even have a reason for leaving town anymore? Why go to Columbia and be alone when I could do that at home?

"You're not doing yourself any favors, you know."

Tim Tokugowa was in my first-hour biology class. He was the only Asian student at Boyer. In fact, aside from a couple of Mexican kids, he was the only minority. As such, he felt he had certain obligations. Namely, he wanted to destroy the stereotype of the clean, hardworking Japanese.

Tim had thick black hair, great teeth, and a smug way of looking at you that made you want to admit that he was right, even if you weren't arguing. Tim's weight, however, was really starting to get out of control.

His eating exploits were legendary. I once saw him eat a thousand M&M's on a bet. Even now, at 7:50 a.m., he was cramming down fistfuls of Fiddle Faddle from a jumbo box. He flopped his ponderous body onto the bench next to me.

"Hey, Tim. Did you see the Rams game last night?"

Tim ignored the question and stared at me with his narrow brown eyes. He would have looked rather mystic and serene had it not been for the flakes of caramel popcorn stuck to his cheeks.

"You're waiting for Brenda's bus, aren't you?" Tim could have accused me of shooting heroin and made it sound like the truth. Every year, the Boyer debate coach would beg Tim to join the forensics team.

"Of course not."

"Yes, you are. You're out here every morning waiting for bus fifteen. It's not healthy."

I turned and faced the dusty trophy case, enraged. It wasn't that Tim had been so dead-on correct, it was that I hadn't even realized what I was doing. I'd convinced myself I was just resting, and if Brenda just happened to pass by . . .

"Look, Logan, I know she hurt you. But you can't sit here every morning panting after her."

I resented Tim for his insight, just like I resented Jack for not realizing how much pain I was in.

"I'm not panting . . ." That was as far as I got. Brenda had arrived.

Brenda didn't turn heads. She was too skinny, too mousy for most guys to notice. But she had a willowy figure, with long, shapely legs and delicate arms. A soft neck that she wouldn't let me kiss. Long black hair that I wanted to run my fingers through (but she didn't like that). And that face . . . that narrow, beautiful face, behind those glasses that she could never keep clean.

That was one of the many things I loved about her. I thought she was perfect. The year before, every morning, I'd wait for her on this bench. When she got off the bus, she'd skip over to me and give me a big hug. And a smile. Christ, that smile . . . She made me feel like a king. A god. Just the way she'd look at me with those brown eyes . . . I would have done anything for her—including nothing. It wasn't easy, but I was content for over three years with just kissing her. Turns out she did want something more, just not from me.

Brenda trotted across the lobby, not looking in my

direction. Maybe she didn't want to deal with her ex. More than likely, she didn't even notice me.

"Logan, shut your jaw," said Tim with his mouth full.

I glared at him. "I wasn't staring."

He threw his empty box in the trash. "Let's get to class," he said with a shake of his head.

When we arrived at the biology lab, a putrid smell nearly made me gag. I mean, it stank. Only when I saw Mr. Elmer opening the crates marked RUSH and PERISHABLE did I remember we were going to start dissecting frogs that day. Tim and I took our seats at our table. I tried to breathe through my mouth until I could tolerate the odor. Tim opened up a bag of mini candy bars.

At that moment, a new student walked in.

Let me say that again. *A new student walked in.*

When I started kindergarten twelve years ago, there were fifteen kids in my class. Looking around the lab, I saw six of them there with me. For more than a decade, I'd been in class with the same few dozen kids. Occasionally, students would transfer in and out (mostly avoiding the Department of Social Services), but for the most part, people didn't willingly move to Boyer. On the rare occasions we did get new students, it was always uncomfortable. They'd come in cowering as the lifers smacked their chops and sealed vile arrangements with cartons of cigarettes.

Not this chick. She stormed into the lab as if she'd been coming there every morning. She had masses of curly rust-colored hair. Thousands of freckles dotted her cheeks and forehead. When she smiled, her green eyes scrunched and her wire-covered teeth were fully exposed.

She was almost amazingly tall. I was used to looking down at most women, but this girl had to be nearly six feet.

Her outfit was kind of strange, too. Her dress was completely black on one side and white on the other. Her earrings were such enormous hoops I thought they might be piston rings. She also wore pointy black boots and a matching beret.

Now, Mr. Elmer, despite his short hair and neat mustache, was kind of a hippie. He didn't stand on formality; when the new girl barged in, he just sort of gestured to the stack of unclaimed textbooks, then to the empty table at the back of the room.

I knew I shouldn't stare, but I couldn't look away. Girls this strange didn't exist in Boyer. They lived in Columbia or Kansas City or places like that.

Just before the intruder reached the back table, Mr. Elmer looked up from the frogs.

"Actually, we're starting a lab today. Why don't you team up with a couple of other people?"

She didn't break stride. Just grabbed a chair from the empty table and, without asking, sat down next to me. I quickly scooted to give her room.

The new girl sneezed three times, then abruptly shoved my books and things to the middle of the table. She neatly arranged her books and binder. Removing her hat, she turned to me. She wasn't a striking beauty. Too many freckles, braces, frizzy hair. She looked like someone who'd model for that photography studio next to Ron's Grill. Like the owner's niece, maybe—presentable enough and would work for free.

But at the same time, there was something very pleasant about her. Maybe it was the way she obviously worked so hard to give the impression she didn't care how she dressed. Or the tiny lines radiating from her green eyes, lines that a teenager would get only from constantly smiling. And what a smile! When she grinned at us, I got the strangest feeling, like she was smirking at something foolish I'd just done but it was okay because she thought it was cute.

She turned to me. "Hi," she said. "I'm Sage Hendricks."

Sage had a deep but sexy, feminine voice, the kind you hear on ads for 900 numbers. I waited for her to say something else.

"Dude," whispered Tim, jabbing me with a chocolaty finger. "Your line."

"Huh? Oh, um, I'm Logan Witherspoon. This is Tim."

Sage smiled at us again. Or maybe just at me. Her lips were covered in bright red lipstick and her grin was mischievous, like my zipper was down but she wasn't going to tell me.

Tim offered his half-empty bag of candy, and she shook her head. Her curly hair fell into her face, and she brushed it aside.

At that moment, the arrival of a chemical-soaked frog corpse interrupted my appraisal of Sage. I stopped contemplating my tablemate and listened halfheartedly to Mr. Elmer's butchering instructions. Elmer was one of those teachers who cracked jokes knowing full well we were laughing at him, not with him. Sage, however, must have thought he was funny. She had a loud laugh and accidentally elbowed me in the ribs more than once.

I wanted to ask Sage about herself, like where she came from. But soon it was time for the first cut. Tim indicated the jaw-to-chest incision that would open our toad like some hideous birthday present.

"So, who wants to go first?" I asked.

Sage scooted her chair back. "This is a man's job."

Tim shrugged. "You heard the girl, Logan."

Suddenly on the spot, I picked up the scissors and did my best to imitate one of those suave surgeons from the TV dramas. My surgery skills were more like something you'd see in a slasher flick.

"Jesus, Logan, you're going to hack into the table at this rate," said Tim, spewing half-chewed Mr. Goodbar. He yanked the scissors from me and made a rather neat incision. I was a little annoyed. He didn't have to talk to me that way in front of Sage.

Sage stared in rapt attention as Tim pried apart the rib cage. I had a hard time keeping my eyes on our work. Without realizing it, I found my gaze drifting back to our new lab partner.

"So, what kind of name is Sage?" I asked, then regretted it. It sounded like I was making fun of her.

She just laughed. "An original name," she replied.

I pretended to be interested in Tim's hacking and slashing, but in reality, I was thinking about Sage. Why? She wasn't any prettier than Tanya, who apparently had a thing for me. Tanya would go out with me. So why could I not stop looking at this new girl?

Okay, she wasn't bad-looking. She was obviously in great shape; she probably worked out. She was really tall, but tall isn't necessarily bad. And she had a nice face. And seemed friendly. I was glad she was at our table.

When the lab was over, Tim and I stood at the sink, scrubbing up. I stared at Sage, hopefully not as obviously as I'd stared at Brenda. She was applying some more lipstick, using what appeared to be a car's side-view mirror to check her reflection. The chick had character, you could say that much.

I thought maybe I should offer to show her around Boyer. Or something that would take more than five minutes.

The bell rang, and I went over to ask her if she had plans after school. I hesitated a bit too long, though. She was packed and out the door before I could say anything.

That day at lunch, Tim inhaled his second meal without using niceties such as napkins or utensils. Jack sat on my other side drumming out some personal rhythm with his fork. This was my life, and there was nothing I could do about it.

I picked at my meat loaf.

"Hey, Tim," I asked. "What did you think of the new girl?" I hadn't been able to stop thinking about her, wondering where she had come from and what she was like. So little ever changed in Boyer; a new student was always a source of interest.

Tim looked up from his tray. He had corn in his hair.

"Sage? She's okay."

Jack stopped drumming, which caused his legs to start jiggling. If Jack was ever put in a straitjacket (and sometimes it didn't seem unlikely), I think his brain would explode.

"Sage?" he asked. "Her sister was in my keyboarding class. Name's Tammi. Freshman."

Two new Boyer students in one day?

"What was she like?"

"Loud," he answered decisively. "I think they're from Joplin or somewhere south. Dad works in Columbia."

"Is Tammi a seven-footer, too?" asked Tim. His tray was empty, but he continued to mop up gravy with his bare fingers.

"Nah," replied Jack. "She's a dwarf. I don't think she's five feet. Cute, though."

Tim shrugged. "Maybe one's adopted."

I didn't reply. I was experiencing my daily 12:13 kick to the nuts.

Figuratively. It was at 12:13 every day that Brenda would walk by my table. Every day, at 12:13, she would walk past our table, pause, and smile at me. Not the great grin that she used to give me. Just a small, friendly smile, like you'd give an old acquaintance you didn't really want to talk to.

And then she'd move on. She was good at moving on.

"Witherspoon!" Jack barked at me, stabbing me in the kidney with his fork. Caught in the act of staring, I turned away. Jack and Tim were looking at me with pity.

"Dude, this is getting sad," said Jack. "She's not coming back."

No, she wasn't. For the first few weeks of our breakup, I didn't give up hope. Every time she walked by, every time the phone rang, I held my breath.

*Logan, I made a terrible mistake. . . .*

Now, I knew it was over. Even if she asked to get back together, I wouldn't want to. But I wished she'd talk to me. I wished she'd apologize. Do something to show me that the past three years had meant something to her.

Jack threatened me with his fork again. "Snap out of it, Logan. Did you ask Tanya out yet?"

Tim shook his head at Jack with a look of fatherly disappointment. Tim, so far as I knew, had never had a date. Jack would occasionally land a girl with his Adam Sandler *I'm so crazy I'm cute* routine, but it never lasted. Since Brenda and I had started dating, the boys kind of looked up to me. And if they both assumed that Brenda and I had gone a lot further than we had, I wasn't about to correct them.

"C'mon, man," Jack began again. "Show the girls around here what runners are made of." With his spoon and two fingers, Jack graphically demonstrated just how I should show them.

Tim sighed, belched, and sighed again. "I think what Jack is trying to say is that you're a really nice guy, and if Brenda couldn't see that, then to hell with her. But you do need to get on with your life."

Jack crinkled his brow. "That's not what I was trying to say."

I gathered my trash. "Thank you both. And screw you both. I'm fine."

I dropped off my tray just as the bell rang. Across the cafeteria, Brenda was carefully gathering her things. My idiot friends thought I was still hung up on her, only they weren't idiots because they were right.

Maybe I should just ask someone out. Find a girl, and if things didn't work out, at least I'd tried. What was the worst that could happen?

I would find that out very shortly.

*chapter four*

WHEN I GOT UP for school the next day, I found my mother in our tiny closet of a kitchen cooking bacon and eggs. Though she probably hadn't gotten off work until one the night before, she was up before seven fixing breakfast.

"Mom, you don't have to do this every morning. I can eat at school." I knew I qualified for the free meals program.

Mom slid two fried eggs onto my plate. She looked tired. Lately, I'd noticed the wrinkles around her eyes and the gray starting to streak her hair. Fourteen years of being a single parent were taking their toll. She got too little sleep. I couldn't remember the last time she'd gone out with her friends.

"Sit down with me and eat," she said, patting the cheap table my grandfather had given us. "I don't get to see you that often anymore."

Obediently, I joined her. It was always kind of awkward, these meals alone with my mother. More and more I felt like we didn't have anything to talk about. Things had been easier when Laura was around. She had enough personality for all three of us.

"So you haven't filled out your application for college yet," she said, pointing to the form still magneted to the fridge. "It's due by January."

I didn't meet her eyes. "I have plenty of time."

"I don't see why you're putting it off; it'll only take half an hour. I could help you, or you could ask your counselor."

"I'll get to it," I snapped. I was sick of talking about this. For years, college and Brenda had gone together. Now that she was gone, I wasn't sure that was the route I wanted to take. What would I do there? Get drunk and party? I could do that in Boyer. And what would I study? I could get a business degree and end up managing a tire place or a motel somewhere. Or get my teaching certificate and wind up coaching and teaching social studies. Neither prospect thrilled me.

"I stopped by the library and picked up some information about student loans," continued Mom. "I have Wednesday off. Maybe we could sit down and . . ."

I threw down my fork. "Mom! Drop it, okay? What's the big deal if I don't go to college? I mean, maybe I could just work for a year, save up some money, and then go."

For a second, I thought Mom was going to cry. The apologies clogged my throat in an effort to get out.

"Aw, Mom, I didn't mean that. It's just . . ."

Mom quickly regained her composure. "Logan, listen to me. I can't afford to send you to school. There's been a lot I haven't been able to give you and Laura . . ."

"Mom!" She'd worked her whole life just to support us. The last thing I wanted was to make her feel like that wasn't enough.

"Let me finish. Logan, it'd be so easy for you just to stay here. You could keep mowing grass. You could probably have your own landscaping business in ten years. And I wouldn't have to miss you like I do Laura. But, honey, that's the same thing I thought twenty years ago. I figured it was okay just to get married right out of high school. I thought I'd still be able to do all those things I wanted to. And now . . . my kids are leaving home, and I realize I'm exactly where I was at eighteen. And I don't want that to happen to you. I don't want you to look back and see a lot of missed opportunities."

I touched Mom's hand. "I know you're right. I promise I'll fill out those forms this week."

She smiled at me. "Thanks, Logan."

I grabbed my bag and stood to leave. There was something else I had to say.

"And Mom? I, um . . . I . . ."

"I love you too, honey."

That morning, I didn't sit around waiting for Brenda. Maybe I was trying to get over her, or maybe I just didn't want Tim to catch me stalking again. As I walked toward bio, I found myself thinking about Sage.

I couldn't remember ever meeting a chick that strange.

Even after an hour of class, I knew that weird girl wasn't like anyone in Boyer. Too colorful, too outspoken, too wild.

Brenda never would have dressed in crazy clothes like that. She always dressed in long skirts and plain sweaters. And she wouldn't have joked around with people she'd just met, either. Brenda was so reserved that she still had a hard time talking to my friends.

Sage, on the other hand, seemed to warm up to anyone nearby. By the time I got to class, she was already sitting at the lab table laughing with Tim. Annoyed, I plopped down next to her.

"And that's when they told Jack he was no longer welcome at Chuck E. Cheese's," finished Tim.

Sage's laughter boomed across the lab. Then she turned to me.

"You've got something on your shirt, Logan."

I looked down and she bopped me on the nose. Kind of hard.

As I pretended to blow my nose to make sure it wasn't bleeding, I looked at Sage. She had forced her spirals of hair into two pigtails. She wore ragged jeans and a short-sleeved sweater. Her arms were almost solidly freckled.

Brenda wouldn't be caught dead in an outfit like that. And she wouldn't have bopped a strange guy in the nose. And she always seemed annoyed around Tim and Jack. I used to think her stuffiness was kind of sweet. Now it just seemed irritating.

The bell rang before I could be charming. Luckily, Tim volunteered to go get the frog, so I had a couple of seconds.

"So, Sage, where are you from?" I asked. It totally

sounded like a pickup line. I might as well have been wearing an open-collared disco shirt.

"Near Joplin. Hey, I forgot my pencil. Give me yours."

I handed her my only pencil. "Joplin's, like, three hours away. Why did you move here?"

Sage ignored the question. "Tim was telling me about you."

I smiled as my brain went into full panic. Tim had known me long enough that he had some real dirt on me.

"What did he say?" I asked with the nonchalance of an FBI interrogator.

Sage was picking through the various plastic bags of candy on Tim's side of the table. "He said you run track. I believe it; you're in great shape."

Sage turned back to me and unashamedly scoped me from top to bottom. I felt like I should be hanging in a butcher's window, the way she was checking me out. It was a great feeling. I tried to flex without making it too obvious.

Apparently, she wasn't content with just looking. "Here, make a muscle."

I obediently showed her my bicep, the result of years of shoving around a lawn mower. Sage clutched my forearm, squeezing me with her painted nails. Her hands were soft.

"Wow!" she said, not letting go. "I'm surprised you don't play football."

When a girl you hardly know starts touching you, it's hard to think about anything else. It didn't seem to be the right moment to explain that I'd tried out for the team but never made it. I didn't have the bulk or the coordination.

Luckily, Tim showed up at that moment with the dead

frog, causing Sage to release me. As Tim feng shuied the frog, the dissection tools, and his food, I tried to get my brain back on track. Brenda was the last girl who had ever touched me for that long (except my sister, but she had had me in a headlock). I'd forgotten how nice it could feel.

"So, do you play any sports?" I asked, trying to keep the conversation going.

"Nope," she said with a shrug.

I tried to be complimentary. "Maybe you should. I think you'd be good at bas . . ."

Sage's smile collapsed into a scowl. Tim, who'd been flipping frog organs around like a master Japanese chef, grimaced.

*Nice, Logan. Tell the really tall girl she should play basketball.*

I tried to recover. ". . . baaass fishing?"

Sage frowned, then suddenly burst out laughing. She shoved me in the chest with her open palm but didn't remove her hand from my chest.

"Sage, Logan, get to work, please," came the warning voice of Mr. Elmer.

Sage sat up in her chair and began pointedly reading the lab instructions. After a few seconds, her eyes crept over the top of the paper. I'd never had anyone smile at me like that before. And I couldn't even see her mouth.

Five minutes before the bell, I stowed the frog in the lab fridge. Tim was packing up his hourly buffet when I returned to the table. Sage was at the front of the room. Despite never touching the frog, she was intently scrubbing her hands.

Tim looked at me, then subtly gestured at Sage like she

was an unruly dog I should be controlling. I allowed myself a grin.

"I thought she was obvious enough that even you might notice," said Tim, placing a licorice stick in his shirt pocket like a pen.

I looked at our lab partner, who caught my gaze and winked at me. That new tall, crazy, and, yes, *cute* girl had been flirting with me.

"You going to ask her out?" prodded Tim.

"I dunno."

The bell rang. Tim leaned over to me. "I didn't say go buy a house with her. Take her to the movies or for pizza or something." He was gone, leaving a trail of Fritos in his wake.

As usual, he was right. I was out of excuses. One date. It would be fun. I looked around for Sage, but she'd already left. I'd have to catch her after school.

Since his first day as a freshman, Jack had been trying to get a free soda from the lobby Coke machine. Three years, five detentions, and a broken finger later, he still hadn't managed to get a free can.

"C'mon, you son of a bitch," said Jack, rattling the machine. "Give it up. You know you want to."

I sat lacing my running shoes for my solitary training. Most Boyer students were gone for the day, but I hoped Sage would pass by. I didn't think she rode the bus.

"Hey, Jack, tomorrow Tim's gonna drive us out to Columbia to see a movie. You coming?"

Jack smashed his fist into the machine's solar plexus. "What's playing?"

"Dunno."

"Sure. I'll see if my brother wants to come."

"Uh, hold off on that." Tim's car would only seat four (actually, we had proven it could hold twelve, but that was another story), and I had just spotted our fourth passenger.

She was standing in front of the girls' restroom. I guessed she was waiting for someone, because she made no move to go in.

"Hey, Sage!"

She turned and smiled. Her braces winked at me as she crossed the room.

"Hi, Logan." She hadn't stopped smiling. Apparently, Sage had psychic brain-draining powers, because all I could see was her mouth. I had forgotten what I was going to say.

Jack had temporarily stopped abusing the vending machine. I suddenly came back to reality and introduced him.

"This is Jack."

He stared at Sage like she was a captive yeti.

"Christ, you're tall. Can I borrow a buck?"

Sage laughed nervously and handed him a dollar. My only consolation was that I'd look better by comparison.

"So, Sage." I gathered up my courage. For the first time since Brenda, I was going to ask someone out. I almost stopped myself. It was only the memory of Sage's hand on my arm that made me rush into no-man's-land.

I took the plunge. "Tim and Jack and I are going out to

the movies in Columbia tomorrow. You want to come with?"

Sage's eyes widened. So did her smile. Her mouth expanded and the lines around her eyes deepened. She had a look of bliss on her face, like I was on one knee, holding a diamond ring.

"Sorry, Logan, I can't." The grin didn't leave her face. I waited for her to follow up with *I'm busy tomorrow*, but she didn't.

Jack, who liked to slow down and watch the aftermath of highway accidents, returned to his vandalism. This was too gory even for him.

I tried to blow off the rejection. "It's cool. I just thought since you're new in town . . ."

Sage shook her head, then hitched up her purse. "Let me walk you to the track."

She trotted to the exit, not looking back to see if I was coming. I considered ignoring her. Why hadn't I asked out Tanya? This strange new girl probably just liked teasing guys, then turning them down. But I followed her anyway.

Sage didn't say anything until we were well out of the building, almost to the football field. Then she stopped, took my arm, and didn't let go.

"Logan, I really would like to go to the movies with you," she said sincerely.

"It's okay," I replied, enjoying the feel of her hand on my arm. At least I apparently wasn't going to get the *I like you as a friend* speech. I was prepared to let things drop, but Sage must have thought she owed me an explanation.

"It's my parents, Logan. They won't let me date."

I tried to look her in the eyes, but she released my arm and looked at the ground.

"Won't let you date? But aren't you, like, seventeen?"

"Eighteen. House rules. I don't date until I'm out of school."

I tried to grapple with the idea. I knew girls who weren't allowed to be alone with boys, kids who couldn't date anyone exclusively, even classmates who had to have a chaperone when they went out. But to tell a high school senior that she couldn't go to the movies with some friends?

"They're that strict?" I asked, disappointed. I realized how eager I'd been to get to know Sage. And now, it seemed, we wouldn't even be allowed to casually hang out.

She sighed. "My dad especially. I never even got to wear makeup until a few months ago."

No makeup at her age? Jesus, what kind of Nazi parents did she have?

"Why not? I mean, they had to know you could put it on at school when they wouldn't be around."

"Uh . . ." Sage looked to the right, like she was trying to think up an answer.

"What?"

"It's nothing." Sage had her back to me. I almost touched her shoulder, but chickened out.

"No, what?" Why would an eighteen-year-old put up with restrictions like that? She was legally an adult.

She bit her lip. "This is the first time I've been to high school. After eighth grade, I was homeschooled." She smiled an embarrassed smile, like she'd just confessed to wetting the bed or something.

*Homeschooled?* That conjured up all kinds of negative images. Puritanical parents who refused to allow caffeinated drinks in the house. Long sessions of Bible reading and cold showers. Private tutors, rows of girls in identical pleated skirts, the cruel whip of the headmistress, secret girl-on-girl bodily explorations . . .

Sorry, lost my train of thought there. But homeschooled? No makeup? Not even allowed to go out to the movies?

We had reached the track. I wanted to say something to let Sage know I wanted to help her. Granted, I wanted to help her sneak out on a date with me, but still.

"Well, if your parents ever *do* let you out of the house . . ." I gestured vaguely.

"Yeah." Sage toyed with her purse. "Logan, what theater are you going to?"

"The Forum Eight," I answered, suddenly interested again. "It's off of Stadium Boulevard in Columbia. We'll probably be there around seven."

She was already walking away.

"See you there?" I called after her, slightly desperate.

She didn't turn around. "Maybe."

*chapter five*

THAT FRIDAY NIGHT, I stood in the cavernous, neon-slathered lobby of the Forum 8 theater and watched the college kids parade by. I felt like a farm boy who'd just driven up on a tractor. Next year was I really going to buy a Mizzou jacket and hang out in bars with these guys?

That was another reason I was worried about college. I mean, Laura could show me around and everything, but I still felt kind of out of my depth. At MU, there were students from Russia, students from Iran, scientists, hippies, anarchists . . . and I'd never even been to Illinois.

Tim was at the snack bar buying his requisite drum of popcorn. He kept insisting on more and more butter grease. Eventually, the girl behind the counter, a colorless teenager with short hair, rammed the bucket into his chest and took the next order.

Jack pounded on a pinball machine with both fists. I

leaned on the air hockey table, knowing I couldn't force the guys to wait any longer. It was already eight-thirty.

Jack tilted his pinball game for the fourth time. "Hey, Logan. Is she coming or not?"

I looked at my watch again. "I guess not. Go get your snacks. I'll be there in a minute."

I shouldn't have bothered. Sage had only said maybe. Her maniac parents probably locked her in the basement. So what? There'd be other girls, I guessed. Probably. Tanya, or maybe some cute college girl next year. Whoopee.

Someone smacked my hand off the table, causing me to stumble.

"Props are dangerous." It was Sage. She was wearing a fluffy white coat that seemed big enough to seat two comfortably.

"Sage! You made it!" Until that moment, I hadn't realized how disappointed I'd felt about her not coming.

She grinned proudly. "My parents think you're the Christian Teens Youth Group, so no funny business, 'kay? Hi, Jack."

We took our seats. As soon as the theater began to fill up, Jack pulled out his cell phone and had a loud conversation. I don't think there was actually anyone on the other line.

"So, how did the prostate exam go? Really? Ouch! Didn't he lube up first? He used a what? Listen, Joe, I don't think real doctors operate out of those U-Store-It bins. . . ."

Sage's body was shaking with laughter. She was the only one in the theater not trying to kill Jack with a glare. He only settled down when the house lights went off.

When the film started, Sage began pulling boxes of

36

candy out of her coat and passing them down the line. Tim looked at her with such rapture I was almost jealous. I wished I could have done this without the guys, but I couldn't really bike the twenty miles to Columbia.

It occurred to me that this was only the second first date I'd ever had since I was fifteen. Brenda and I had come to this very theater. Since neither of us drove, her dad had come with us and sat two rows back.

And now here I was with an extroverted girl who had to sneak out just to see me. I looked over at my companion, who now had her feet propped up on the seat in front of her. Was this really a date? Maybe Sage wouldn't be able to sneak out again. Or wouldn't think I was worth it.

The premovie commercials ended. Sage put her feet down and placed her hand on our shared armrest. She elbowed me in the ribs. Then harder. Then she flopped halfway into my seat, crushing me against Jack. When she finally settled down, the side of her hand was pressed against mine.

I ignored the movie as I enjoyed the physical contact. Should I try to put my arm around her? I decided to play it safe and wait.

It happened about halfway through the film. We'd been swapping boxes of Milk Duds, gummi things, and Dots the whole time. I went to take the Junior Mints from Sage, and her hand was empty. My hand in her hand. I didn't pull back.

Slowly, imperceptibly, her long fingers wound around mine. We sat unmoving for half a minute. It was no first base, but at least I was out of the dugout.

Out of the corner of my eye I could see Sage staring at the screen, her eyes large and white in the dark. Apparently, this was the first time she'd held hands with anyone. She looked almost terrified. I took a risk and squeezed her hand.

A bright scene projected on the screen, and in the light I could clearly make out her expression. She had such an innocent, frightened smile that I wanted to grab her and hug her. And not just because she was cute. Because at that moment, even though I barely knew her, I really liked her a lot.

Sage bit her lower lip and tilted her head down, still keeping her eyes off me. We both leaned closer. And then some more.

The movie changed to a night scene, and I could no longer see her face. Impetuously, I moved forward.

It's embarrassing to try to kiss a girl only to have her lean back. Brenda used to do that to me all the time, even when we'd been dating for years.

It's downright humiliating when your date forcibly shoves your head away.

It wasn't a playful shove, or a *Back off, Don Juan* rejection. Sage pushed me so hard my neck kind of hurt.

Ashamed and upset, I tried to think of a way to quietly apologize. Sage was sitting there glowering at the film, her arms crossed and her leg jiggling. Damn, I'd totally misread her. When she had let me hold her hand, I thought she was encouraging me.

I waited a miserable forty-five minutes for the movie to end, wondering whether I should say I was sorry or just not mention the incident. With Tim and Jack hanging around, apologizing wouldn't be easy. But I didn't want Sage to think I was just after one thing. After three years with Brenda, I was used to a chaste existence.

The second the credits started rolling, Sage jumped up. She rushed to the exit so quickly she bopped Jack on the head with her huge purse. It took me longer to escape from the row, but my years of running paid off, and I caught up with her in the lobby.

"Sage?"

She didn't turn around. "Thanks for the movie, Logan," she said in a monotone.

I didn't follow her into the parking lot.

I got home around midnight, annoyed and confused. Why did Sage have to get so upset when I tried to kiss her? I didn't totally buy that story about her parents not letting her date. What kind of senior puts up with that? Maybe I'd gone a little overboard, but was I really that out of line? I didn't have enough experience to be sure.

Mom was asleep on the couch, a muted infomercial casting the only light in the trailer. After I turned on the light and said good night to Mom, I vanished into my room and pulled a cardboard box out from under my bed. When I had realized it was *over* over with Brenda, I'd grabbed all her pictures, all her letters, and crammed them in here. I had planned to burn them in the backyard when Mom was at work. Instead, I kept them under my bed, looking at them more often than I wanted to admit.

The tickets to every school dance we'd gone to. The

movie stubs from one of our first dates. The purple-inked love letters she'd left in my locker. And the pictures.

I found the dog-eared photo that I used to keep in my wallet. It was bent and faded from the months under my butt, but I could still see the figures clearly. It was right after a track meet the year before. Brenda's father had taken it.

I was sprawled, exhausted, on the bleachers, all block-headed, ham-fisted, and sweaty. Next to me sat Brenda: lithe, graceful, and beautiful. She was smiling, but not at the camera. At me. She always smiled at me. Looking at her grin, you'd think she was the luckiest girl in the world.

I turned the snapshot over and read the inscription.

*All my love, Logan*
*XXX*
*Brenda*

I ripped the picture to shreds. *All my love.* Nothing but words. Nothing but bullshit.

It was funny. Tonight I had been prepared to let that all go. To start dating again. And I hadn't expected to get anywhere with Sage. So why did her rejection hurt almost as badly as Brenda's?

*chapter six*

ONE OF THE FEW ADVANTAGES of small-town schools is they're easy to get into. No gates, no metal detectors, no ID badges. That's why I was free to use the track on weekends when there was no football game.

After stretching, I began to run. Normally, I didn't do cross-country, but there's a kind of Zen to running. Round and round and round, back to exactly where I started, day after day. There's a metaphor for ya.

The problem with running is it's a solitary sport. After ten minutes, your internal voices start bringing up the questions you try not to think about.

*Could I find happiness away at college?*

*Were Brenda and I just not meant to be, or did I drive her off?*

*Why did Dad leave?*

*Am I really abnormally small, or was that spam e-mail just exaggerating?*

*Why did Sage get so upset when I tried to kiss her?*

She just ran out on me. Why did that bother me so much? One bad date. Most guys had dozens. Jack could write a book. But every time I thought about Sage, I felt like I owed her an apology. Or she owed me an apology. Somehow, one of us had gotten the wrong impression.

And suddenly, like a root beer stand in the desert, there she was. Sage sat on a bench on the other side of the track, decked out in a fake-fur coat, fake-fur hat, and fake-leather boots. Her face was expressionless, but then, she was an eighth of a mile away.

I did not speed up. I did not slow down. I just kept running in her direction, expecting her to vanish like a bag of Doritos near Tim. But she was real.

I leaned on my knees in front of her, trying not to wheeze.

"How did you know I'd be here?"

She didn't smile. A light breeze picked up, blowing hair in her face. I wanted to reach out and brush it away.

"What makes you think I'm here to see you?"

Instantly, I felt like an ass. She must have been out for a walk.

Sage cracked a tiny smile. "Tim said you usually came here on weekends. I took a chance."

She removed her hat, letting her hair blow wild and tangled in the rough November wind.

I placed my hands on my hips and leaned back. I was trying to act impatient, like I was doing Sage a favor by talking to her but I really wanted to get back to the track. Let her know how it felt to have someone run away from you.

Sage got up and started to walk toward the parking lot. For a horrible second, I thought my plan had actually worked and she really was leaving. But Sage turned and gave me a brief yet kind smile. I followed her.

We didn't speak until we'd reached the crumbling cement basketball courts we shared with the middle school. As we walked, I wished I had a chance to duck into the locker room and grab my deodorant. I knew I smelled like sweat, and I didn't want Sage to get a whiff of my lumberjack odor.

Someone had left one of the underinflated PE basketballs on the court. Sage stooped to pick it up, bounced it a couple of times, and tossed it at the basket. She missed it entirely. Either she was terribly uncoordinated, or she was just trying not to enforce stereotypes about tall people.

I retrieved the ball, steadied myself, and shot. Nothing but net. I waited for the applause, but Sage was removing her coat. She was wearing a fuzzy white sweater that was so tight I could see the outline of her bra.

Watching her attempt another basket, I suddenly felt incredibly lonely. Most nights, I lived alone. I worked alone. When I ran, I was essentially alone. That was how it had been for the past couple of months. It hadn't bothered me before. I'd never asked Tanya out, or tried to get a regular job, or joined a club or anything.

So why did I want to be with this new girl so desperately? She was cute, but that didn't explain everything. I hardly knew her. But it felt like if she didn't want my company, then I was better off alone.

That was a weird attitude. It bordered on obsessed. Sage was just a girl, after all. One who obviously didn't see me like I saw her.

When Sage missed her shot, I snatched the ball in the air and almost dunked. Sage caught the rebound, then dropped the ball. The semiflat ball scooted along the cracked concrete. Sage pinned it with her foot, then gave it a kick. She had an intense frown on her face. The kind of expression a girl wears when she really wants someone to say, *Tell me what's wrong.*

I wasn't sure I wanted to ask that. Not because I didn't care, but because I just wasn't used to hearing about people's problems. Mom was a martyr; no matter how hard her life was, she never complained. Tim and Jack were guys, and therefore showed no feelings. And Brenda, pardon the pun, never let me inside her.

"Sage, what's the matter?" I wondered how I'd managed to transform my offended dignity into deep concern in less than ten minutes.

Sage shook her head. I wondered if I should prod her, but she didn't need coaxing.

"Want to hear something funny?" Her tone told me that she meant the sad type of funny, rather than Jack's *one-legged Japanese woman named Irene* brand of funny.

I mumbled some sort of answer. Sage began to walk the circumference of the court. She paused and touched the huge metal crank that had been attached to a tennis net decades ago.

"I used to have a normal life, Logan." She let go of the

gears. Facing the fence, she wrapped her arms around her sides, as if hugging herself.

I wasn't sure if I should say anything or just let her go at her own pace. When she didn't continue, I asked her what she meant.

"What I mean is, up to maybe seventh grade, my parents were normal. I could visit my friends, go to public school, just like any other kid. But at the beginning of eighth grade, they decided I shouldn't go. Made me learn at home. They said it was for my own good, that I wouldn't be safe at school, that I'd end up getting into trouble. Maybe they were right; I don't know. But that's not the worst part."

I scooted up next to her. Sage turned to me and smiled sadly. There was hair in her face again. This time I did gently brush it away, and she didn't stop me.

"The worst part is, I wasn't allowed to go out. At all. Not to visit friends, not to go to the mall, nothing. At home, all day. We'd go out as a family, but that wasn't the same."

I was horrified. I'd just pictured Sage's parents as being overly strict, but not allowing your daughter to have friends? That was psycho. I wondered what sorts of memories were hidden behind Sage's smile. How bad was her home life?

"They thought they were protecting me, Logan, but for over four years I've been a prisoner. When Dad got transferred here, I told them I wanted to go to school. They said no. But, like you said, I'm eighteen. I think they know they can't stop me."

She grabbed the crank and tried to turn it, but it was rusted in place. With great deliberation, I placed my hand lightly on hers. We stood there, not looking at each other, doing nothing but breathing, for quite some time.

"Logan, I guess what I'm trying to say is that I could really use a friend right now. I'm not trying to blow you off. It's just . . . be my friend. It's been so long since I've had one."

I squeezed her hand and let go. Of course I'd be her friend. The poor girl had never been to high school, never hung out with other teenagers, never had a guy hit on her. If she needed a pal, then that's what I'd be. And hey, sometimes friendship developed into something more.

Sage smiled. I retrieved her coat and, with uncharacteristic suaveness, helped her with it.

The wind picked up as she stuck her arms through the sleeves, giving me a faceful of her dark hair. For the first time I could see the back of her pale neck (it was just above my eye level). I was tempted to kiss her there in a friendly, platonic fashion, but decided I was deluding myself.

By the time she turned around, she was smiling again, her inner turmoil hidden.

"Thanks, Logan." She held out her hand.

When I attempted to shake, she grabbed me by the wrist. With no warning, she yanked me toward her and engulfed me in a bear hug. Her fur coat made me feel like I was being mauled by a grizzly. Then she released me and walked off without another word.

I watched her go. I felt a bizarre mixture of friendship, lust, fear, pity, lust, confusion, panic, and lust. Brenda had been served an eviction notice. Sage now occupied most of my brain. I'd traded a girl who seemed to like me but secretly didn't for a girl who . . . what? Sage and I had just met. She didn't know my father was gone. I hadn't met her sister. We hadn't visited each other's houses. We didn't know each other's birthdays. And yet, she seemed to really want my friendship. And not the usual female *I want to be your friend so you'll never try to sleep with me* definition, either.

I needed to stop thinking like a sprinter and start thinking like a marathon runner. There was no rush. Just take things slow and steady. And if Sage and I wound up only as friends, well, there was nothing wrong with that.

When two guys are friends, it means they are free to fart and scratch themselves in each other's presence. Well, you don't actually have to be friends for that.

When a guy and a girl are friends, it means either the girl is ugly or the guy isn't cool. Otherwise, the balance would be upset and they'd be more.

Sage was cute. Not in the head-turning, blond, flat-stomached way a magazine model is cute. And not in the quiet, understated, pretty-in-spite-of-herself way that Brenda had. Sage was beautiful like a sunset. There was no one part of her that especially stood out, but viewed as a whole, there was no room for improvement.

Except that didn't matter. Sage just wanted to be my friend. If she'd been ugly, no problem. But she wasn't. And I had to spend the first hour of every school day being her friend. Nothing is harder than acting normal around someone you think is hot.

Strike that. Nothing is harder than acting normal

around someone you think is hot, and then dissecting an amphibian together.

I wonder if anyone has ever said that sentence before.

At any rate, when I walked into the lab that Monday, I expected to find Tim, Sage, and a tray of fish bait. It should go without saying that I was not expecting a plate of home-made cookies.

And yet there they were, at my section of the table, cheerily wrapped in red cellophane. I looked over at Sage, who pointedly took out a compact and began reapplying her lipstick.

"Thanks," I ventured. She grinned and turned away.

Tim was already eyeing my treats like Wile E. Coyote looked at Road Runner. I slipped the plate into my back-pack.

Soon we were busy hacking and slashing at our dead buddy. As Tim wielded the scalpel (Sage absolutely re-fused to cut, and Tim refused to let me), an odd assortment of thoughts hit me.

*So does she like me?*

*What, exactly, is going on at her house?*

*Is she flirting? No girl, not even Brenda, has ever baked me anything.*

*Is that a kidney or a spleen?*

*Why is life so complicated?*

*Why did I think first-hour biology was a good idea?*

Sage left the room five seconds after the bell rang, while Tim and I were still washing our hands. It occurred to me that since we'd met, I had never heard her say good-bye. She'd just up and leave.

Tim was staring at me. At times, I had the upsetting impression he was wondering how I'd taste with fava beans and a nice grape Crush.

"She baked you cookies," he whispered.

"Yeah." I wiped my hands on my pants. Tim probably thought I was still hung up on Brenda, too dim to take Sage's hint.

"*She baked you cookies!*" he repeated as if I'd missed the importance.

"So what?" I turned to get my bag, but Tim blocked my way.

"She wants to have your babies."

I ignored that. He was insistent.

"The way to the heart is through the stomach, Logan!" I didn't respond, but Mr. Elmer, who was passing by our table at the time, looked crushed. I guess he thought the anatomy lab had been lost on Tim.

"Tim," I said, squirming around him. "She doesn't like me like that." Right? I mean, she said so yesterday. The cookies were probably just a way to say thank you. She just wanted to remind me that we were buddies, that she was there for me, and to forget about asking anyone else out; I was hooked.

Tim fingered a crumb on the table, sniffed it, and decided it was part of the frog. "Then can I have the cookies?"

Tammi was a lesser version of her sister. It was like someone had turned a strange knob and all aspects of Sage had decreased by about twenty-five percent: her height, the thunder of her voice, even the number of freckles. It was only in the area of chest size that Tammi beat out her sister; she had an almost impressive rack for a freshman.

I saw her after school that Monday, outside the cafeteria. She was tying her shoe in front of the butt-ugly mural that had been painted by the Class of 1982. A crowd of badly painted students (much more ethnically diverse than Boyer ever was) stood around an enormous bear, which was clad in Roman-style armor. The scene always reminded me of some sort of cult gathering; it was like the Boyer mascot was about to order a mass suicide.

Even though Tammi was dressed in conservative jeans and a sweater, there was no mistaking that this girl was Sage's sister. When she stood up, I went to introduce myself.

"Logan?" she asked before I could say a word.

"How did . . ."

"It's stitched on your jacket." Her voice was much softer, much less intense, than her sister's.

"You must be . . ."

"Right." Tammi was staring at me like I was a used car with bad shocks and no radio. I regretted trying to start a conversation.

"So, Tammi, what do you think of . . ."

"It's okay." Tammi's gaze made me feel like I was standing in front of a two-way mirror with five other guys as she decided which of us had snatched her purse. If I stared at a girl that way, she'd be justified in smacking my face. Eventually, she made eye contact.

"You and Sage snuck out together Friday, didn't you?" She wasn't accusing me. It was like when a cop asks you if you knew how fast you were going. It doesn't matter how you answer.

"Uh . . ." I wasn't sure what to say. Was Tammi planning on snitching to her parents? And why would she? I'd covered for Laura before; you never ratted out your own sister.

"It's okay, Logan," continued Tammi. "Sage told me she went to the movies with you."

Great. I pictured the two sisters sitting in a darkened bedroom discussing my aborted kiss.

*I dunno, Tammi, I guess he likes me, but, well . . . he rides a bike, and he actually grew up in a trailer. I think I'll tell him I just want to be friends.*

Tammi sucked in her cheeks, then peered up and down the hall and into the abandoned cafeteria. She motioned for me to lean in close.

"Logan, Sage shouldn't be doing things like that. I think my parents know she lied. She could wind up in real trouble if she gets caught."

If Tammi had been a hulking twenty-year-old marine I would have quailed at the warning. Coming from a fifteen-year-old semidwarf, it was just weird. Was she really such a goody-goody that she wanted to make sure Sage didn't violate her parents' insane restrictions? Didn't she realize that she'd be forced to obey the same rules as her sister?

Tammi wasn't finished. She spoke in such a soft whisper, I nearly had to bend at the waist to catch what she said next.

"Logan, I don't mean that I want you to stay away from her. She says you're a nice guy, and she needs a friend. But don't convince her to sneak around. You might think it's no big deal, but Sage can't afford to get in trouble right now."

I nodded, and Tammi left. What had she meant by that cryptic remark? She made it sound like something awful would happen if Sage ever broke the rules. Like her parents were *waiting* for an excuse to punish her.

Once again, I wondered what was going on at her house. Could it be that her parents weren't strict, but abusive? Or maybe Sage had messed up big-time when she was younger and her parents no longer trusted her.

Well, Sage had asked that we be friends. And if I was really her friend, maybe someday she'd tell me what was wrong.

# chapter seven

BY WEDNESDAY, our frogs were nothing more than skeletons and scraps; sad carcasses of use to no one but the sausage factory. Last cuts tomorrow, test Monday.

For the first time since this lab began, Tim wasn't in charge of the surgery. He was having some kind of stomach problem and spent most of the hour slumped in his chair.

"How often does this happen?" whispered Sage as we filled out our lab report.

I watched Tim drop two tabs of Alka-Seltzer into his Coke. "Less often than you'd think. He must have accidentally eaten a vegetable."

Sage got up to return the animal to the lab fridge. Tim focused his bleary eyes on me.

"I shouldn't have come to school."

"Don't I tell you that every day?"

Tim gave me a thin smile and looked over at Sage. "So what's going on with you two?"

"I told you, nothing. Just friends."

Tim hauled himself to a semiupright position. "How convenient."

"What the hell's that supposed to mean?"

"I think you're afraid. It just occurred to me, you haven't asked a girl out since you were fifteen."

I glanced over at Sage, who was still waiting in line to store the frog. She saw me looking and gave me a wave and a smile.

I turned back to Tim. "Big talk, coming from you. You've never had a date."

I instantly regretted bringing that up. It was pretty obvious why Tim never went out. But he didn't look offended.

"I may just surprise you one of these days, Logan."

Sage sat down in her chair. Then, without warning, she swung her long legs around and flopped them onto my lap. She grinned at me defiantly. Tim, who was now clutching his stomach and sweating, still managed to look at me smugly.

Sage's pants had scrunched up a bit, leaving her pale shins uncovered on my lap. Without thinking, I laid my hand on her bare skin. She didn't object. She also didn't seem to mind when I rubbed my palm down her bladelike shin and tickled her ankle. In fact, she closed her eyes and wrinkled her nose in what I hoped was an expression of pleasure. As Mr. Elmer reviewed what we'd covered in the lab, Sage kicked her shoes off. I began to massage her toes.

I felt strangely guilty, like I was giving a foot rub to a friend's girlfriend. Sage had told me she wanted me as a friend. Her sister had warned me off. If I was ready to start dating again, I shouldn't waste time hitting on a girl with all these issues.

And yet, here I was, kneading her feet and probably enjoying it more than she was. Maybe later, she'd like a shoulder rub. Or a back rub. Or a front rub.

I knew I needed to stop. In spite of his dysentery attack, Tim was watching us. After the cookies the other day, Tim was convinced that Sage wanted me for a boyfriend. He'd think I was lying if I tried to tell him otherwise.

Was it really time to stop pursuing Sage? What had Mom said the other night about missed opportunities? Something told me that if I gave up on Sage, I'd end up regretting it.

When Mr. Elmer finished his review, I removed my hands from Sage's foot. She shot me a fake scowl.

"Uh, Sage," I began. "We're all going to the basketball game Friday. Want to join us?"

*There. Friends go to sports events together. There's nothing wrong with my asking.*

She tilted her head and scratched her chin as if she was contemplating the mysteries of the universe. "Sure!" she said after a minute. "I think I can get out. I'll meet you there."

The bell rang. Sage carelessly retracted her feet across my crotch, momentarily causing me a flash of blinding pain. She was out the door in seconds.

I turned to Tim, ready to gloat that I wasn't afraid of Sage. Before I could say anything, he let out a loud fart so stinky that it covered the odor of the frog preservative.

He leapt to his feet with a grin on his face. "I feel like a new man!"

I hoped Sage really would show up at the game. I needed a change of company.

Time seemed to stand still as our center threw a desperate, longer-than-half-court shot with no time left in the half. For an agonizing second the basketball seemed to hover directly over the rim. Then gravity took effect and the shot went wide.

No big deal; we were down by twenty-four points.

Half the town had turned out for Friday night basketball. The tiny gym was stuffed to the gills as the Moberly Spartans wiped the floor with the Boyer Bears. Moberly was large enough that people actually had to try out for their team. At Boyer, anyone interested was pretty much guaranteed court time.

The cheerleading squad assembled at half-court and proceeded to perform the same three cheers they did at every game. I could see Tanya at the bottom of the pyramid.

For the third or fourth time, I scanned the seats for Sage's lanky form. She had said she'd meet me here, but it looked like she had other plans. Maybe her parents had refused her, or maybe Tammi had tattled. Or she just didn't want to go.

It didn't matter. It's not like I'd been looking forward to this all day. Not like I'd rushed home in order to take a shower and shave before the game. Not like I'd spent my emergency fund on a new shirt. Not like I'd spent the past hour barking at anyone who tried to take the seat next to me.

"Hey, Logan." Tim had joined me. And, shockingly, he had what appeared to be a female with him.

She was a skinny girl with deep blue eyes, the only feature that kept her from being a true albino. Her short hair was almost white and her skin seemed to have no pigmentation at all. She was the sort of person who might catch fire on a sunny day.

"Logan, this is Dawn. Dawn, this is Logan." Tim was grinning as if he'd just pulled her out of a hat.

I shook her hand. "Don't I know you?"

"Maybe. I work at the Forum Eight snack counter."

Ah, so that was where Tim met her. With the amount of money he poured into that place, I was surprised they didn't provide him with a wife.

The cheerleaders eventually finished their routine, and the basketball team thundered back onto the court. Jack, who was not a starter, had been put in for the second half. He wasn't especially good at passing, but the guy moved like a gas molecule and could dribble the ball like a jackhammer.

The cheerleaders had converged near the exit. I recognized Tanya's circular shape. I watched as a strange boy approached her from behind and wrapped his arms around her neck. She turned and kissed him for an entire Boyer time-out. Apparently, I'd missed the boat with her.

Five minutes into the third quarter, Jack's wildly flailing elbow connected with a Spartan's face. A couple of the

Moberly players didn't seem to think it was accidental, and for a few seconds, it looked like there was going to be a brawl.

After the two coaches defused the situation, I turned to Tim to make a joke. Then I quickly turned away. For once, Tim had his lips wrapped around something besides a corn dog.

That was my cue to leave. Not only had Sage stood me up, but now Tim and Dawn were exchanging closed-mouthed little kisses and giggling. I grabbed my jacket.

"Hey, you leaving?" asked Tim when I stood up.

"We're getting stomped. I'll see you guys later."

"You sure? We're going to Mr. Pizza after the game."

That had *third wheel* written all over it. I slouched out of the gym building and into the cold autumn night. The whole parking lot was filled to capacity with pickup trucks and vans. Every other vehicle had an NRA bumper sticker or one of those decals of Calvin pissing on something. I buttoned my jacket and prepared for the mile-and-a-half walk home.

I recognized Brenda's car parked alone over by the middle school. That ugly gold Saturn with the unnecessary spoiler and the little clown head on the aerial. I allowed myself a sad smile, remembering the backseat. Parking lots, dirt roads, Brenda's driveway—our lips never separating, even as Brenda firmly shoved away my exploring hands. I'd been patient; I'd figured someday she wouldn't man the defenses. I just kind of assumed I'd be there when it happened.

Brenda was around here somewhere. I thought maybe I should try to find her and say hi. Just walk by her and say, *Oh, hey, didn't see you; how's it going?* Let her know I was okay and bury the hatchet. Unless she was here with that new boyfriend. Then I'd just bury my fist in his face.

I was eighteen, alone, unloved, broke, and, I suddenly realized, seconds away from being hit by a car.

The driver didn't have his lights on. I only realized he was barreling toward me by the sound of his squealing tires and the shadow of the vehicle against the parking lot lights.

I deftly went sprawling into a handicapped space as the car, a Chevy with one busted headlight and no grill, fishtailed to a stop behind me. I leapt to my feet, wondering if I was about to threaten a bad Boyer driver or have my ass pounded by a carload of insane Moberly fans.

Before my adrenaline rush kicked in, the driver rolled down his window. I knew the guy, a redheaded sophomore named Rob. He was a big oaf, the kind of guy you read about in the paper who'd accidentally shot himself in the butt or burned down his house trying to remove a wasp's nest.

"Sorry, Logan."

It was impossible to stay mad at Rob. I remembered the time he congratulated a girl undergoing chemotherapy on her successful "diet."

"Did you just get your license?"

"Soon."

He wasn't alone in the car. There was a short girl sitting next to him. She looked familiar.

"Hey, Logan."

I squinted into the darkness. It was Sage's sister, Tammi.

From the rear of the car came a familiar feminine voice. "Get in the car, Logan."

I joined Sage, who was sitting cross-legged in the backseat. She didn't scoot over to make room for me, so I was wedged in comfortably close to her. If this was a normal relationship, I'd have leaned over and kissed her. However, I remembered what had happened the last time I'd tried to merge lips, so I just patted her knee.

"Sorry we're late," she said. "Is the game over already?"

"No," I replied. "We were just losing real bad—"

Rob peeled out, then immediately slammed on the brakes for some reason, giving me my first taste of whiplash. Sage nearly toppled over. I realized she was having trouble fitting her long legs in the backseat, and I wondered why she wasn't riding shotgun. Only when I saw Rob awkwardly drape his arm over Tammi's shoulder did I realize what was going on. I grinned internally. So Tammi was sneaking out with a guy, too! So much for her high-and-mighty attitude.

"So, where are we going?" I asked. Not much was open in Boyer this late.

"Let's head out to the rock quarry," suggested Rob. He started to massage Tammi's neck, which apparently distracted him from driving. After crossing the yellow line and nearly plowing head-on into a van, he kept both hands on the wheel.

Sage took several deep breaths to avoid hyperventilating. "Why don't we just go to the park?"

Veterans Park was on the outskirts of Boyer (anything not actually on the town square was the outskirts). It boasted a war memorial, some decrepit playground equipment, and a baseball diamond. When Jack and I were in junior high, the cops constantly used to bust us for skateboarding in the parking lot. The year we entered high school and lost interest, the city installed a half-acre skating facility.

Rob managed to park across three spaces in the empty lot, then left with Tammi to go on the creaking swings. Sage sat on a park bench and patted the seat next to her.

The town council wouldn't pay to keep the park lit up at night, so we sat silently for a bit, waiting for our eyes to adjust.

"Sorry I had to bring Tammi and Rob," Sage said after a while. "Mom wanted me to chaperone."

I didn't say anything, but my mind was racing. Sage's mom knew Tammi was out on a date? Then why did Sage have to sneak out to the movies with us the other night? If her parents let their fifteen-year-old daughter go on dates, why didn't they allow her older sister to just hang out with a boy?

The groaning of the rusty swings stopped. Sage squinted blindly into the darkness, trying to see what her sister was doing.

"Is Rob an okay guy?" she asked, worried.

"Yeah. I don't know him that well, but I haven't heard anything bad about him."

Sage was squirming in her seat. "That doesn't mean anything."

"You really aren't from a small town. Trust me, if he'd done any shit, everyone would know."

Sage giggled. "Damn, I have to get used to living in BFE. Tammi didn't really date at her last school. She said all the boys . . ."

Sage suddenly stopped. I could see her braces reflect the dim moonlight as she gritted her teeth. She hadn't meant to let that slip.

"Sage?"

She didn't answer.

"Sage?" I insisted. "Tammi went to public school? Why didn't you? And how come she's allowed to go on dates?"

Sage shifted on the bench until her broad back was toward me. I think she was tired of my questioning, but I wasn't going to let it drop. There was something weird going on at her home.

"Hey, talk to me."

"Fine." She swiveled and faced me. She was smiling, but it was sort of a cruel smirk. "Tim told me you just broke up with someone. Do you feel like talking about *that*?"

I scooted away. "No, I really don't." Why would she bring that up?

Sage scooted after me. We were now both scrunched on the extreme left side of the bench. I was in danger of falling off. Sage leaned over to me.

"Then you understand that there are some things I don't want to discuss, either. Could we just leave it at that for now?" Her smile was friendly again.

"Okay." My mind was racing. What the hell was the big deal? Why had Sage been homeschooled all those years? Maybe she'd done something bad—broken the law and wound up in juvie for half a year, so her parents kept her at home. Or what if she'd gotten pregnant when she was, like, twelve, and her parents yanked her out of school so she could have the baby . . . or an abortion. That would explain why she wasn't allowed to date. Or she could be HIV positive. Or . . .

"Logan, whatever you're imagining, it's not that bad."

"Okay, but you've got to admit—"

"Shut up."

There was a pause, and then we both laughed. We hadn't moved apart on the bench, and we were close enough that Sage's face was clearly visible in the darkness, just a little above mine. The night was cool, and I could see our breaths mingling. I could even make out the freckles on Sage's nose. Her bright lipstick and shiny braces. Her doubly pierced ears. And the steam from our breathing continued to get heavier and closer.

A dark figure suddenly lunged at us from the darkness. Before I could react, it had slammed between us into the bench, almost knocking me to the ground. The attacker's hand grabbed at both of us, reaching for our necks, attempting to subdue both of us at the same time.

It was Tammi. She wedged herself in the middle of the bench, a friendly arm around each of us. Rob was approaching across the gravel playground looking rather disappointed. Maybe the moment had been ruined for him, too.

"Time to go home," ordered Tammi. I couldn't read

Sage's expression over her sister's head. Not only did Sage's parents not want her to date, but neither did her little sister. Tammi was chaperoning Sage, not the other way around.

But Sage had told me she wasn't going to answer any questions. As curious as I was, you don't badger your friends when they don't want to talk. Sage hadn't known me that long. Once she realized she could trust me, I felt sure she'd open up.

I never dreamed Sage's secret was about to become my secret, or how desperate we'd both be to keep it.

*chapter eight*

IT NEVER FAILED to amaze me how the one sizable tree in our yard could produce so many leaves. Fall after fall, I'd end up raking ten bags or so. I dumped the last load into the charred oil drum at the rear of our property, squirted some lighter fluid, and dropped a match. The pleasant smell of burning leaves filled the air.

Thanksgiving was the next day. Jack was in Iowa, celebrating with his extended family. Tim was probably sitting in front of his parents' stove, watching the turkey and drooling. There were never any leftovers at his house. Sage was vague when I asked her about her plans. She said she didn't visit her grandparents anymore, but she didn't elaborate. She told me she might call if she got bored.

My grandfather was spending the holidays in St. Louis with my uncle and his family. Mom couldn't get a lot of time off work, so we were staying in Boyer. Just the three of us.

I smiled when I saw the trail of dust approaching down

our gravel road. I made sure the fire was burning okay, then ran to meet my sister.

I'd never seen her car before. She'd saved her pennies from her job at the MU library and bought it from a friend. It was a white Taurus that had seen better years. As she parked, I realized that Laura now drove the nicer car in the family.

I whistled when Laura stepped out of the car but mentally did a double take. Laura looked stylish! She was wearing a long brown coat, a scarf, and leather boots. Her dark hair was much shorter than when I'd last seen her over the summer, and she was wearing makeup, which was unusual for her.

It was hard for me to picture this sophisticated woman as the same girl who used to have water balloon fights with me. The same sister who knocked out two of my baby teeth during a softball mishap. And here I was wearing torn jeans and leaning on a rake like some hillbilly.

"Aren't you going to help your sister with her bags?" Laura said with a smile.

"Nice to see you, too." We laughed and hugged.

I hauled Laura's suitcases into her old room.

"So are these full of bowling balls, or what?" I asked, dropping the bags at the foot of her bed.

"Just wanted to give you an opportunity to show off those muscles, studly."

Laura removed her boots and sat on her bed. She looked around her old room like she was expecting big changes since she'd left. Actually, almost nothing was different. Her gymnastics and softball trophies were still on her dresser, the pictures of her old friends were still on the walls, and, I suspected, the little metal pipe and box of rolling papers were still hidden in the back of her closet.

"I thought you and Mom would have taken over my room by now."

I straddled Laura's desk chair. "Desecrate your shrine? Never. At least, not until I figure out how to remove that wall so I can I have a big room."

My sister lay back on her pillow with her arms folded behind her head. "Your small room is good training, Logan. The dorms at Mizzou are even tinier, and you'll have to share with someone. Are you still thinking of rooming with Jack?"

I didn't answer. As I tried to think of a way to change the subject, I realized Laura had sat back up and was staring at me.

"Logan, you *are* still planning on going to college, right?"

It was funny. I could look my mother in the eyes and tell her the biggest whoppers and sound as sincere as a minister on Easter morning. But when my sister suspected I wasn't telling her the truth . . . She'd realized Brenda and I had broken up long before Mom had even suspected.

"Yeah, I'm going. I guess." I'd sent in the application the week before. According to Tim, I qualified for several grants and interest-free loans from Uncle Sam. All that was left was deciding that I really wanted to go.

Laura patted the bed, and I sat down next to her.

"Logan, I know how you feel. I grew up here, too. And it's not easy to leave. But think about next year. You won't be at school for eight hours a day. Jack will be gone, and so will Tim. And me."

"Twenty miles away. You're practically on Mars."

Laura punched me in the arm. I think she assumed it didn't hurt me. "Listen to me. Not a week goes by I don't hear about some concert that I think you'd like, or meet some guys you'd get along with, or do something fun and wish you were there to enjoy it with me. You could work out in a real gym instead of a shed. Get a job where you get paid with a check instead of a handful of quarters. You always talk about taking guitar lessons; do you have any idea how many shitty guitarists there are on campus? You could have your own band in two weeks!"

I bit my lip to keep from grinning. Laura could probably make Greenland sound like Club Med if she wanted to. And I knew I'd end up bowing to the inevitable and going to Mizzou, at least to see what it was like. But there were other things going on.

Laura placed her hand on the back of my neck. I tensed until I realized she wasn't about to put me in a wrestling hold. "You're still thinking about Brenda, aren't you?"

"Maybe. The main reason I wanted to go to MU was because she'd be there. And now it doesn't matter."

Laura was about to say something when we heard the door to the trailer open.

"Laura!" Mom called. "Laura, honey, where are you?"

My sister smiled at me. "We'll talk more later."

For the next few hours, we enjoyed an evening together, just like old times. Mom badgered Laura about her classes, her roommate, and her social life, while making the final preparations for supper the next day. Laura sat at the dining room table grating carrots or preparing stuffing (there wasn't room for two people in the kitchen). I didn't bother to offer my help. The laws of chemistry didn't seem to apply when I attempted to cook, and I knew I'd be stuck with most of the dishes the next day, anyway.

That evening, as the Thanksgiving ham slowly baked, we all sat on the couch, ate popcorn, and chatted. Mom kept dozing off, and eventually we hustled her off to bed.

"So how's Mom doing?" asked Laura after Mom's door closed.

"Okay, I guess. She's working too hard. If I move out next year, I hope she'll ask for fewer hours."

Laura flicked a kernel at me. "You mean *when* you move out."

"Gosh, I could live in a tiny room with Jack and see you all the time. Sounds great."

We both laughed, then fell silent, lost in thought for a minute. Laura sifted through the duds in the bowl.

"Do you want to talk about it?" asked Laura eventually. She didn't mean college. She meant Brenda. My sister was the only person who realized that my relationship with my girlfriend had been more to me than some stupid teenage crush. She was the only one who knew the true story of my breakup.

I shrugged. "I haven't talked to Brenda in over a month. She's moved on."

"I really don't give a shit about how she's doing," said Laura without pausing. "I want to know how you're holding up."

"Eh," I grunted.

"That's not an answer. That's not even a word." Laura scooted closer to me. She laid her bare feet on the coffee table. This was the sister I remembered.

"She's gone and I survived. I hope she'll be happy. I also hope her boyfriend will slip in the shower, fall face-first into the toilet, and drown. One or the other."

Laura didn't feed me any lines about getting back on the horse or looking to the future. She just gave me a one-armed hug.

"So you haven't asked anyone out, I guess."

"No." I paused. "Well, once."

"Really?" asked Laura with interest. "Who?" As a former Boyer Bear, she still knew everyone at school.

"New girl, no one you know. And she turned me down."

Laura rolled her eyes. "Then she's stupid. But at least—"

I cut her off. "It wasn't like that. There's something going on with her parents. She says she's not allowed to date. She's been homeschooled since junior high."

"Sounds like she has personal issues, and you're probably better off. But now that—"

"It's weird, though. Her younger sister can date, but she can't. And her sister went to regular school."

Laura was giving me a perplexed look. "Well, that's her problem, isn't it?"

"Yeah, but . . . I dunno."

Laura suddenly grinned. "So you *do* like her. What's her name?"

I blushed a little. It's not like I was ten years old; I

could admit to liking a girl. "Her name is Sage. She transferred to Boyer a couple of weeks ago."

"What's she like?"

"Weird. Dresses like she's been in a paint factory accident. But she's funny and cute and puts up with Jack and Tim. And sometimes she acts like she can't keep her hands off me. But she freaked out when I tried to kiss her. And then she baked me cookies. She won't tell me anything about her family, but she sneaked out to be with me twice. And it's not like I couldn't get a date with anyone else. It's like . . ." I tried to figure out how to explain it.

Laura finished my thought. "Like as long as you think you might have a chance with Sage, then you aren't interested in anyone else."

I nodded. "If she'd just say she didn't like me, I could deal with it. But there's some other reason why we can't go out. I don't buy her line that it's because of her parents. She's nearly as sneaky as you were."

My sister shrugged off the compliment. "I'm glad you're dating again. For your own sake, and for the women of the world. Sounds like Sage just doesn't trust people very easily. Give her some time. Either she'll come around, or she'll end up regretting it." Laura picked up the popcorn bowl and walked the three steps to the kitchen. "I'm just glad you're getting over a certain slut."

Two weeks ago, I might have taken offense at Laura insulting Brenda like that. Now I just chuckled.

*chapter nine*

LAURA STAYED for two days before returning to Columbia, land of indoor plumbing and 'lectricity. That Saturday I helped her load her bags in the trunk. Mom was working the lunch shift, and I'd spent the day hanging out with my big sister. It was funny, but she hadn't gotten together with any of her old friends while she was in town. Most of them were still around. I wondered if Laura was trying to forget about Boyer. I wondered if I would.

"Guess I'll see you at Christmas," I said. I was already starting to miss her.

"You know, you could come up and visit me some weekend. Have Jack drive you. I've got friends you could crash with."

"Maybe. Um, thanks for talking with me the other night."

Laura smiled. "My pleasure. Keep being nice to Sage.

Maybe she got used by some guy and wants to make sure you're as great as you seem. But if it doesn't work out, I know about ten girls in my dorm I can set you up with."

Laura hugged me, then hopped in her car and took off. I suddenly felt desperately lonely. I wanted to talk to someone. But Jack was still out of town and Tim was probably in a food coma. I remembered how I'd talk to Brenda when I was sad.

Then I realized I was having false memory syndrome. I never talked to Brenda about my father. Or my fears about the future. In three years of dating, we'd only ever had one serious discussion. Our last one. Now that I thought back on it, Brenda had never once told me when she was sad or scared or lonely. Every time I asked, she'd just smile and say she was fine. And she'd never really wanted to know how I was doing.

I returned to the trailer and started to pick up some of the mess that Laura had left behind. I was making the bed in her old room when the phone rang.

"Logan? This is Sage."

I grinned into the receiver. I didn't know why she was calling, but I suddenly felt joyous. Even if she hung up after two minutes, it would still mean she'd been thinking about me.

"Hey, Sage." For the first time in five years, my voice cracked.

"How was Turkey Day? Did you get a drumstick?"

I remembered the foil-wrapped ham slices in the fridge. "Uh, no."

"So, what have you been up to? Watching football?"

"I did the other day." I got to see my favorite team, the St. Louis Rams, have their collective ass handed to them.

I could hear Sage munching on something over the line. "Did anyone hit a home run?"

I snickered. "Sage, that's baseball."

"I know. I just wanted you to feel superior for a minute."

"Oh."

"So, are you doing anything? Mom and Tammi are shopping and Dad ran in to work. Feel like a picnic? I understand if you can't come."

I think I would have chewed my own leg off to go meet her.

"I'd like that."

"Great. Meet me at the gas station in half an hour." She didn't say goodbye and hung up.

I don't think Sage realized how far from "town" I lived. I had to haul ass on my bike to get there on time. I found Sage sitting on a curb reading a copy of the *Randolph County Recycler*, the free paper that advertised farm auctions and cattle for sale. She was wearing a fake-leather jacket studded with rhinestones.

She grinned when she saw me ride up. As soon as I parked my bike, she enveloped me in a bone-crushing hug.

"I missed you," she said, still embracing me. Her arms wrapped completely around my back and her chin rested on top of my skull.

I didn't answer. I figured if I said anything, she'd release me.

Eventually, she let me go. I contemplated kissing her cheek or gently touching the back of her neck. Something to bust me out of this impossible neutral situation I found myself in. But Sage had bent down and was picking something up off the ground.

"Here." She handed me a large convenience store bag filled with plastic-wrapped sandwiches, mini bags of chips, and some bottled fruit juice.

"Now, where should we eat, Logan?"

I was rummaging through the bag. Sage had bought four different types of sandwiches, and I didn't like any of them. But we'd known each other less than a month, after all. Why did I have such a hard time remembering that?

"We could go to the park."

Sage pulled one of her curls, then let it boing back into place like a spring. "Uh, maybe we could go somewhere a little more . . . you know, isolated?"

That got my heart pounding until I realized she was referring to her dating ban. She didn't want us to be seen eating together. Why? Brenda's parents had liked me. When she'd gotten her license, they'd allowed us to go out alone together.

But Sage's parents . . . She couldn't even sit in a public park with me! What did they think would happen?

*Mrs. Hendricks, I hate to be the one to tell you this, but I just saw your daughter eating a ham and cheese sandwich with a boy. Right out on the playground, where anyone could see them! I don't know how they do things in Joplin, but we have rules in this town.*

Well, at least Sage was willing to eat in secret with me, which was something. I remembered an isolated place where Jack, Tim, and I used to set off fireworks. "There's the old Arborville Road Cemetery. Are you up for a walk?"

It was a glorious cold, late-autumn afternoon. The sky was a deep, cloudless blue. Flocks of geese honked their way from horizon to horizon, off to Texas or Mexico or wherever. You could feel the bite of the coming winter in your ears and lungs. It was the sort of day that made you want to run outside, take a deep breath, and then go back in and watch TV all day.

Sage literally skipped as we made our way down County Road 1124. She seemed inclined to stop and inspect every rock, blade of grass, and shattered whiskey bottle beside the road.

"This is so neat!" she said, laughing. "Back in Joplin, you had to drive everywhere. You couldn't go twenty feet without passing a Burger King."

I thought that actually sounded kind of nice. "Watch out for hypodermic needles," I warned.

Sage stopped prancing around and started walking next to me. "So, did you have a good Thanksgiving?"

"Yeah. My sister was in town."

"She goes to Mizzou, doesn't she?"

Hmm. Sage had actually been paying attention when I'd mentioned Laura. With Brenda, I'd sometimes gotten the impression she listened to me just to be polite.

"Yeah, she's a freshman."

"I bet that's hard on your parents, her moving out and all."

"Um, I guess I never told you. I don't have a father."

Sage froze. "I'm sorry, Logan. I didn't know. When did he pass away?"

She was looking at me with such gentle compassion that I didn't want to tell the truth. "He actually ran away. I never really knew him."

Divorce was part of life in Boyer. Half of everyone's parents were divorced, and the other half had never been married in the first place. But Sage didn't look any less sorrowful than when she'd thought my father was dead. For a moment I thought she was going to hug me again, but instead she offered me her arm. I slipped my hand over her elbow, and we began walking. I wanted to wrap my arm around her waist. I wanted to tell her she was pretty. I wanted to reach up and kiss her.

We arrived at the cemetery before I could do anything stupid. It consisted of about three dozen ancient tombstones, mostly too eroded to read. Whatever farmer owned the property kept the small plot mowed.

Sage found a bare patch of earth and spread out our post-Thanksgiving feast. I choked down a prepackaged corned beef sandwich while Sage gulped down two sandwiches and a bag of chips.

There was something very natural and insanely frustrating about being here, quietly eating with Sage. I tried to put my finger on it. Maybe it was the silence. When was the last time I'd just sat quietly with someone? Certainly not around Jack. Or my mom. Or Brenda. Silence with her had always been awkward; I'd always felt like she was bored.

But with Sage, we didn't talk and it was okay. Two good friends, enjoying each other's company.

"Penny for your thoughts, Logan." Sage leaned against a tree, smiling at me. Her reddish-brown hair contrasted against the yellow leaf that was stuck on top of her head. With her freckles and tomboyish ways, she looked like something out of an Outdoor Missouri ad. Maybe without the purple jacket.

"C'mon, Logan, what are you thinking about?"

And that was the frustrating part. I didn't want to be friends. I didn't want to be the guy she leaned on, the rock in the storm, the best pal who was always there for her. Well, I *did*, but I also wanted to kiss her. I wanted to take her face in my hands, press our lips together, and enjoy another type of silence.

"It's nice out," I said. "Warm for this time of year."

Sage stood up and dusted off her legs. Then she joined me, sitting back against the rotten rail fence around the cemetery.

"Logan, can I ask you a personal question?"

Never, ever a good sign. "Yeah?"

"Tell me what happened with you and your old girlfriend."

"That's not a question."

"*Will you* tell me what happened?"

I didn't want to talk about it. I'd only ever talked about it with Laura. "Why?"

Sage touched my cheek lightly. "Because you're my friend, and I want to know."

I could have reminded her that she was keeping secrets,

but I didn't. "She cheated on me. We broke up. End of story." *C'mon, let's play the quiet game.*

Sage tucked her long legs up under her chin. "There's more to it than that," she prodded.

"You really want the whole sorry episode?" When I'd told Laura what happened, I'd summed everything up in one sentence: *Brenda cheated on me.* Why did Sage want to know more than that? And why was I about to tell her? Maybe I wanted her pity, or I thought that if I told her my secrets, she'd be more open with me.

Mostly, I think I just wanted to vomit out the whole humiliating incident. Lance it like a boil. Purge my breakup like a bout of diarrhea. The fact that I was thinking of my ex in terms of gross bodily functions was probably a sign that it was time to move on.

Sage nodded, staring at me with wide eyes.

"Okay." I tried to keep my voice steady. If I was going to tell this story to Sage, the last thing I wanted was to sound whiny. "Brenda and I started going out in ninth grade. We'd never dated anyone else. She's the only girl I've ever kissed. And that's all we ever did."

Sage's eyes got wide. She must have thought I had more experience with girls. I wished I'd kept that detail to myself. Sage might not be a virgin. I'd just made myself look inexperienced and awkward.

"Anyway, we'd been together for three years. We were going to go to Mizzou together. Live in the same dorm." I paused. "I thought, you know, we were in love. I was stupid." I let out a fake, sarcastic laugh. This was sounding a bit too much like *poor, poor Logan.*

"You weren't stupid!" yelped Sage suddenly. "Don't ever think that."

I reddened at the compliment. But Sage was wrong. I'd wasted almost all of high school feeling giddy and in love with a girl who didn't even like me enough to tell me she didn't like me.

I walked away from Sage and sat down near Ida Woodlawn (*1899–1960, loving wife and mother*). I closed my eyes to the world and continued.

"Then I was a fool. Every time I saw her, I couldn't believe how lucky I was. We'd hang out all the time. We went to dances; she'd go to my track meets. It was like I'd won the lottery."

I paused for a minute, remembering Brenda. Our first kiss. The first time she told me she loved me. Those nights after basketball games when I tried to get her to go out to the rock quarry. When did she start having second thoughts? How many times had she told me she loved me when she didn't mean it? How many kisses? I hoped to God I'd never find out.

I sighed. Sage had asked for the whole story, so I might as well tell her everything. Opening my eyes, I braced myself for the best part. The really funny part.

"So back in October, Jack came up to me. He was all nervous and stammering, but it was Jack, after all. He said that he was cruising downtown and saw Brenda in a car with some guy out behind the Dollar General."

Sage no longer looked compassionate; she looked furious. It was probably for the better that she hadn't been around during the breakup. Brenda might not have been safe.

ᴏʀᴇs in Boyer put up their Christmas decora-
ay after Thanksgiving. The town council
ᴅded Nativity in Vets park, political correct-
ᴇd. The first week of December, I made
ndred dollars shoveling walks when we got
urned half of it over to Mom and saved the
ᴅing.

season ended with a surprising victory
ᴁing Boyer with a 2–8 record. Tim and
be seen together.

ᴅd the time when I shucked my self-
ᴃ with Brenda for a self-destructive
ᴂ still spent every morning hanging
now Sage joined me, snacking on
and making fun of the other stu-
ogether and spend the whole hour

"So what did you do?" she asked.

"I punched Jack. Right in the gut." Not very hard, but enough that he'd lost his footing and fallen on his ass right in front of everyone in the parking lot.

Sage looked at me with awe. "You *punched* him?"

I flicked a dandelion, causing the seeds to spray everywhere. "My best friend. I was that sure he was lying. Brenda and I had never . . . you know."

"I know."

"She'd always stop me. Kept telling me that the time wasn't right. Telling me that we should wait, that then it would be all the more special when it happened. I never even got to second base. Not that I minded. I mean, I *minded*, but I was willing to do whatever she asked. And then, one night, she just jumps into the backseat with some prick from Moberly. She'd known him less than a week, and was willing to . . ." I couldn't finish. Three years of convincing myself what a great, wonderful guy I was for respecting Brenda like that—never pushing, never insisting, never demanding. What a sap.

"Maybe they didn't," offered Sage, as if the idea might not have occurred to me.

"They did. She told me the next day. She tried to be nice about it, but once your girlfriend gets naked with some guy . . . I haven't talked to her since." I stood and began picking up our trash.

"Logan. Listen to me—"

"Please don't say anything. Seriously." I didn't want to talk about it anymore. In fact, I didn't want to talk about it ever again. Or think about it. Or about Brenda. Maybe that was for the best. There was more to life than wondering what I'd done wrong. Maybe telling the story had helped drive that home, just a bit.

"But . . . thanks for listening, Sage. I . . . it was good to get that off my chest."

Unlike most girls, Sage didn't force conversation. When we were ready to go, she paused and took my hand.

"Remember, you can always talk to me if you need anything. I promise, Logan." She smiled and moved in for a hug.

I knew I shouldn't ask. She'd told me not to talk about it again. But I'd just opened up. Now it was her turn.

"Why were you homeschooled, Sage?"

Sage's expression didn't change. "So how are the Chiefs doing this year?"

"I know you told me not to ask . . ."

"Or the Rams? What's your favorite team?" She was grinning like a funhouse clown.

"I just thought maybe you'd talk to me."

"How about baseball? You like the Cardinals?" There was a defiant smirk on her lips. Obviously, her life was still a closed subject. We started walking back to the road.

"Hey, Sage?"

She turned and gave me a real smile. "Yes, Logan?"

"You've got leaves on your butt."

We didn't talk all the way back to town. It wasn't the serene silence of earlier. It was heavy. It was like our thoughts had congealed and were hanging in the air like humidity. I wanted to thank Sage for listening. And I almost wanted to holler that she could trust me and tell me

her secrets, to let her know that I was worthy of dence.

Maybe Sage was thinking her own heavy

When we reached the highway, Sage "I'm going the other way. See you at schoo

"Yeah." I felt like I was standing on a and it was my turn to speak but I'd tota to say.

"Logan, I . . ." Sage's jaw was fro been paused. She stood there, imm minute. There was something frigh ture. It was almost like she was fea disaster. She looked as if someth ing. There was no reason for nearby.

"Sage?"

She spun on her heels an

giggling and poking each other under the table. Mr. Elmer threatened to separate us more than once, but he never did.

Sage had a different lunch hour, but we'd run into each other between classes. I'd find little notes in my locker, pink stationery covered with smiley face stickers, wishing me a good day. After school, Sage would walk me to the track, or the gym, or my bike, often under the scowling gaze of Tammi. But that was where it ended. Once we left the high school grounds, Sage vanished. No walking me home. No heading out for a bite to eat. No going over to Jack's to watch monster movies on Friday night. It was like we were in a long-distance relationship, even though we lived less than five miles apart.

It's not like Sage forgot about me after school. Two or three times a week, she'd call me at home, asking forced questions about biology and trying to get a rise out of me by saying she was phoning from the shower. Mom never commented on her frequent calls, though she would gaze at me slyly over the top of her *Soap Opera Digest.* It was obvious Mom thought I'd landed a new girlfriend. But when I invited Sage over for an innocent study date, she'd always change the subject.

I should have been happy, or at least resigned. Sage was a good friend. I enjoyed hanging out with her. If that was all there was, then that was all there was.

But that was not all there was. Because sometimes she'd let me hold her hand, provided her sister wasn't around. She'd place her hand on my knee and leave it there for most of first hour. She pinched my butt on more than one occasion. But when I tried to put my arm around her or give her a little kiss, she'd jerk away.

Sage's other maddening habit was her absolute refusal to talk about her home, her past, or why she was treated so differently from her sister. Tammi already had a boyfriend, was in the French club, and had found a group of friends. But Sage couldn't date, didn't participate in any after-school programs, and hung out only with me. It was like I was dating a woman in prison. I could visit her, but she lived under someone else's strict rules. It didn't matter how much I cared for her; she feared the warden more than she liked me.

Why wouldn't Sage talk to me about anything serious? Was she waiting to see if I could be trusted, or was something else going on? There was no one I could talk to about this. Asking my mother for dating advice was a tad too Norman Bates for my liking. Tim would accuse me of being too chickenshit to put the moves on Sage. Jack had already decided that Sage and I were secretly doing it; he'd given me a graphic description of the problems we'd encounter due to our height difference.

If this was an ideal world, I'd have a father I could ask for some advice. If this was a sitcom, there'd be some young black teacher I could confide in. But life is not ideal and is only occasionally a situation comedy.

I sat in the commons after school bouncing the gift-wrapped package on my knee like it was a toddler. The school was almost deserted. Christmas break had begun with the last bell, and not too many students wanted to hang around.

I had no reason to be nervous. I'd left a note in Sage's locker asking her to meet me here. I wouldn't see her for almost two weeks and wanted to give her her present. I'd spent the afternoon before at the Wal-Mart in Moberly trying to find something I thought she'd like. A little something to let her know I'd been thinking about her. But nothing too fancy, so she wouldn't feel like I expected a gift (or anything else) in return. Since I only had thirty bucks, it was easy not to go overboard. I'd finally settled on the third-most-expensive body lotion for sale. I'd seen it on TV, endorsed by an actual celebrity, so it must have been good.

I looked at the clock. I'd been waiting ten minutes. What if Sage hadn't gotten my note? Gift exchanges hadn't been nearly this nerve-racking with Brenda. I'd always flat-out ask her what she wanted, and she'd always tell me. Usually a CD or a DVD. She knew my limited budget. And knowing my love of football, Brenda would always buy me some Kansas City Chiefs memorabilia because it's the most popular team in the area. I never had the heart to tell her I was a Rams fan.

"Is that for me?" Sage sat close to me even though the bench was empty.

"Just a little something." I shrugged, wishing it could have been a big something.

"What lovely paper you picked out!" she said, examining the obviously store-wrapped box. "Should I open it now or wait till Christmas?"

"Whatever you want."

"Good!" She greedily tore open the package. When she saw what the gift was, she froze.

"Like it?" I prompted, worrying that I'd accidentally picked out some sort of feminine hygiene product by mistake.

"Logan, it's wonderful," she whispered, staring at the bottle. "Thank you." Her eyes glistened. I couldn't tell if she was tearing up.

"Well . . ." I tried to shrug it off but was mentally patting myself on the back. I'd done good.

Sage sniffed loudly. "Okay, open yours." She passed me a large brown paper bag, stapled shut. Inside was some sort of a blanket or comforter. It wasn't the size of a standard bed; in fact, it was more of a trapezoid than a rectangle. It was made of strips of black and yellow material. A picture of the University of Missouri tiger, clipped from an old sweater, was inexpertly stitched to the middle.

Sage had made this herself. She must have been working on it for weeks.

"It's for your bed at Mizzou," she explained. "Someone said the heat doesn't always work in the dorms."

"Sage . . ." Cookies were one thing, but a handmade blanket? No one had ever sewed me anything. *Thank you* didn't seem sufficient.

"Just make sure you don't spill any crap on it," said Sage half mockingly. "And wash it occasionally. I'll be there to check up on you."

She must have noticed my baffled look. "Didn't I tell you? I got accepted to Mizzou."

It hadn't occurred to me that Sage would be leaving home after high school. But she was going off to college, where her parents had no control, where their rules didn't apply. Where Sage and I could do anything we wanted. The idea made me smile. Sage smiled back. We just sat there smiling at each other, and it wasn't awkward.

"You know," she said after a while, "I kind of wish we were sitting under the mistletoe right now."

*Score!* My grin got bigger. I tried to place my hand on her cheek.

Sage abruptly looked up at the bare ceiling.

"Hmm. Too bad." She stood. "See you in January, Logan." She walked away, not looking back.

Christmas at the Witherspoon trailer didn't involve a huge turkey, roasted chestnuts, and spiced oranges, but I preferred it that way. To me, the holidays would always mean a raggedy fiberglass tree, Mom's green bean casserole, and gifts from the clearance aisle at Target. I couldn't remember ever really believing in Santa Claus. I just enjoyed Mom having the day off and spending time with Laura. If Norman Rockwell never painted a family eating Christmas brunch from TV trays while still in their pajamas, then it was his problem.

Laura was pleased that I'd finally decided I'd join her at Mizzou. When I showed her Sage's blanket, she told me to name our first daughter after her.

I spent New Year's Eve at Jack's house with Tim, Dawn, Jack's younger brother Matt, and a few other people. We watched movies and played Ping-Pong. It wasn't a wild party, but I didn't care. Friends and food. There was just one thing missing.

At eleven-thirty, Tim and Dawn announced they were

going for a walk. We didn't see them again until one in the morning. At midnight, we counted down to the new year and drank a couple of shots Jack had filched from his dad's liquor cabinet. The only couple there kissed.

I was sitting alone on a sofa when we rang in the new year. The years I'd been with Brenda, she'd give me a brief, closed-mouth kiss at midnight (she'd never give me a real kiss when we were around other people).

Jack blasted a paper noisemaker right in my ear. "Happy fucking New Year!" he yelled.

"Yeah."

Jack vaulted over the back of the couch and sat next to me. "So, how come Sage isn't here?"

"She had a family thing." I had invited her when she called me the day after Christmas. She just said she couldn't come. No explanation. She couldn't even go out on New Year's Eve.

On the TV screen, the Times Square lunatics screamed and waved at the camera. For the first time since the last president, I was entering a new year by myself. Next year, after a semester in college, would I be watching the ball drop with Sage? Or would we drift apart and I'd be here with some new girl? Or alone again?

"So, I sent in my housing application the other day," said Jack.

Jack was also going to MU. We'd decided to be roommates, though the idea of living in the same room as Jack sometimes seemed frightening.

"Logan, don't take this the wrong way, but I'm glad Brenda's gone." He winced slightly, worried that he might set me off. When I didn't respond, he continued. "You never had any fun around her. Now you can start college, no strings attached. We're going to have a blast. It'll be a year you never forget."

I didn't realize it at the time, but that was one of the most profound things I'd ever hear Jack say.

I biked home at five a.m. At nine, the phone woke me up. I wanted to ignore the ringing, but I knew this was one of the few mornings Mom got to sleep late, and I didn't want her to get out of bed to answer it. I stumbled blearily to the living room.

"What?" I barked into the receiver.

"Happy New Year to you, too!" said a familiar, throaty voice.

"Sage!"

"Listen, Logan, are you up? I need a big favor." She was her usual abrupt self.

"What do you need?" I asked. I'd had three hours of sleep, it was ten degrees out, and I had two driveways to shovel. But I knew that I'd be out the door in ten minutes, ready to do whatever she asked.

"Tammi and Rob went out last night," Sage explained. "They were supposed to stay at our house, but they snuck out. And Tammi let Rob drive our truck."

"Christ, he didn't wreck it, did he?"

"No, but he left the lights on. I just noticed this morning when I tried to move it. The battery's dead. Tammi will get grounded for a month if Dad finds out what she did. I need to jump start the car."

I wanted to ask why Tammi could run around with the human crash-test dummy but Sage couldn't date. I didn't, though. I knew I wouldn't get an answer.

"So what do you want me to do? I don't have a car." New Year's or not, Mom was working the lunch shift, and I couldn't risk leaving her without a ride.

"Logan, please!" Sage sounded desperate. "Everyone's in Columbia today. Dad needs the truck tonight. He's going to kill Tammi unless we can get it started."

I sighed. "Where do you live?"

Two minutes later, I was pulling on my coat. I would have done the same if Jack or Tim had been in trouble, though with much more cussing.

Grandpa had given us one of those jump start batteries a few years back. The family car was pretty pissy about starting, especially in the winter, and we'd gotten a lot of use out of the thing. Trudging through the drifts in the backyard, I managed to crack open the frozen shed doors and load up the battery and cables. Then I realized I couldn't carry them on my bike. I went back into the trailer, strapped on my boots, and began trekking to Sage's house.

Sage lived in one of Boyer's few subdivisions, with newish houses owned by people who worked in Columbia. It was a nearly three-mile hike. Even with my track experience, lugging the heavy battery nearly killed me.

I had always pictured Sage's house as some sort of gray, imposing structure, a place where laughter went to die. After all, her parents wouldn't allow her to date, didn't let her wear makeup until recently, and kept her away from public school. They had to be humorless Puritans, right?

When I found Sage's house, I was almost convinced that I'd gotten the street number wrong. It was a blue ranch house, probably less than five years old. But what caught my eye was the gaudiest display of Christmas decorations this side of Branson.

The struggling saplings in the yard bent under the wads of tinsel and lights. An inflatable snowman billowed in the front yard, powered by a portable air compressor. Two ugly wire reindeer flanked the front door like some kind of hellhounds. There were enough lights on the roof to rival Busch Stadium.

I hauled the battery up the driveway, which was lined with giant plastic candy canes. These people weren't dour religious nuts. They were tacky at a level you usually only saw at Graceland.

I found Sage in the garage smashing aluminum cans for the recycle bin. She dazzled me with her braces when she saw me approaching.

"You're a lifesaver, Logan. I told Mom and Dad I'd keep an eye on Tammi, but she really wanted to go for a drive with Rob. Now we'll both get in trouble if Dad finds out they weren't here all night. The keys are in it. You get it started, and I'll make you some hot chocolate." She winked at me as she headed into the house.

As I unrolled the cables, I felt like John Wayne rushing in to save the day. It was a good feeling, and not just because of the sprig of plastic mistletoe I'd noticed over the front door. I just liked the idea of helping Sage. Liked knowing that she'd been in trouble and I'd been there for her.

The truck was so old that it was almost, but not quite, a classic. I knew enough about cars to know that it was one of those models that would suck a battery dry if you tried to start it wrong. I hooked up the cables and crossed my fingers.

The engine roared to life when I turned the key. I gunned the gas. I could see why Rob wanted to drive this beast. They didn't make 'em this big anymore. Maybe I could convince Sage that we needed to charge up the battery by taking a quick drive.

"Logan Witherspoon, you're my hero!" said Sage with only a little sarcasm. She was leaning on the driver's door, a mug of cocoa in her hand.

"Take you for a spin?" I asked, grinning.

"Get out of there," she chided. Disappointed, I left the engine running and hopped out.

Sage handed me the chipped I GOT BLOWN IN THE WINDY CITY—CHICAGO, ILLINOIS mug. I sipped the watery hot chocolate as Sage went back to crushing the cans.

"So, how was Christmas?" I asked.

She shrugged, not turning toward me. "It was okay."

The truck coughed and shuddered but didn't die. "This will take a few minutes. Want to go for a walk?"

Sage turned to me and shook her head. "Logan, please don't take this the wrong way, but I'm not supposed to have anyone over. I don't know when everyone's going to be back, and I don't want them to catch you here."

I set the cup on a workbench and pretended to check the cables. Sage had made me a beautiful gift but couldn't or wouldn't hang out with me. Sometimes she acted like I was great, but she had this weird phobia about her parents knowing about me. She'd begged me to come out here, then practically ordered me to leave.

Smoke began to wisp up from the battery terminals, so I turned off the truck. As I unhooked the jumper cables, Sage quickly bent over to contain a mini avalanche of cans. Her sweater rode up her back, revealing her pale skin and the tops of some bright yellow panties.

My world froze, but unfortunately, my body didn't. I absentmindedly grabbed the positive clip, and like many wayward teens, was grounded.

When I yelped, Sage jumped up as if she was the one who'd been shocked. Grabbing me by my good arm, she hustled me into the kitchen and thrust my hand under the sink. The ice-cold water caused the electrical burn to hurt worse, but I didn't let on. Sage didn't ask if I was okay as she dried the wound.

"Have a seat. I'll go get you a bandage."

I made my way into the living room and sat on the couch. There was more evidence of the family's bizarre decoration style here. A framed print of dogs playing poker. Mismatched furniture and drapes. Various souvenir ashtrays and other knickknacks.

On a table next to me stood a picture frame with a bunch of slots. I leaned over to get a better look. There was a bald, unpleasant-looking man, who must have been Sage's father. And a woman who must have been her mother because she looked exactly like Tammi. Just as short, too. And there was Tammi in elementary school. And there . . .

A large hand shot out and slammed the frame down on the table so hard I heard glass crack. I looked up to see Sage towering over me, a look of fury on her face.

"What the hell are you doing snooping in here?" she bellowed.

I was dumbfounded. All I'd done was look at a picture that was out where anyone could see it. "I was just looking . . ."

For a moment, I thought Sage was going to punch me. Then she calmed down. "Just get out, Logan. My parents will kill me if they find you here."

I stood to face Sage, but still had to look up. "Find me here doing what? Sitting on the couch talking? Drinking hot chocolate? Helping you with your car trouble? Why is that such a big damn deal, Sage?"

"You wouldn't understand!" She didn't say it like a spoiled thirteen-year-old. There was a catch in her voice, something that told me her personal problems were greater than I'd imagined.

"Try me!" I was almost begging.

Sage didn't answer. She just extended her finger toward the door. I had been dismissed. She needed me when she was in trouble, but God forbid she talk to me. God forbid she let me help her.

I stomped toward the garage door to collect my cables and battery. I fought back an urge to turn the truck's lights back on and drain the battery again.

"Logan?" I heard Sage call softly. I turned.

She was sitting on the couch, her head hung over her lap. Her body was shaking lightly. I realized she was crying.

"Sage?" I returned to the living room and sat down next to her. She didn't stop me.

Little wet drops appeared on the legs of her jeans. A sick, sick feeling grew in my gut. My friend was miserable, but she wouldn't tell me why. Why did girls have such a hard time telling me the truth? First Brenda, not wanting to admit she'd stopped loving me. Now Sage, with whatever secret was torturing her.

"Hey, Sage, c'mon." Gently, I touched her cheek.

She lifted her face toward me. Tears streamed down her nose, and her eyes were red.

"Logan, I'm scared."

"Why are you scared, Sage?"

She didn't answer, just continued to look at me. At a loss, I tried to wipe the tears from her cheeks. Soon, I was holding her face in my hands.

She didn't move away when I leaned closer. She didn't stop me when I put my face level with hers. She didn't resist when our lips met.

For ten wonderful seconds, we kissed. The world vanished. Sage's father could barge in at any second, and it wouldn't matter. All I knew was that the attraction wasn't one-sided. Sage was kissing back. Hard. I had to brace up my back to stay completely vertical. I felt her mouth open, then immediately clamp shut. Then again. Then it stayed open.

I was aware that Sage was holding my left hand with

her right, our fingers interlaced. And still we kissed. When Sage decided to let down her barriers, she didn't hold back! Although, a nagging voice in the back of my mind reminded me that she still hadn't told me what was bothering her, still hadn't let me into her brain.

And suddenly, Sage pulled away. When I opened my eyes, I found her staring at me with a look of abject fright on her face.

"We shouldn't have done that," she gasped.

"Why not?" I asked with a sinking feeling. It doesn't bode well when a girl regrets kissing you *during* the kiss.

"Logan, we can't do that again. Ever. You need to leave now." The fear in her voice was intense. There was something I wasn't getting. Something she hadn't told me.

"Is this about your parents, Sage? Because they'll never find out."

Sage just shook her head, her eyes growing wider.

"Then . . . do you not like me? Just tell me, if that's it."

She shook her head again. "I've liked you since that first day in biology, Logan."

I was delighted and terrified. What was this mysterious *thing* she was dancing around?

"Then talk to me, Sage. I deserve to know."

She shook her head, then stopped. Almost imperceptibly, she nodded.

"Logan," she croaked, real fear in her voice. "The reason I can't date . . . the reason we can't kiss . . . the reason why I was homeschooled . . ."

I suddenly didn't want to know. Somehow, I realized

that I was going to regret asking her to reveal this much. But I couldn't stop.

"Yes, Sage?"

"I . . ." She swallowed, took a deep breath, and closed her eyes. "I'm a boy."

## chapter eleven

I WASN'T SURE how long I'd been running, or how far. Seven or eight miles, probably. I didn't remember going to the track. I just knew I was there, running at a dead sprint in my jeans and sneakers.

*Sage is a guy. A boy. A MAN!*

I had never been so disgusted. How could I not have known?

Her large hands. Her height. Christ, her husky voice.

And I'd fallen for it. Jesus, I'd fallen for it completely. I'd kissed a boy. French-kissed a boy! That made me a fag, didn't it?

For a month, I'd fantasized about Sage. Her cute face, her muscular, athletic body. Now my mental image of her naked body filled me with horror. Big, hairy balls. An eight-inch cock. Flat, hairy chest and hairy back. And I had kissed her.

No, not her. *Him.*

In spite of the cold, sweat had soaked through my shirt. I was dimly aware of a splitting pain in my side and blisters forming on my feet. Still I ran.

When Sage had told me, I froze. Just for a second. And then I pulled back my fist to punch her. I was going to break her . . . *his* nose.

Sage didn't move. Didn't duck. It was like she knew the punch was coming. Expected it.

I don't know why I didn't hit her. I don't know why I didn't put that sicko in the hospital. Sage certainly had it coming.

No wonder she had been homeschooled. No wonder she wasn't allowed to date but her sister was.

My breath was coming in painful gasps. A pair of middle-aged joggers tried to flag me down every time I passed them. I was oblivious. I ran faster.

And here I had thought maybe Sage didn't like me. She liked me, all right! Just as I'm getting over Brenda, just when I think about dating again, the first girl who likes me is a guy! I never thought anything could hurt me as badly as what Brenda had done. But Sage made Brenda look like an amateur.

Then a thought blindsided me. An idea worse than Sage's confession. Worse than the knowledge I'd made out with a boy.

I'd believed Sage was a girl. *But does everyone else?*

Now that I knew, Sage's true sex was fairly obvious. Did anyone else guess? What if Jack or Tim figured it out? What if they thought I already knew?

The pain in my side turned to agony, and I went sprawling. On my hands and knees, I vomited all over the rubberized surface of the track.

"Logan?"

When you live in a trailer, you can't sneak in. Mom was sitting on the couch in her waitress uniform watching a soap opera. I pretended I didn't hear.

"Logan, are you okay?"

I kept walking. Just a few more steps to the bathroom.

"Logan! Answer me!"

She was my mother, and there was no ignoring her.

"I'm fine, Mom. I just went running and pushed myself too hard."

Mom stood and looked at me with a mixture of concern and suspicion.

"Mrs. McGarvy called. She said you were acting funny at the track, and then you threw up. She said you were crying."

*Was I?*

"Mom, I just ran a little too fast and a little too far. I hit the wall."

Mom clearly didn't believe me. I knew my limits, and I never went running in street clothes. She didn't push the issue, though.

"A young lady stopped by when you were gone."

My mom must have heard my horrified gasp. No. Not Sage. What had she said to my mother?

Mom continued. "She said her name was Tammi."

I commenced breathing. "I gave her . . . sister a jump this morning."

"Well, she looked upset. She said you really need to call her sister. Said it's urgent."

I grunted and headed for the bathroom.

"Logan, what happened?"

She was talking to the door.

The scalding water of the shower brought me somewhat back to reality. I had to stop acting like this. People would wonder what was going on. Start asking questions . . .

I scrubbed myself raw. Too bad I didn't have some lye or some ammonia to burn Sage's touch away.

She'd ruined my life. For the rest of the school year . . . hell, for the rest of my goddamned life, I'd be worried someone would find her out. And then everyone would know that I liked a guy. It didn't matter that we'd never really dated. Just the flirting in biology would be enough to paint me pink for the next twenty years.

There was only one option. Sage—no, the entire world—would have to know she was dead to me. That I felt nothing but hatred for her . . . him . . . her. Even after her little revelation, I still could not think of Sage with masculine pronouns.

I'd call Sage, all right. Tell her I never wanted to see her again. Not even at school.

Tell her if she ever told the world what she really was, or if anyone ever found out, then I'd hurt her. I would.

\*  \*  \*

That evening I sat alone in the abandoned Arborville Road Cemetery. I had called Sage and told her to meet me there. It was the most isolated place I could think of.

She showed up just as the sun was going down. For once, she wasn't dressed outrageously. Just plain jeans and a gray sweater. I guess she realized that it was the wrong time for fancy dresses and gaudy jewelry. I tried to picture her as a boy, picture her as a man. Couldn't do it. Even with the height, the voice, the shoulders . . . she was still Sage.

A beautiful, zany, sensitive girl who liked me. Truly liked me. Who'd be going off to college with me. The girl who was going to help me move on with my life. The girl who just happened to not mention that she had a dick growing between her legs. Did she think that wouldn't matter to me? Did Sage honestly expect me not to care?

"Logan . . ." Her husky voice was cracked and hoarse.

In response, I threw something at her feet. It was the MU blanket she'd given me for Christmas.

Sage sat on a log and stared at it for a long time before picking it up and folding it carefully. Then she spoke without looking at me.

"Logan, I'm not going to apologize, because I know it wouldn't matter. And I'm not going to try to explain, because I know you don't care. But I have to ask you something."

I didn't respond. She went on.

"Are you going to tell anyone my secret?"

The idea that I'd actually tell anyone that the girl I liked had a penis struck me as perverse. I laughed.

"Be serious, Logan! You may think I'm sick. Fine. But you used to treat me like a friend. So I'm asking you . . . please don't tell. I'll drop out of bio so you won't have to see me there. But if anyone here knew that I'm not a full woman . . . I'd have to quit school. My family would have to leave town. Think of Tammi. Please, please, keep this between us."

I kicked a tombstone. "Sage, do you think I want my friends to know I kissed an ass pirate like you? Just stay the hell away from me. I don't ever want to see you again, faggot."

Sage stood. For a moment, she looked at me. The afternoon sun caught the moisture in her eyes. Then she gained control. She tossed the blanket onto the snowy ground and quickly left the cemetery. I stood there alone as it started to get dark.

Grabbing a handful of snow, I molded it into a ball and hurled it at a tree. It hit with a satisfying *splat*, leaving a white star on the trunk. I pictured Sage's head splattering against the tree, her brains spewing everywhere.

The thought gave me no pleasure. I'd spent nearly two months thinking warm and fuzzy thoughts about Sage. If I was going to hate her, it would take some work.

I threw another snowball, nailing the tree inches from my first hit. Sage had said she liked me. If that was true (and I was very close to not believing anything any girl ever told me), then she should have left me alone. But hugging me and fixing me food and making me a present—she had to realize what that was doing to me.

Maybe she assumed I'd never find out. Or that I'd somehow understand. But I didn't understand. I'd never be able to erase the memory of kissing a guy.

I looked down at the crumpled, wet blanket in the snow. I started to pick it up, then stopped. I ground the black-and-yellow fabric into the mud with my foot.

*I wish I'd never met you, Sage.*

## *chapter twelve*

I HADN'T BEEN so scared to go to school since my first day of junior high. I thought about pretending to be sick, but I needed to be there. What if Sage decided she wanted to cause trouble? I had almost hit her, after all. What if she wanted revenge? She could tell any sort of lie about me, knowing I'd never be able to admit the truth.

Sleep hadn't come that night. I kept having nightmare visions: Sage's shirt accidentally being pulled off (hey, it could happen). Someone in the office realizing her birth certificate said *male*. A thousand scenarios that ended with Sage's secret exposed and me branded as a homosexual. If word of her true gender got out, it wouldn't matter that I didn't know. No one would believe it. They'd think I knew Sage was a guy and didn't mind. Or liked it! Shame never dies in a small town. Everyone would think I was gay. Jack, Tim, Brenda, even my mom.

I was relieved to see Sage wasn't in biology that morning. Maybe she'd changed classes like she'd said. Tim had already eaten himself into a food coma, so I was free to internally panic as Mr. Elmer discussed the boring botany unit we were starting.

I didn't see Sage at all that day; she must have skipped school. Tammi wasn't around, either. She was probably home consoling her "sister." Maybe this incident could work to my advantage. Sage would come to her senses and realize how stupid she'd been for trying to attend school as a girl. She could go back to being homeschooled, and I'd never have to see her again.

My entire future rested on what happened in the next few months. If Sage didn't get found out until we were both out of high school, then I was safe. Provided I never talked to her again, so no one would remember how we used to hang out. I promised myself I would just play it cool. Be smooth. Not let on that I was more scared than I'd ever been in my entire life.

I didn't blow it until the end of the school day.

Jack and I sat in the commons after the final bell. Mr. Bloch, the principal, was casting a wary eye on us from his office, so Jack wasn't attacking the soda machine. I'm not sure if Mr. Bloch knew of Jack's vandalism, but at six feet two inches, and three-hundred-plus pounds, the principal was not a man you deliberately antagonized. Rumor had it that the only meth dealer ever to find his way onto the Boyer campus left in an ambulance.

Jack was making an elaborate paper airplane out of the school newsletter.

"Hey, Jack?"

"Yeah?"

I wasn't sure I wanted to ask this, but I had to know.

"Did you, um, ever notice anything kind of . . . *strange* about Sage?" If Jack had even the slightest inkling that Sage was a boy, I was completely fucked.

Jack threw the airplane. It did an impressive loop-the-loop and bounced off the glass-fronted office. Mr. Bloch glowered but apparently had other things to do than throttle Jack.

"Strange? Hell, yes!"

I tasted bile. "What do you mean?"

"She likes you, Logan. That's pretty weird."

My stomach unknotted. "Yeah."

Jack retrieved his aircraft. "So what's up with you guys?"

"Nothing," I said bluntly.

"You sure?" asked Jack, missing the warning in my voice. "I mean, I know she wouldn't let you feel her up in public, but I thought you might be friends with privileges or something."

"Shut up, Jack!"

He prepared for another launch. "Don't try to tell me you're not hot for her. Nothing wrong with that. She's got that jungle woman thing going on. Maybe she'll drag you by your hair—"

I grabbed Jack roughly by the arm, causing him to drop his airplane. *"I said shut up!"*

My friend looked stunned for a moment. Then his eyes narrowed and, for one of the few times since I'd met him, I saw a look of true anger on his face.

"Get your hands off me."

I realized I was crushing his toothpick arm in my hand. I let go. Across the commons, Mr. Bloch was trying to decide if he needed to intervene.

Jack stared me down. "Logan, I don't know what the hell is going on with you. But I am not your personal punching bag. Understand?"

I looked at my shoes. Two months ago, when Jack had told me Brenda was cheating on me and I'd hit him, he had let it pass. I had never apologized, and he had never brought it up. He knew I was hurting. But you could only push your friends so far.

"Jack, I . . ."

He was already gone.

The weight bench had been a gift for my fifteenth birthday. Mom had gotten it at Goodwill or a garage sale or something. I'd set it up in our old shed, and I got quite a bit of use out of it.

I'd been staring up at the metal bar for almost two hours, since I got home from school. I hadn't even stopped at the trailer. Mom had left for work a few minutes before, probably wondering where I was.

I lay there, counting the mud dauber nests on the ceiling, reflecting that my life was in the toilet. Jack and Tim thought Sage and I were dating. Before New Year's, I would have gladly fueled that rumor. Now what? If I acted like I was mad at Sage, people would think we were having a lovers' quarrel. And if I acted like nothing was wrong, they'd still think we were a couple.

*And all this is Brenda's fault!* If she had just broken up with me before she cheated, maybe I would have gotten over her more quickly. And asked Tanya out when she still liked me. Or maybe Brenda and I could have worked things out if she'd tried to talk to me. And we'd still be together.

But no. She had cheated on me at exactly the right time for me to fall for Sage. To fall for a boy. I'd spent over a month trying to get another guy to go out with me.

I could make all the excuses in the world. I could tell myself Sage had lied to me, that anyone would have been fooled, and it didn't count.

*But when it comes down to it, you kissed a man. And really enjoyed it. And that makes you . . .*

"I'm not gay!"

*Maybe not, Logan. But you liked kissing Sage. You wanted to do more.*

"I didn't know she was a guy!"

*So? You thought Sage would be your girlfriend if you were patient enough. You could have gone out with a real girl, but you were holding out for Sage. You were going to take him to prom.*

I leapt to my feet. "She tricked me!"

*You wanted to screw him. Don't deny it.*

"I DIDN'T KNOW! IT DOESN'T COUNT!"

*Logan's a queer! Logan's a fag!*

"I didn't know!" Suddenly, to my horror, I realized this dialogue wasn't going on in my head. I'd been screaming out loud. Terrified, I looked out the door of the shed. Our yard and the road in front of it were deserted.

I returned to my weight bench and began hefting the barbell.

*I thought Brenda was the one. But she wasn't.*

Sweat rolled down my face, into my ears.

*I thought Sage would help me forget her. But she was a liar, too.*

A lone June bug, still alive in spite of the frost, buzzed around the roof.

*All I ever wanted was for a girl to like me. I got so excited when Brenda liked me, I never noticed she was having second thoughts. And I was so into Sage, I just assumed things would work out. That I could help her with whatever was bothering her.*

The barbell clanked against the brace as I lowered it too far.

*What is that expression? Fool's paradise. When I was happy, I just thought everything was going okay. But things weren't okay. How can I ever ask a girl out again? Sage's betrayal tops Brenda's. Christ only knows what the next girl I date might do.*

I let the weight fall back into the rack.

*It's never going to work out for me. I came so close, but close only counts with horseshoes and hand grenades.*

*chapter thirteen*

THAT WEEK, it warmed up and most of the snow melted. That was a good thing; I was not in the mood to shovel driveways. In fact, I wasn't in the mood to do much of anything. After school, I'd go home and lock myself in my room and listen to music, or go to the shed and lift weights. I went three days without seeing Mom. Jack called me a couple of times, but I pretended like I wasn't home.

Sage came back to school the next Monday. Not to bio, thank God. I saw her in the hall between classes. For a moment, I mistook her for Tammi. She seemed like she had shrunk. Maybe it was because she was hunched down. Or walking slowly, less sure of herself than before. When she noticed me, she immediately hurried away.

I grinned as I opened my locker. Sage was afraid of me. Scared. Timid. She'd think twice before treating a guy like that again. If she knew what was good for her, she'd keep to herself from now on. Not be so friendly, so joking. No longer be herself.

I paused. *No longer be Sage.* Was that really a good thing? Did I really want her to become something else because of me?

I slammed the locker. Whatever she was going through, she'd brought it on herself. I was the one who'd been wronged. It was all her fault.

That Sunday, Jack stopped by the trailer to remind me that we were playing touch football that afternoon. I told him I didn't feel good, but he refused to take no for an answer. Eventually, I let him drive me out to the game.

Once or twice a month, about a dozen of us would gather in the dirt lot that might or might not have been part of Veterans Park. We called it touch football because sometimes a junior higher or a girl would join us. However, every game eventually descended into all of us pounding on each other in the mud.

We'd stand in a huddle as Jack barked off plays more elaborate than the Normandy invasion. Then we'd run out on the field and plow into the other team until someone crashed into the bike rack that marked the end zone.

I normally loved these games. I'd convinced myself that playing in these pickup matches meant that it didn't matter that I couldn't make the real team. Today, I was just bored. What was the point of all this? I wanted to go back home and be alone.

I glumly took my place opposite a big blond nineteen-year-old named Chad. Jack's brother threw a pass to Tim. Tim wasn't expecting that (normally, all he did was block).

He stared at the ball for a second before being dog piled by the other team. First down.

It happened when we were about to score the first touchdown. Chad tried to tackle one of our guys, and I blocked him a little roughly. His nose banked off my forehead.

"Ouch!" he yelped, clutching his bleeding nose.

"Sorry." I was already wandering back to my position.

Chad had pulled a wad of tissue from his jeans pocket. "Just watch it, faggot."

He probably hadn't meant anything by it. When you're a teenage guy, you pepper your conversations with *faggot*, *butt munch*, and *douche bag*. In the strange world of male bonding, questioning someone's sexuality and hygiene was a way to demonstrate friendship and camaraderie. Unfortunately for Chad, I was overly sensitive about my sexual identity that day.

"What did you call me?" I bellowed. Chad, who was blowing his bloody nose, looked back at me with surprise.

"What did you call me?" I shouted again, enraged. Chad took a step backward.

The other players were staring at us. Chad, unsure of why I was screaming, blinked at me.

"I, um . . ."

I balled my hands into fists. "Don't you ever call me that, asshole!"

If Chad had apologized, I might have realized how much I was overreacting. But you don't show weakness. Not at a football game with your friends.

"What's the matter, pussy?" he taunted, unsure of how he'd been roped into this. "The truth hurt?"

I grabbed him by his nylon jacket so hard I heard fabric rip. "Take that back, you son of a bitch! I swear, I'll fuck you up."

Chad pulled away, and for a second we almost went at it. When Jack laid a hand on my shoulder, I nearly jumped him.

"Whoa, whoa there, guys," said Jack with a forced laugh. "Let's calm down. No harm, no foul." Chad started to back off.

"He's beggin' for it!" I yelled, pointing at Chad.

"You want some of this?" he countered. His eyes darted toward one of his teammates, who shrugged. He didn't know what the fight was about, either.

"Then let's do it!" I started to pull off my jacket when Jack put his hand on my shoulder again. This time it wasn't a friendly tap, but a restraining grab.

"Walk away, Logan." He was not smiling. Tim had quietly joined us and was standing at my other side.

"But . . ."

Jack suddenly sounded quite serious. *"Walk away."*

Jack didn't release my shoulder until we were almost to the parking lot. Then I twisted free. I turned to my friends. Tim looked at me with concern.

"Uh, Logan, what the hell was that about?"

"You heard what he called me! I ought to go back there. . . ."

Jack frowned. "Jesus Christ, Logan, so what? I've called you worse than that. He was just talking."

"So that's the way it is?" I hollered back. "You're taking his side?"

"No one said that. Would you calm down?"

"Fuck you. If you won't stand up for me . . ." I waved my arm vaguely and stomped off.

When I arrived home, I was ready to punch something. But everything in the trailer was too cheap to stand up to any abuse. By the time I got to the backyard to kick the hell out of the burn barrel, my anger had subsided. I now lay curled up on the couch.

So some guy called me a faggot and I went nuts. You didn't exactly have to be Freud to make sense of that. If I didn't get myself under control, and fast, Sage's secret would be the least of my problems. I had to remind myself that Sage made a very convincing girl, convincing enough to totally fool me. She was no taller than a lot of women, and that was really the only giveaway. How had she achieved that? How long had she been pretending to be female? Her parents must have allowed it, at least at home. Why on earth would a boy want to be a girl? I almost wished I was still talking to her so I could find out.

When someone knocked on the door, I knew who it had to be. Tim and Jack stood on the concrete slab that passed for our porch. They had looks of grim determination on their faces. Kind of like furniture repossessers: they had an unpleasant job to do, but they'd see it through nonetheless.

Jack was holding the football, twisting it in his hand. "Can we come in?"

That drove home how crazy things had gotten. They

hadn't asked permission to come into the trailer since elementary school.

"Yeah."

We all sat down, and for a minute, there was nothing but silence. Jack stood up and began pacing like a small dog on a short chain.

"So who won?" I asked after a bit.

"The game kind of ended when you left. Logan, what the hell were you trying to prove?"

I attempted to smile. "Lost my temper. Sorry."

Now, normally, that's all a guy needed to say. Men don't discuss their feelings. *Sorry* usually covered just about any mistake.

Jack and Tim didn't smile. Tim sat in the recliner looking solemn. Jack tossed the football into the air until it almost kerbonged the ceiling fan.

"Logan," he said, still looking up. "Your mom called me yesterday."

"Very funny." But no one was laughing.

"He's serious," said Tim. "She called me too."

My eyes widened. "Why would she call you?"

For the first time in years, Jack stood motionless. "She wanted to know if you were on drugs."

"What would she think that for? She knows I'm not into that shit."

Jack and Tim exchanged glances. "That's what we told her," said Tim. "But she said that for the past week you've been hiding in your room. Said you were acting all angry and wouldn't talk to her."

Jack spun the football on the coffee table. "We thought

you were just pissed off. But today at the game . . . Logan, you're not doing meth, are you?" He wasn't kidding. That was a serious question.

"No, I'm not on meth." I was too embarrassed to pretend to be indignant. "I guess I really went nuts back there."

Tim smiled, just a bit. "I wouldn't go back to the game next month if I were you. Listen, Logan. We know what's bothering you."

I had been getting up to get some sodas, but I froze. *They can't possibly know.*

"So she lied to you," said Tim. "You're not the only guy that's ever happened to."

I leaned against our entertainment center, trying to act like I wasn't bracing myself. The trailer suddenly looked unfamiliar, like this was all some sort of post-enchilada nightmare I was having. Jack and Tim wouldn't look at me. They knew Sage was a guy. They thought I was gay. Now I was going to have to run off and join the navy so I wouldn't have to spend the rest of my life living this down.

"Who told you?" I shrieked.

Tim suddenly looked uncomfortable. "Jack did. It's not exactly a secret at school."

I was about to cry. Everyone knew Sage was a boy. She must have told. Or they'd figured it out.

"Logan," said Jack in a tone like someone trying to communicate with a drunk. "She's not worth it! I hate to be the one to tell you this, but Brenda wasn't even all that pretty."

*They aren't talking about Sage. They think this is still about Brenda.*

I managed to smile, my first real smile in over a week. "Yeah. I know. Listen, thanks for being worried. But I'm not on drugs, and I promise I'll try to calm down. And, um, you know. Thanks."

After Jack and Tim made their escape, I propped my feet up on the table. Sage was gone, and my problems were more in my head than anywhere else. The solution was never to think of her again. In a few months, I'd leave Boyer forever, and she'd be less than a memory.

Mom was working the lunch shift. She arrived home at about six looking like she'd spent the past ten hours slopping pigs. In a way, she had; I'd eaten at Ron's before.

It took Mom a minute to compute that the dishes on the table weren't just a mess I'd left for her. For my first attempt at cooking dinner, it didn't turn out too badly: slightly burned burgers, undercooked vegetables, and rolls that didn't look nearly as fluffy as the picture on the can.

"What's all this?" asked my mother warily. She was torn between her joy that I'd cooked and her fear that I must have done something *really* bad.

I finished tossing the salad, hoping she wouldn't notice that I'd accidentally made it with cabbage rather than lettuce. "Dinner," I replied, and she left it at that.

We didn't talk much as we ate, though several times I caught Mom looking at me with a mixture of relief and curiosity. I hoped this made her realize that her drug fears were unfounded. Things were finally returning to normal.

*chapter fourteen*

JANUARY WAS a good month. I stopped hanging out in the shed and got back to work. I earned so much money shoveling snow and doing odd jobs that I was able to pay for the repairs when the trailer's furnace died. Mom hated to take the money, but . . . well, you know. I think the fact that I was working and showing responsibility again was what convinced her I didn't have a drug problem.

As for Sage, the only time I ever saw her was in the halls. I'd look away every time. She never made an effort to talk to me, either. I'd see Tammi, too. She'd usually sneer at me, but she never said anything.

I wanted to banish Sage to the corner of my mind reserved for those I hated, along with Hitler, Bin Laden, and whoever stole my weed eater last year. But I found myself remembering her at odd times, wondering what she was doing and what she was thinking about me. Whenever I caught myself, I'd mentally replay that scene in her living room. I had to remind myself of how she had betrayed and deceived me.

Still, I couldn't help but wonder why Sage wasn't honest about her . . . situation right from the start. She could have told me the truth when I asked her out the first time. Or after the movies, when I tried to kiss her. Or at the basketball courts. Or a thousand other times. Then we could have just been friends. I never would have made a move, had I known.

Then again, how do you tell a friend something like that? *Could you pass the salt, Logan? Oh, and by the way, I'm really a boy.* Shit, I would have run for the hills! I wouldn't have been able to think of anything else. I would have asked Mr. Elmer to move me to a different table in biology.

It was bad enough to know that when things had gotten rough and I'd found out Sage wasn't what I thought she was, I was so hateful to her. Jesus Christ, I'd almost punched her! I'd never imagined I was capable of that. It scared me.

I guess no one could blame me for my initial reaction— all things considered, I'd kept my cool. But later, at the cemetery, I'd called Sage some names . . . said some things that I shouldn't have. Looking back, it would have been better if I'd just kept my mouth shut and let her talk. Then, when she was done, I could have said, *Sage, under the circumstances, I don't think we should see each other anymore.* We wouldn't have parted as friends, but there wouldn't be all that hate. And I regretted throwing away the blanket she'd made me. That was a dick move, no matter how you looked at it.

Recently, I had begun contemplating whether I should talk to Sage again. I could take her to some isolated place and explain why I'd been so disgusted.

The only problem with that was I had no idea how to put any of my feelings into words. All I knew was that Sage brought out something in me I didn't like. A violent, paranoid man. Whatever she was trying to do with her life was none of my concern. We'd avoid each other from now on. It was better that way.

On the day after Valentine's Day, the skies opened and it poured. Missouri rain can be harsh, second only to (<u>your state's name</u>). Mom insisted I take her old station wagon to school; she had a friend drive her to work.

Using our English books as hats, Jack and I hurried to my car. The windshield instantly fogged up. Rather than wait five minutes for it to clear, I sailed my way off school grounds, peering blindly though a tiny patch just above the heater vents.

Through the flapping, erratic movement of the wipers, I spotted a pedestrian. A girl. Someone in a glaring yellow rain slicker. She carried a folded umbrella by her side and stared up at the clouds like a drowning turkey. There was something familiar about her; in fact, she kind of looked like . . .

"There's Sage," said Jack, wiping his window with his sleeve.

I made no comment and just kept driving.

"Aren't you going to give her a ride?" Jack realized Sage and I were no longer close, but he didn't think I was going to let her stand out there in the rain.

"No." I wasn't going to offer, and I doubted she would accept.

"It's pouring," he said as if I hadn't noticed.

"She won't drown."

"Lemme put it this way," said Jack. "Give her a ride."

There's a fine line between being hurt and being an asshole. Maybe by giving Sage a lift I could show that I'd calmed down. Even though she'd hurt me worse than Brenda had, I'd gain nothing by making her live in fear of me. Just one final, friendly gesture to the girl who'd baked me cookies. Sage would realize that so long as she kept her mouth shut about what she really was, I could let bygones be bygones.

I waited until we were about ten yards away, then braked so hard we almost spun out. Sage jogged to reach my car.

She looked uncertain as she opened the back door, though she did smile warmly at Jack. We drove in silence. Bitter, uncomfortable silence. All I could think about was her tear-streaked face on New Year's Day, her telling me the secret I wished I had never found out. And I'm sure Sage had her own nasty memories of me as well.

Jack began to squirm. I think he realized Sage and I were happier not seeing each other. He nervously crossed and uncrossed his legs.

"So, Sage . . . what's new?" he asked, breaking the silence.

"Nothing." She paused. "What's new with you?"

I think at that point, Jack was ready to throw himself from the moving car, but he still forced conversation.

"Well, my church is doing some major renovations. Painting the whole building."

"Since when do you go to church?" I asked. He ignored me.

"We didn't think we were going to have enough money, so we bought some cheap paint and watered it down. Didn't look the greatest, but it got the job done."

"What the hell are you talking about?" Jack never got up before three p.m. on Sundays.

"Well, we spent all last Saturday painting the outside. Unfortunately, right when we were finished, this rain started. Washed everything away."

"Oh no," said Sage, sounding genuinely concerned.

"The funny thing is, right when we were all running inside, I could swear I heard a voice from the clouds."

I sighed. "Saying what, Jack?"

*"Repaint! Repaint and thin no more!"* Jack waited for Sage to laugh. Then, without warning, he opened his door and leapt out onto the street. We were stopped at Boyer's only traffic light at the time, but knowing Jack, that might have been a coincidence.

Sage's home was still a mile away. I began to speed. If we were alone in the car too much longer, one of us would have to say something.

"Pull over, Logan," said Sage after a minute. "I can walk from here."

"It's pouring, Sage. I'll take you home."

"Don't do me any favors." She spoke like she was dying of thirst and I'd offered to let her lick the outside of my water glass when I was done.

In the rearview mirror, Sage was looking at me with contempt. I pointed the mirror to the ceiling. A little too roughly, actually. Luckily, there's a special kind of glue for that sort of thing. Five minutes later, we turned onto Sage's street.

The Christmas ornaments were gone from her house. All that was left was a fir tree painted silver and some rain-sodden tinsel.

She opened her door and grabbed her umbrella.

"Sage, wait." I don't know what made me stop her. Maybe I realized it would probably be the one time we'd ever be alone together. If either of us had anything to say, it was now or never.

She paused, one foot out in the rain.

"What?"

*What? What do I have to say to her?*

"Sage . . ."

"What?"

*What?*

I turned in my seat. She glared at me. Whatever she had once felt for me was gone. Maybe I didn't like that. With all the hatred I'd felt for her in the past month, it never occurred to me the feeling might be mutual.

"Sage. I'm sorry." My words fell flat, like when the teacher forces you to apologize to the kid you hit.

She shrugged. "You've got nothing to be sorry for," she responded bluntly, swinging her legs out the door.

"Maybe . . . ," I began.

"Maybe what?"

I took a deep breath. "Maybe if you explained things, I'd understand."

She stood in the rain and slammed the door. Great. I try to make peace, try to make some damn sense out of whatever the hell Sage was doing, and she runs off.

But a second later, she was sitting next to me in the front seat. She had to push it back to fit her long legs.

"Do you really want to know, Logan?"

For the first time in a month, I looked Sage in the face. I desperately searched for something masculine. But there was no beard stubble, no unibrow, nothing but Sage. Just as pretty as she'd been when we met.

A drop of rain dangled off the end of her nose. Her wet locks lay plastered all over her face. Two months ago, I would have reached up and smoothed her hair. Touched her cheek. Tried to see cleavage through her wet shirt.

"I really want to know." That was a lie. I certainly didn't want details about how she shaved her shoulders and padded her bra. But then again, maybe that was why Sage hadn't told me in the first place.

Sage brushed the hair from her forehead. "What?"

I had questions. Questions I wasn't sure I wanted answered.

"Is your name really Sage?"

"Yes."

*Okay. At least it's not Steve.*

"Why . . . why are you pretending to be a girl?"

Sage snorted. "I fooled you, didn't I?"

I revved the engine. "Goodbye."

"Wait." She touched my arm, then immediately pulled away. "I guess this is all new to you."

It was my turn to snort.

"Logan, I've never thought of myself as a boy. Not since I knew the difference. I *am* a girl. It's some sick damn joke of nature that I wasn't born with a female body. And you're not going to see anything there, so stop staring."

I realized I'd been looking at her crotch.

"Sorry."

"I don't expect you to understand. You don't owe me anything." She was bitter.

"You weren't ever going to tell me, were you? Just drag me along, laugh at how you fooled some guy?" Picking up Sage had been a mistake. We were both getting angry and defensive.

Sage turned to me, and I was suddenly very aware that I was not the most powerful person in the car.

"Logan, you think that's all it was to me? You think I didn't feel guilty?"

I leaned against the driver's door. "No . . ." I cleared my throat. "No. You lied to me."

"Well, I felt like shit for doing that. I wanted to tell you. Remember when I dragged you out to the cemetery? I was going to tell you then, but I couldn't."

"Why the hell not?"

Sage seemed to shrink. "I thought you might beat me up. And I wasn't being paranoid, was I?"

I recalled, how for the only time in my life, I almost hit a girl. Or almost a girl. I couldn't excuse that. I should have just stormed out. The second I balled up my fist, I became the bad guy.

"You didn't hit me, Logan. And, in my defense, I could have let you kiss me a lot earlier. I wanted to."

"Why did you have to kiss me at all?" I felt like I was grasping for reasons to be pissed. I had to remind myself of Sage's huge lie.

"You're not the easiest guy for a girl *not* to kiss." Sage abruptly turned away, and we sat for a moment. My earlier feelings for Sage were apparently not one-sided.

Sage spoke again. "Logan, I would have liked to be friends. I guess that can't happen. But thanks for keeping your cool, and thanks for not telling anyone. I wish I could take back that kiss, but honestly, I'm not sorry." She turned back and stuck out her jaw defiantly.

"Sage . . ." This was the end. Our friendship was over, but I was glad it was ending here, now, calmly.

"Logan . . ." Sage looked like she had more to say, but she didn't say it.

We looked at each other for a long moment. This was the last time we'd ever talk.

Sage opened the door. The rain had let up. I pulled out as soon as she entered her house.

Brenda's home was exactly the way I remembered it. Two stories, three-car garage, no abandoned appliances in the yard. Aside from Brenda's Saturn, I counted three other vehicles in the driveway, but I didn't think they were having company. A neat row of rosebushes, covered with protective plastic for the winter, lined the side of the house. Their inground pool, the only one in Boyer, was empty.

I never really understood what Brenda's father did for a living, but he earned a lot. At this home, a trailer was what you used to pull your boat, not something you lived in. It was funny, but her parents had always treated me nicely. This was one of the few places where I hadn't felt like a poor boy.

The rain had stopped, and I'd been standing in the street for ten minutes trying to swallow my pride and go up and knock. It shouldn't have been hard; I'd banged on that door every weekend for three years. Eventually, I ran up and pushed the doorbell, fighting an urge to run off giggling.

"Logan!"

I'd forgotten what it was like to be this close to her, to look her right in the face. That long black ponytail. The high cheekbones, the pale skin. Those filthy glasses.

"Hey, Brenda."

Her surprise turned to worry (or suspicion). "Would you like to come in?"

"Uh, no. I was just passing by. Feel like a quick walk?"

Brenda grabbed her jacket, and we took off down the road. Neither of us spoke. For years, I'd spent every free moment with this girl, and now I couldn't think of a thing to say. I think the last thing I had told her was that she was a whore, so it was hard to start a conversation.

She ended the silence. "How are Jack and Tim doing?"

"They're fine. Jack and I are going to Mizzou in the fall. And Tim's got a girlfriend."

"So the rumors are true." At Boyer High, it was hard to lose track of anyone, even after breaking up with their friend.

I stopped suddenly. We were in front of a large stump at the end of Brenda's street. It was the spot where we'd first kissed, back when we were freshmen. God, I'd felt so awkward. But she had giggled and hugged me and told me I was the cutest guy she knew.

I placed a foot on the stump and stared off into a fallow field. "Brenda, why did you leave me?" I said the words quickly, like diving into a cold pool. I would have lost my nerve if I'd waited.

"Logan . . ." Brenda's tone was almost whiny. Maybe she was afraid I wanted to fight some more. Or wanted another chance.

"I'm not trying to rehash this, and I don't want to get back together. But you owe me this. Why?"

She didn't say anything for a bit. "I guess you wouldn't believe it if I said I didn't mean to cheat on you."

I gazed off into the distance.

"Logan, look at me."

I considered disobeying, but only briefly. She stared at me with the same sad intensity as she had on that awful day in October. The same look that had made me realize even before she said a word that Jack hadn't been lying.

"Does it really matter at this point?"

"Yes. I need . . . what's the word?"

"Closure?"

I nodded. After dropping Sage off, I'd found myself driving out here. I wanted to finish things with Brenda, to try to finally close up the wound she'd left. And I had to know where we'd gone wrong before I could do that.

"Okay, but this was your idea." She took off her glasses and polished them on her shirttail, leaving them even more smudged than before. "I cheated on you because I was weak. But, Logan, I would have hurt you more if I'd stayed."

I almost convinced myself I'd misheard her. "Brenda, what—"

"Let me finish. When we started going out, you'd always go on and on about how smart I was. And how pretty I was. And how wonderful it was to be with me."

"Excuse the hell out of me." Jesus Christ, did every woman make no sense?

"It was wonderful for me, too. For a while. But I kind of just thought of you as my high school boyfriend. I figured you saw me the same way. We'd date for a while, then get on with our lives."

Recalling my reaction to Sage's revelation, I forced myself to count to ten before saying anything. "I *did not* see you like that, Brenda. Remember when we said we loved each other? I'm not sure what you were talking about, but I meant it."

She smiled a frosty smile. "Logan, I tried to tell you I was having second thoughts, but you'd just gloss things over, act like nothing could ever end our eternal romance." Her tone took on a slight sarcastic edge that I did not care for. "Remember when we went mini-golfing on Labor Day? You kept talking about the fun we were going to have at Mizzou. How could I tell you I wanted to go to Washington U instead?"

Wash U is a private college in St. Louis. Even with student loans, it was well out of my price range.

Brenda continued. "I think that was the day I decided I didn't really love you."

"Labor Day?"

She nodded.

"My *birthday*?"

She winced, then nodded again, not breaking eye contact.

"Then why didn't you just dump me? Why didn't you tell me I was being a romantic fool?"

"I didn't want to hurt you."

I actually laughed. "You didn't want to *hurt* me?" A little slobber ran down my chin.

Brenda turned away. Her body went rigid for a moment. She took a deep breath and turned back to me.

"Or maybe I didn't want to hurt *me*. I knew if I tried to break up with you, you'd convince me to stay. I wasn't strong enough to tell you that your feelings and my feelings weren't the same. They were close, but close isn't always good enough."

"You certainly came up with an interesting way of telling me."

Brenda opened her mouth with an angry look on her face, then stopped. "I didn't mean for it to happen. I swear I didn't. But Blake offered to give me a ride, and one thing led to another—"

"You know what?" I interrupted. "I'm sorry I wasted your time."

I used to think Brenda might be my wife someday. I never thought we'd end up being strangers to each other. It hurt more than I wanted to admit.

Brenda was standing there staring at the stump. When she finally looked up, there was a defeated look in her eyes. As much as I didn't want to acknowledge it, she was hurting, too.

This was one of those Hollywood movie moments where the hero says something profound before walking off into the sunset. Of course, my attempt at cinematic greatness was anything but profound.

"Blake?" I asked, my voice tinged with sarcasm.

"Huh?"

"You dumped me for a guy named *Blake*?"

Brenda looked confused. I continued.

"I mean, I could understand you leaving me for a Doug, or a Johnny, or even a Brian, but *Blake*?"

Brenda glared at me through the distinct thumbprint on her right lens. "He's a nice guy."

"I'm sure he is." I turned on my best Homer Simpson mocking voice. "Ooh, my name's Blake! Would you like to have some tea and go to the opera?"

"Logan, shut up."

"My name's Blake! I enjoy romantic movies and walks on the beach!"

"Stop it!"

I began to skip about. "I'm Blake! I like ponies and Cinderella and rainbows!"

Brenda suddenly shoved me in the chest with both hands, and I went sprawling. I hadn't been expecting that, and I stared up at her in shock as muddy water trickled into my underwear. Brenda looked so angry I thought she was going to kick me in the face.

But five seconds later, we were both laughing, hard and loud, just like we used to. As Brenda helped me up, I smiled like a total goofball. For the first time since the summer, I wasn't mad at her.

"Logan . . . ," began Brenda.

I couldn't bear to talk more about what had gone wrong between us, so I decided to make a quick exit.

"I'm going to head out now." I put my hand on her shoulder and gently squeezed. "Be happy, okay? And I hope you find what you're looking for." I walked off toward my car, still giggling. *Blake?*

As I spread newspaper on the front seat to avoid leaving a muddy butt print, I thought back to what my ex-girlfriend had said. She'd lied to me about so many things. Nurturing my hate wouldn't do anyone any good.

When I started the car, I thought about Sage. She hadn't lied to me about our relationship. She had flat-out told me she couldn't date me and that we could only be friends. In fact, she had only ever lied to me about one thing. Granted, it was a pretty important thing.

Did I really want Sage out of my life? Maybe. At least that way I wouldn't have to face what had happened between us.

## chapter fifteen

SINCE I WAS no longer stalking Brenda or hanging out with Sage in the mornings, I actually began to arrive at biology before Tim. When he entered the lab the Monday after I'd tried to exorcise the demons from my past, I noticed something different about him.

For starters, he wasn't hauling around his usual convenience store's worth of candy, chips, and other junk food. Just a sixteen-ounce soda and a small can of Pringles. Was he fasting? But there was something else.

"Tim? Do you have a job interview today or something?"

For years, Tim's wardrobe had consisted of a highly distressed pair of jeans and a baggy sweatshirt, even in the summer. But today he was wearing khaki pants, a T-shirt that wasn't a size too small, and a stylish-looking sweater vest. He'd even traded his sneakers for some loafers.

Tim flipped through his bio book. "Dawn's picking me

up after school today. Thought I'd dress up." His olive cheeks flushed red.

I fought the urge to tease him. If Dawn could convince Tim to watch what he ate and not to be a slob, then more power to her.

"That reminds me," continued Tim, trying to change the topic, "my eighteenth birthday is this weekend."

"Oh yeah! What's the plan? Buy some cigarettes, lotto tickets, and a rifle?"

"Vote and register for the draft," countered Tim. "Actually, Dawn wanted us all to go out and see this comedian in Columbia on Saturday. It'll be fun."

"Yeah, okay." That sounded like something college kids would do. It would be good training. "Jack can drive me."

"Jack's still grounded."

"Oh yeah." I'd tried to warn him that constructing a potato cannon was not the greatest idea, but he and his brother were determined. Luckily, no one had been injured in the explosion, though Matt had nearly become another spud-related statistic.

"I think Mom has to work Saturday night. Can I ride with you and Dawn?"

Tim, for once, wasn't seething with self-assurance. Something was bothering him. Finally, he spit it out.

"Logan, do you think you could, you know . . . bring a date?"

"Huh?"

Mr. Elmer was sifting through his notes. Class was about to begin.

"Listen," said Tim rapidly. "We can drive you to

Columbia, no sweat. But . . . Dawn said she wanted to . . . I mean, after the show . . . wanted to go somewhere and be alone." Tim had turned completely away from me and had nearly buried his face in his hands.

"Oh, uh, yeah. I'll find someone. Someone with a car."

Tim shot me a thankful smile as the first bell rang. I, on the other hand, felt uncomfortable. After Brenda and Sage, my next date would probably turn out to be an ax murderer. Oh well, as long as she could drive.

I stared at our rotary dial phone, trying to will myself to pick it up. Mom was gone. For the first time in over a year, she was spending one of her nights off out drinking with some friends. She'd been apologetic when she brought it up. I almost had to push her out the door.

Arranging a date for Tim's birthday had proved harder than I'd expected. Tanya was off the market. Brenda was dating Blake the Flake. The few dozen girls I knew well enough to ask out either were dating someone, didn't like me, or were girls I didn't especially want to go out with. It was starting to look like I'd have to either not go or try to bum a ride home from someone.

I tapped on the phone. Of course, there *was* one person who liked me. Sage would probably like to see the comedian. And she had access to a car. We could go to the club and wouldn't really have to talk to each other.

And afterward we could put tinfoil in the microwave and clean some loaded guns. What in the world was I thinking? After the pure hell Sage had put me through, why would I want to see her again? We'd both apologized, and though we weren't pals again, the hate was gone. That was the best we could hope for. If I asked her to join us, she might think I wanted to be friends again. I didn't want that.

I smacked the phone so hard the bell dinged. *I don't want that!* Because Sage would still be nice, still be funny, and still be—pretty. And still be a boy. I could forgive myself for my earlier attraction. But now if I looked at Sage and thought she was cute, even for a moment, then I'd have no excuse.

I thought it would be so easy not to think about Sage. Denial is powerful. With practice, I could just pretend that I'd never kissed a boy, never almost hit a girl, and never been so gaga over Sage. While I was at it, I could pretend I was rich and a football hero. Maybe that's what my father had done. Convinced himself that his kids were better off without him. Being a dad is hard, so why try? Being friends with Sage was hard, so why bother?

I got up to pace, but there wasn't room. Maybe Sage deserved more than this. Maybe I deserved more. If Sage and I could just go out and see a show together, then maybe there was no reason to end our friendship. We'd be going to college together, after all. Now that I'd never try to kiss her again, we could hang out every now and then. And if things were too awkward at Tim's party, then I could honestly say I had tried.

This was all just an elaborate way of saying I missed Sage and wanted to see her again.

I felt the same knotted tension in my gut that hit me

before every track meet. She probably would just hang up on me, anyway. I dialed her number, almost hung up, then involuntarily smiled when she answered.

"Hi, Sage."

"Logan!" I could hear her gasp on the other end. Then there was a pause. I heard her walking, then heard a door slam.

"You still there?" she asked.

"Yeah. Um, how are you?" I asked in a monotone.

"I-am-fine," she mocked in a robotic voice. I smiled, remembering the many times she'd made me laugh.

"Hey, listen. Tim is turning eighteen tomorrow. And some of us are going to a comedy club in Columbia." I said this so rapidly I expected her to ask me to repeat myself.

"Yes?" she asked warily.

"I dunno. If you wanted to meet us there, it'll be tomorrow, at eight. The Bipolar Comedy Club on Cherry Street." I didn't offer to drive her because that would be too much like a date. And I didn't have a car.

Sage didn't jump at the chance, but she did hop. "Okay. Yeah. I'd like that."

"And could you give me a lift back to Boyer afterward?"

Sage laughed. Had she guessed that Tim and Dawn wanted to be alone after the show, or did she think I was only interested in her car? "Sure, Logan."

"Okay." Christ, I hoped I wasn't making a huge mistake. "Just remember—"

"I *know*, Logan. This isn't a date."

"Uh, yeah. See you there." Actually, I was just going to

remind her that parking was bad in Columbia and to get there early. But I was glad we were on the same wavelength about the other thing, too. It was kind of funny. She used to be the one who told me our outings most certainly were not dates. Now we'd flip-flopped.

The Bipolar Comedy Club was located in downtown Columbia. It was just a hole-in-the-wall joint. Any big-name comedian who came to this area would play the Déjà Vu Lounge or at the university. Bipolar would probably never get a headliner, unless it was NIGHTCLUB FIRE KILLS 23.

I stood in the freezing-cold parking lot, watching college couples file in to claim the best tables. Tim and Dawn had gone inside already. Tim said he'd get us a good spot, which probably meant one near the kitchen.

Sage was twenty minutes late. She'd seemed willing when I'd called her, but she could have changed her mind. A lot had passed between us, and maybe Sage had decided some things were better left buried.

Why had I called her? We'd kind of made peace. She wouldn't blame me for disappearing. And yet here I was, waiting in the bitter February cold, about to take a she-male to an evening of *Didja ever notice . . . ?*

I spotted Sage a block away. Even if you ignored her enormous white fake-fur cap, matching muff, and fleece coat, she still stood nearly half a foot higher than the tallest pedestrian.

She didn't wave or acknowledge me. Just walked up and leaned against someone's car. Even slouched over like that, we were still almost eye to eye.

"Sorry I'm late. I couldn't find a place to park."

"Yeah."

We just stood there for a few seconds. Back when we were friends, we'd have already been laughing and joking. Now things were tense and awkward. There was no way I could ever be relaxed around this person again. To me, Sage would never be just Sage. She'd be Sage-the-boy-who-pretended-to-be-a-girl-and-who-I-kissed-that-one-time. No friendship could survive with that many hyphens. I wondered what she was thinking. I leaned against a cement wall, not looking at her, not talking.

"Well, we better go on in," I said eventually. I avoided eye contact.

"Okay," Sage said with resignation. It was like she was about to tackle some dull chore she'd been avoiding. "Who's performing?"

"Chip Durham." We joined the line that snaked out the door.

"Who's that?"

"I don't know. They're billing him as 'the guy from the Bud Light commercials,' so I'm not optimistic." Sage giggled a little.

"Have you ever been here?" I continued.

She shook her head.

"It's supposed to be pretty fun. My sister says the food's good and you can sometimes get beer if you're not too obvious about it."

"I don't drink," she said pointedly.

The guy taking money at the door could have quelled a prison riot with a glance. He was even taller than Sage, with a shaved head and a torso that bulged from beneath his SECURITY T-shirt. Along with paying fifteen dollars, all patrons had to show ID.

I was fishing out my wallet when Sage grabbed my arm.

"Why do we have to show our license if we're not drinking?" She had a funny look on her face.

"You have to be eighteen to get in. Don't worry, sodas are still five dollars apiece, so they won't lose any money on us." She didn't laugh.

We were almost at the door, but Sage wasn't moving forward. "I . . . forgot my ID in the car."

There were still, like, twenty people behind us. I wasn't sure if they'd let Tim save seats. At this rate, we'd be sitting in the men's room.

"How far are you parked?" It was our turn, and the people behind us were pushing.

"I . . . Logan . . ." Her faltering voice brought me back to reality. Of course. It didn't matter if she had her license with her or not. She wouldn't dare show it to a stranger because it would list her sex as male.

"Hey, move it!" hollered the guy behind us. I stepped out of line.

"Fine time to remember this detail," I snapped at her.

Sage bit her lip and shook her head. I'd never seen her look so ashamed, not even on the day she'd told me her secret.

"Just go without me, Logan."

"I can't. Tim wants to be alone with Dawn later, and they don't need me sitting in the backseat looking at my watch. I was counting on you to drive me back."

"Then I'll go wait in that coffee shop until you're done. I can take you home after."

It annoyed me that she was being so accommodating. That meant there was no reason for me to be angry.

"I'm not going to have you sit alone for two hours. Let me tell Tim we're not coming, and we'll get some food or something. We can meet up with them later." I sounded bitchy; I wanted to make sure she knew I was annoyed. Not so much about missing the comedian, but that she'd messed up our plans.

"Wait, Logan, you don't have to—"

I turned and glared at her. "It's okay, Sage. I just wish you'd thought of this first."

They were just closing the doors when I arrived at the ticket counter. The heat wave from the crowded club nearly knocked me over after the cold parking lot.

"I've just got to go in and tell a friend something."

The doorman was as unimpressed as Tim at a vegetarian restaurant. "If you want in, you buy a ticket. Fifteen bucks."

"I just got to . . ."

"Fifteen bucks. We're closing the doors here. You coming or not?"

I was tempted to tell Sage just to go on home, but Tim wanted to be alone with his date later, and his plans didn't include me. I forked over some of my snow-shoveling cash, had my hand stamped with the UNDER 21 seal of shame, and hunted down my friends.

They'd managed to get a great table by the stage and

had saved two empty seats. Tim had ordered the house specialty: a platter of hot wings surrounded by White Castle hamburgers. I really wanted to join them.

"Guys," I loud-whispered, "Sage forgot her ID. We can't get in."

Dawn, whose pallid skin almost glowed in the dark, started to get up. "We can do something else, if you like." Tim began eyeballing the food, probably wondering if he could shove it all in his pockets.

"Nah, just call Sage's cell phone if you want to do something after." I wrote her number on a napkin. I didn't even know if Sage had her phone with her, but I knew Tim wouldn't be calling.

Chip Durham took the stage. Before he said a word, I could tell he was the *I'm a redneck and that's funny* type of comedian (as opposed to the *I'm black/Hispanic/female/overweight/homosexual/loud and that's funny* type). I briefly considered just sitting down and watching the show. After ten minutes, Sage would figure I wasn't coming back, right?

No, she'd wait for me for an hour in the cold parking lot. I grabbed a burger, wished Tim a happy eighteenth, and left.

Sage half smiled when I returned. "You don't have to do this, Logan."

Actually, I did. The doors were closed and the security guy was gone. "C'mon. What do you want to do?" My voice was flat. She'd ruined the evening, and I wanted her to know it.

"Um, I'm cold. Let's go back to the truck."

We walked past the crowded bars and clubs on Ninth Street.

"Logan, I'm sorry. I should have known they'd ask for identification." She didn't say *Please tell me you're not mad*, but her tone betrayed her thoughts.

I shrugged, walking quickly so she'd have to jog. "You'd think you'd remember something like that."

We stopped at the corner to let some traffic pass. "Well, if I ever do forget, I know you'll remind me." Her voice was just slightly hostile.

"What's that supposed to mean?" The light changed and Sage hurried across. I ran to follow her. "Sage?" I called angrily. "What did you mean by that?"

We were on the Mizzou campus now. She stopped in front of the empty journalism building. "What do you think it means? When you called me, I thought we could put what happened behind us. Thought we could really be friends. But I can tell this still bothers you. And I can't guarantee that this is the last time I get put in an awkward position. In fact, I know it won't be the last time. So let me drive you home, and that's it. I'd like it if we could be friends, but we just make each other too uncomfortable."

"Look who's talking! I'm not the one who was dishonest. I'm not a . . ."

Sage was standing in the shadows, and I couldn't see her face. The restrained fury in her voice was unmistakable. "Not a *what*, Logan?"

I wasn't sure how to answer that. "A . . . you know . . ."

Sage swiveled on her heel until her back was facing me.

"I know exactly what you'd call it. I changed my mind. Have Tim drive you back." She passed under the journalism arch and onto the college quad.

Shit. This wasn't exactly the *let's show Sage what a wonderful, nonjudgmental guy Logan is* evening I had in mind. I wanted to try to get back to normal with Sage, and instead I'd insulted her. I ran after her.

"Hey, wait!" She didn't stop. I don't think she knew where she was going, just as long as it was away from me. I could have easily caught her, but I didn't think chasing her down in the dark would be the best idea.

"Sage! Please!"

She froze but didn't turn. Slowly, I approached her. "We could talk," I suggested lamely.

She turned to me. "You don't have to act like you want to know, Logan. You want forgiveness, fine, you're forgiven. There. Stop feeling guilty. Go away." She was trying to be angry, but even in the shadows, I could see the look on her face. The last thing she wanted was for me to leave.

"Sage, I'm not going to lie to you and say I'm not freaked out by your . . . lifestyle. Because I am. I thought I could forget about it, but seeing you tonight, it's all I can think about. I guess that means I'm a horrible person. Or perfectly normal, I don't know. But if we just sat and talked for a while, maybe you could help me kind of understand." I wished there was a teleprompter behind Sage's head with much more articulate words.

"Is that what you really want?" The anger in her voice was forced.

"I want to be your friend." I wasn't sure if that was the

truth. The thought of what Sage was doing still made me squirm. But at least Sage couldn't say I wasn't trying to make sense of her. For some reason, I had to let Sage and, more importantly, myself, know that I was trying.

In the center of the quad stood six huge limestone columns, remains of a building that had burned down a hundred years ago. Floodlights illuminated the concrete bases. Wordlessly, we each jumped onto a block opposite each other.

Sage smiled a weary smile, and again I checked her face for masculine characteristics. But there was no five o'clock shadow, no Adam's apple, nothing that would clue anyone in to her real sex.

"So where should I start?" she asked.

"Whatever's on your mind."

The quad was empty and silent. Across from us, the domed administration building was lit up like a jewel. We sat quietly as Sage composed her thoughts.

"I'm not going to tell you the psychology behind what I'm doing. But I want you to know, I can't live any other way. It's just not possible. And you're the only one I ever voluntarily told my secret."

"I'm sorry . . ." I started to apologize for my reactions.

"It's not that. I expected it. And you reacted more calmly than my parents. They pulled me out of school when I was thirteen. Said it was for my safety. But that's not the real reason. They were ashamed of me. For almost four years they kept me in our house in Joplin. I mean, I'd go out, but only after we got in the car and drove fifty miles so no one would accidentally recognize me. It was like I was some kind of crazy relative they had to lock in the attic."

"Jesus, Sage." I'd never thought about that end of it.

"When I turned eighteen this year, I told them I was going to go back to school. They couldn't stop me. So just like that, my dad quits his job, pulls Tammi out of school, and moves us halfway across the state. So no one would ever realize what had happened to his . . . son." Sage had to force herself to say that last word.

"Logan, I promised myself I wouldn't make any friends in school, and I wouldn't date. I just wanted to have a normal semester in high school before college. But then I met you. And you asked me out that first week. And I thought, 'Wow! This cute, athletic, funny guy, who could probably date any girl in school, wants to go out with *me*! I'm really a woman!'"

I reddened a little at Sage's stream of adjectives. Then she continued.

"I could have snuck around and been your girlfriend. I wanted to. I didn't, so you have to give me credit for that. I wanted to tell you the truth. And I had this stupid fantasy that when I did, you'd understand. I knew if you accepted me, then maybe other people would."

A college couple crossed the quad, holding hands. I pretended to be waiting for them to pass before answering. Did Sage honestly expect me to be some new age, politically correct hippie who thought you could just choose your own gender? I was from central Missouri, for Christ's sake!

"That was a lot to spring on a guy." I left it at that. Sage was apparently getting enough shame from her family.

"We shouldn't have kissed, Logan. I'm sorry."

We sat in silence for a minute, thinking. Sage didn't have to be *totally* sorry. I allowed myself to remember our kiss. It still kind of got me in the gut, and not 100 percent in a bad way, either. Just 99.9 percent. I couldn't deny that last fraction, that forbidden decimal of enjoyment. Like that time when I was twelve and accidentally walked in on one of Laura's friends changing in our bathroom. I'd been too embarrassed to come out of my room that night. But I wouldn't have taken it back, either.

Sage was no longer looking at me. She was staring off into the distance, kicking her feet against the column, looking bored.

"Let me drive you home," she said, sounding disappointed. Maybe she'd been hoping I'd say something more.

"Sage, listen. I was really messed up over Brenda. Ask Jack. All I wanted to do was sit around and feel sorry for myself. And then you came along, and I started getting over her, and suddenly, I'm gay!"

"You're not gay, Logan," she chastised.

"I know that now. I'd never have kissed a guy on purpose."

Sage frowned. "I'm not a guy," she whispered.

For the first time since New Year's, I looked at the tall person next to me without prejudice, without fear. The long-legged, long-haired, defeated, lonely person on the base of the column next to me. This was not a guy. Not a girl, maybe, but certainly not a guy.

"Sage?"

She turned and looked at me, sad and a little tired. "Yes, Logan?"

How in the hell could I tell her what I was feeling when I didn't even know? "You . . . want to get some food or something?"

Sage stared at me blankly. Then the faintest trace of her old smile crept across her face. I'd spent the past couple of months trying to destroy that grin. I was happy that I'd failed.

"I'm starved."

We hopped down from the columns and walked toward town. It took us about ten minutes to get back to Sage's truck, the old monster I jump-started on New Year's. When we were seated in the cab, we turned to each other and opened our mouths to say something. Then we sat there gaping like a couple of drooling mental patients. Sometimes there just aren't words. Eventually, Sage started the truck and we drove away.

We were friends again. Sort of. Which meant I'd have to face the consequences if her secret got out. But Sage was hurting. Her family was ashamed of her. I was the only other person she'd been honest with. She'd opened up to me in a way that Brenda never had. The least I could do was have a burger with her.

And maybe I didn't want to do just the least I could do.

## chapter sixteen

I GUESS it was about midnight when we got back to Boyer. Sage and I had stopped at the Columbia Steak 'n Shake for some burgers and malts. Like any place that sells greasy food at night, the restaurant was loaded with college students in various states of sobriety. The more I thought about it, the more I was looking forward to going off to school.

Sage and I didn't talk about anything important. We sat in a corner booth drinking milk shakes and laughing behind our hands at the drunks. I managed to go nearly ten minutes without thinking about Sage's sex. It was a start. By the time we left for college, maybe I could think of Sage simply as my friend. Just like Jack or Tim. Sage would just be one of the guys.

What an amazingly bad analogy.

By the time we returned to Boyer, the town was almost

totally dark. Only a couple of bars cast illumination onto the silent streets.

"Hey, I still don't know where you live," said Sage, slowing down as we pulled into town.

"Yeah." Now that Sage had told me her secret, it seemed kind of silly that I'd been ashamed of living in a trailer. "You know, you still have my car battery." Mom had asked about it a few days earlier.

"That's right. Okay, we'll stop by my house and pick it up. It's in the garage, so we won't wake my parents."

Agreeing to this was one of the stupider things I'd ever done.

He was standing in the garage when Sage hit the automatic opener. I don't know how long he'd been waiting. He just stood there in the glow of the headlights like some demon from a slasher movie. Indestructible and immortal.

Sage's father.

Even if I hadn't recognized him from that photo in Sage's living room, I would have from the striking family resemblance. This was where Sage got her height, her big hands, her Y chromosome.

He was not pleased to see us.

Sage gripped the steering wheel so hard that her knuckles were white. I waited for her to say something, to show me the situation was not as bad as it appeared.

"I wasn't supposed to be out tonight. Especially not with a guy." Her hand lingered over the gearshift like she was contemplating throwing the truck into reverse.

So much for that hope. Without looking in my direction,

she exited the vehicle. I contemplated locking the doors and starting a new life as a hermit inside the truck, but I decided it wasn't feasible. I followed Sage.

Mr. Hendricks was not more attractive close-up. He had lost most of his hair, but his baldness somehow made him look manlier. His hands were hairy and his teeth were crooked and yellow. He was looking at me like I was a neighbor's dog who'd just crapped on his lawn.

"Dad," began Sage.

"Get in the house, Sage." His one eyebrow crinkled over his misshapen nose.

"But, Dad . . ."

"Now." He didn't raise his voice, but he was not to be argued with. With a sad backward glance, Sage went inside.

It occurred to me that if I put my head down and ran, he wouldn't be able to catch me. I was a sprinter; I'd be down the street before Sage's father realized what was happening. But then Sage would be screwed. I had to stick around for damage control. Act like for all I knew, Sage was just a normal girl and we'd just been out eating, nothing more. Then I'd stand there and take my lumps. I just hoped the lumps would be metaphorical.

Mr. Hendricks spit on the oily floor. Then, to my horror, he hit the garage door button, sealing me in. This was bad. Maybe he wanted to punctuate his displeasure with a couple of punches to my gut and didn't want the neighbors to hear.

Sage's father pulled up a bench and did not invite me to

sit on a nearby lawn chair. Instead, I stood at rigid attention while he picked up a lawn mower blade and began to methodically sharpen it.

"So you're Logan," he said eventually. He said it like being Logan was some sort of dark perversion.

"Yes, sir." So he knew I existed. At the moment, I kind of wished I didn't.

The blade rhythmically scraped on the stone, its shadow dancing in the harsh glow of the garage light. This was worse than the time Jack and I had to return his father's car minus the passenger door.

Mr. Hendricks raised the blade and stared at it with a critical eye. "Sage isn't allowed to date."

"This wasn't a date!" I babbled. "We just went out for some food, that's all."

"Sounds like a date to me." I didn't dare argue. He was still armed.

"Logan, Sage tells me he let you in on a very private secret. He told you something you have no right to know."

Oh, crap. Sage had left out this little detail! Why the hell had she told her father? What if he knew how I'd threatened her?

"Mr. Hendricks . . ." That was as far as I got. Good thing, since I had no clue what I was going to say next.

"Logan." His voice was louder, angry. "Do you have any idea how hard it is for me to see my own son going to school in a goddamn *dress*?"

"No, sir." Probably as hard as finding out the girl you were hot for is actually someone's son.

Mr. Hendricks stood and began to pace. "He acts like this is the only way he can be happy. Says he wants to be a girl. That he wants . . . to have one of those operations."

He picked up a wrench and began toying with it. I think now he was just talking to talk. "Every day I hope he'll stop. Every day I pray he'll go back to being my son. And every day that I see him prancing around in a skirt and giving Tammi advice about boys, I feel like I failed. Like I'm a bad father."

He violently threw the tool down on the bench. He stood there gripping the table, facing the wall.

"Sir?"

Sage's father turned and glowered at me, as if Sage's lifestyle was my fault. "Sage says you two are just friends. Just a couple of *buddies*. Is that true?" Obviously, he didn't buy it.

"Mr. Hendricks, I know what this looks like, but . . ."

"That's not answering my question."

"I'm not interested in Sage like that, I swear." I said this as forcefully as I dared. I wasn't sure if I was more worried about Sage getting in trouble or her father thinking we were more than friends.

Mr. Hendricks looked at me for a long time. Perhaps he was deciding if he should just yell at me or beat me unconscious.

"Logan, when Sage started acting like this, we pulled him out of school. He wouldn't have lasted a day. He didn't argue. But now he's insisting on taking his last semester at your school. I didn't want to let him, but it was important to him. But the rules were that he couldn't date and he couldn't tell anyone he's really a boy. Sage promised, and now he's broken that promise. I should pull him out of school for that."

That would break Sage's heart. "Sir, I don't think—"

"I didn't ask for your opinion. Logan, do you know what happens to guys who go to school dressed like girls? Do you know what happens when people think the guy's really a woman and then they find out the truth?"

I shook my head. The year before, I didn't think people like that really existed.

"They get killed, Logan. I'm not kidding. I've done my research. This happens more often than you think."

"Mr. Hendricks, no one is going to find out. She only has a few more months."

He hocked up a wad of phlegm, thought for a moment, and then spit it on the floor instead of in my face.

"I know *he* only has a couple of months. But Sage told you his secret. How do I know I can trust you?"

"I swear, I won't tell."

Mr. Hendricks's hostile face softened for a moment. "I know you think you won't tell anyone, but that's not good enough. You have to swear to me, if you care about Sage, you won't let anyone know. Someone might hurt him. Would you want that, Logan? See someone take a baseball bat to Sage's head?"

I'd never really thought about the serious trouble Sage could get into. I remembered how I'd flown off the handle. Someone else might have really hit her. Or done something much worse.

"I won't tell," I repeated.

He towered over me. I only came up to his neck. "Not even if you fight. Not even if you get mad. The second I doubt you, Logan, Sage is gone from school."

"Yes, sir."

We didn't shake hands. He just hit the garage door button and walked into the house. I ran nearly the whole way home.

*chapter seventeen*

THE COLD WEATHER BROKE that Sunday, and for the first time in months I could believe that spring might come back to Missouri. Mom was working the breakfast shift. Unable to think of anything else to do, I spent the morning cleaning out the shed.

The shed wasn't huge, but we'd managed to cram ten years' worth of junk inside: my lawn care stuff, old clothes of Laura's, cartons of Mom's old possessions. It took me nearly three hours, but I managed to pull everything out, sweep, and restack all the boxes. By the time I was done, the outbuilding was even more of a mess than before.

I hadn't spoken to Sage since my Friday night confrontation with her father. He'd rattled me. Not just because of the insults and threats. It was the way he'd talked about Sage. He'd acted like she was making pipe bombs in the basement or something. I guess I didn't expect him to understand Sage's motivation. But that shame he felt, how could Sage deal with that?

Around noon, I was trying to get my lawn mower started in preparation for spring business. I'd mown most of the lawns in this neighborhood for the past five seasons. The next year, someone else would take over. Yesterday I'd received my official letter of acceptance from MU. I'd be in Columbia, pushing a mop or stacking boxes for a lot more than I made now. And when I graduated . . . I tried to imagine myself renting an apartment, driving my own car, filling out a tax return . . . When did I suddenly grow up?

I'd nearly thrown out my back trying to tug the mower to life when I heard a car barrel down our road. It was followed by an ominous thud and a crunching noise from the vicinity of our front yard. When I ran around the trailer to investigate, I found Rob trying to remove one of our garbage cans from under his front bumper. He smiled the apologetic smile of the perpetual screwup.

Sage leapt from the rear seat, either excited to see me or relieved to be out of Rob's car. Maybe both.

Sage had on jeans, a tight sweater, and a denim jacket. In one hand she held the jump start battery, and in the other she clutched a purse the size of a briefcase.

"I snuck out," she announced proudly. "My parents think we're picking up Tammi from her piano lesson."

"I'll be back in fifteen minutes," said Rob. He shot me a conspiring wink, tripped over the trash can lid, and fell into the ditch. I led Sage behind the trailer as Rob was still trying to back out of the driveway.

Sage strutted across the yard as if she'd been to my

home a dozen times already. She didn't seem to notice that I lived in a glorified RV. Or maybe she didn't care.

*I could tell her to leave, tell her she shouldn't be here. It's not my job to deal with Sage's hostile father. I don't want to have to question my own sexuality every time she smiles at me. But I won't ask her to leave because I don't want her to.*

"Here!" Sage suddenly barked, thrusting the car battery into my chest. The thing must have weighed forty pounds, and I nearly staggered over backward. I chuckled internally as I put it down. Sage made a believable girl, but she definitely had a guy's stamina.

Sage sat down on one of our ancient lawn chairs. I sat opposite on the warm concrete plug of the septic tank.

"I was worried about you, Sage." It hadn't occurred to me until I said it, but I really had been concerned. Had her father yelled at her after I'd left? Reminded her that she wasn't a girl? Maybe I should have stood up to him more, though that probably wouldn't have helped.

Sage giggled. She had a powerful laugh. Not masculine, but it certainly was in keeping with her height. "I was worried about you, too, Logan. I hated to leave you with my dad. But I knew he only wanted to yell at you for a while. If I'd stayed, he would have gotten a lot angrier."

"Gee, thanks."

"Dad's all talk. He . . ." Sage suddenly glanced around the yard, gripping her purse, as if fearful she'd be overheard.

"Logan, can we go in your house?"

"No, sorry. Mom would kill me if she knew I had a girl in there when she was gone."

Sage shot me her full-force wiry smile. I think she was as touched that I'd called her a girl as I was that she'd called my trailer a house.

"Then can we go in there?" She pointed to the shed.

The outbuilding was wooden, and not too cold inside. I sat on an oil drum. Sage perched on my weight bench. She removed her jacket, revealing her bare, freckled arms. I'd never noticed how well defined her biceps were. Did they look like a man's arms, or the arms of a girl who was in excellent shape? It was the same with the bulges in the front of her tight sweater. They looked real but must have been a padded bra or something.

"Sage, when did you tell your dad that I was 'in the know'?" Even after our heart-to-heart, I still couldn't come right out and say *you're secretly a boy.*

"Right after the basketball game. Rob accidentally let it slip that I'd been out with a guy. Dad was all ready to yank me out of school, so I lied and told him that you knew. That we were just friends."

"But I didn't know!" I sniped. "And your dad thinks we were doing more than hanging out."

Sage glowered, and for a second I thought she was irritated with me. Then she spoke.

"Dad always tries to think the worst about me whenever possible. Tammi spent New Year's Eve alone with Rob, and that was okay. But I go for a ride with you, and he calls me a . . ." She didn't speak for a while. "It's always been like that. For the past four years, it's like everything I do is about gender issues. When I first told him—" She suddenly stopped. "Sorry. Let's talk about something else."

I could have changed the subject. Told Sage about the time Laura had locked me in this shed when I was eight. Or speculated about what Tim and Dawn had been doing after the comedy show. But that would have been kind of chickenshit of me. Sage wanted to talk about her family problems. Either I could let her know I didn't want to hear about them, or I could listen.

"No, you can tell me." I almost sounded totally sincere.

Sage braced her elbows on her knees and placed her chin in her hands. "Seriously? I don't want to freak you out."

"Way too late for that." I shrugged. "Look, you told me earlier that you hoped I'd understand. Well, I'm trying."

Sage didn't smile, but she had such a warm look in her eyes, I had to remind myself that she was a boy. How come real girls never looked at me like that?

"You've never met a transgendered person, have you?"

"No." Growing up in Boyer, I'd also never met a homosexual, a Muslim, a Jew, a Communist, or a New Yorker. Up until this year, people like Sage were just perverts who appeared on talk shows. And now I was friends with one, and she wasn't even as perverted as Jack.

"I guess it started when Tammi was born. I had just turned three. I was so excited about having a little sister. She was so cute. Mom dressed her up like a little baby doll, in these little pink dresses, and bows, and the most adorable—"

"This is thrilling, Sage, but we're not talking infant fashion here."

"Right. So it wasn't long before I started asking Mom and Dad why I couldn't wear dresses and be pretty. They thought I was jealous, so they bought me new toys, new clothes. Mostly sports stuff." She gagged. "But I wasn't jealous of Tammi. I just wanted to be beautiful like her." She looked at me. "I didn't think you'd be so shocked already."

I realized how surprised I was. "Sorry. I guess I assumed you were a lot older when you decided you wanted to be a girl."

Sage's forehead wrinkled. "It wasn't a decision, Logan. Tammi was what showed me that there was a difference between boys and girls. I realized I was a girl. I told Tammi I was her big sister. Told Mom and Dad that I was going to grow up to be a princess. That didn't go over well, especially with Dad."

"I can imagine." I couldn't imagine that at all. Mr. Hendricks seemed like the type of guy who'd explode if he caught one of his children smoking or staying out past curfew. Having a son who wanted to be Cinderella? I was surprised he didn't have a stroke.

"Well, the more I wanted to be a girl, the more he was determined I would be a man's man. Every day from when I was, like, five, Dad would make me play baseball or basketball with him. Every birthday I'd ask for a doll or an Easy-Bake oven, and I'd get a catcher's mitt or a T-ball set." She paused. "By the way, do you know anyone who wants some unused sports equipment?"

I shook my head.

"So I decided to be a girl in secret. Tammi helped me. She let me wear her clothes, though they were always too small. She'd help me borrow Mom's things, and we'd play house. I'd always be the mommy. I thought that if I tried hard enough, I'd grow up to be a woman. It wasn't until I was a lot older that I realized how impossible things would be."

Sage sat, spinning the empty weight bar on the bench, lost in thought. "One day, my dad caught me wearing Mom's bikini." She laughed with the voice of someone remembering something that wasn't funny. "He signed me up for Little League. Jesus, I hated that. I told him so, but he forced me to play. He thought it was good for me. He would have enrolled me in kickboxing if he could have. It took me two years to convince him to let me quit. When I was ten, I was already really tall, and he tried to get me to try out for peewee football."

I laughed; I couldn't help it. She glared at me.

"Thank you for laughing at my emotional baggage, Logan."

"Sorry. Just the thought of you playing football . . ."

She rolled her eyes. "Anyway, it went on like this until sixth grade. Remember those stupid human development films we had to watch?"

I thought back. "No. Jack and I got kicked out for making rude comments."

"Shocking. Well, it was then that I realized I was going to grow up to be a man, no matter what. So that night, I locked myself in the bathroom and took out Dad's razors."

"Christ, Sage, you didn't try to cut off your wang, did you?" She'd just crossed the line into uncomfortable territory. But what she said next floored me.

"No, Logan. I tried to slash my wrists."

The shed suddenly became ice cold. I almost touched Sage on the shoulder, but I stopped myself. I knew being a girl was important to her, but suicide? Jesus.

Sage wouldn't look at me. "It wasn't as bad as you think, Logan. I freaked out as soon as there was blood, and I started bawling. Dad had to force open the bathroom door. It was a real mess. Luckily, I'd only scratched myself.

"My parents made me go to a psychiatrist after that. And even then it took me a month to get up the courage to tell my parents why I'd tried to kill myself. But there was no going back. I told them I was going to be a girl, or I didn't want to live. I think they were afraid I'd slit my wrists for real if they didn't let me.

"So they pulled me out of school right before eighth grade. Who knows, it was probably the right thing. And I've been living as a female ever since. Now please say something!"

I stood up and began to pace nervously in the narrow confines of the storage building. I pictured an effeminate junior high boy who needed to be a girl so badly that he wanted to die if he couldn't. "Sorry, sorry. I just didn't know how serious you were about this."

She cocked a disbelieving eyebrow.

"Okay, I guess I did realize it. This is just weird. I'm sorry, but it is."

She didn't look offended. "At least you're willing to listen, Logan. I wish my parents would just let me try to explain things. Especially my dad."

The fact that they let Sage be a girl showed they were

more open-minded than a lot of people. "How are they taking it?"

"Mom's resigned. I think she's terrified that I'll do something crazy, or run away if she tried to stop me. But she wishes I wouldn't do this. Dad . . ." Sage rapidly turned to the wall and didn't say anything for about two minutes.

"Dad," she continued hoarsely. "He's disgusted by me. We never talk. He works constantly. I'm not allowed to visit my grandparents. I know he didn't want to transfer out here, but I think he liked the idea that no one he knew would realize his son was now a girl." A sob racked her body, but she got control of herself. "Do you have any idea what it's like to have your father so ashamed of you, Logan?"

"No," I replied bluntly. "I don't."

"Sorry, I forgot."

I idly stacked some empty crates. "Sage, um . . ." How could I put this delicately?

"Just say it, Logan. Whatever it is."

"Okay. Why do you have to, um . . . change?"

"Transition," she corrected.

"Transition right now? I mean, why didn't you tough it out for a few more years? Wouldn't it be easier to do this after you were out of school? When your parents weren't watching you?"

Sage contemplated her polished nails. "You'd think so, wouldn't you? But transitioning is something you can't put off. The younger you start, the easier it is." She reached into her purse. "Let me show you something."

She handed me a color printout of a photograph. I almost laughed before I realized she wasn't trying to be funny.

It was a picture of a middle-aged guy in a blond wig and a dress. He was wearing makeup and sitting with his legs crossed. Obviously, he was trying to be pretty. There was no way. He was a man in a dress. You could even see his beard stubble.

"Um, Sage, this isn't how you hope to turn out, is it?"

"Of course not. That's what I want to avoid. That's a picture of Sylvia. I know her online. She didn't transition until she was fifty, and married with kids. If you think my parents didn't understand, you should hear her talk about her family."

I handed Sage back the picture.

"The point is, Logan, I don't want to turn out like that. I've been living as a girl for almost five years. I don't think anyone at school suspects. Next year, I'm going to enter college as a woman. I let myself deny that I was a female for over ten years. That's ten years wasted. And it'll probably be another ten years before I can afford the surgery."

In my entire life, I'd never wondered about how a sex change worked. "So you're really going to have some doctor cut it off?"

She shook her head. "They won't actually remove my penis," lectured Sage. "They'll slit it laterally to create . . ."

*"O say, can you see? By the dawn's early light!"* I sang at the top of my lungs. *"What so proudly we hailed . . ."*

"Sorry," she snickered. "Too much info there."

I pulled my fingers out of my ears. "You think?"

"Okay. Yes, I do want to have sexual reassignment surgery, or a sex change, as you'd call it. When they're done, you could see me naked and still think I was born female."

My testicles shrank up into my body as if they were in danger. "And it's really that expensive?"

Sage held her head in her hands. If I didn't know better, I'd think she was staring at her crotch.

"Over thirty thousand dollars. Mom and Dad won't help, of course. They'll pay for college but won't pay for me to become a full woman."

I wanted to spout some pearls of wisdom. Fat chance. Sage had just told me that being a woman was so important to her that she'd almost killed herself. What do you say to that?

"Sage, it'll happen someday. And for now, no one knows." Except me.

She balled her fists and rubbed her eyes. When she spoke again, there was hurt in her voice. "Logan, *I* know. And every time I go to the bathroom or take a shower . . . I want you to imagine that instead of a penis, you had some sort of deformed tentacle, or a gaping, oozing sore. That's how I feel. It's like I have a terminal disease, and there are doctors all over the place who can cure me, and my parents could help pay for it, and they won't! I can't live, *I can't live*, until I don't have to pretend. The only one in the world who even cares is Tammi."

"I care." I really did. I didn't understand, but I didn't like to see Sage in pain. And it was all the worse because there was nothing I could do to help her. I couldn't give her the money. I couldn't make her family accept her. I couldn't completely accept her myself.

Sage sniffed, then smiled. "I know you care. And that's important to me." She wiped her eyes and pulled her hair back into a ponytail.

I stood. "Let's get some air." We'd been talking about this for about ten minutes, and I'd kind of reached my limit.

"Logan? I printed out some information about transgendered people. Would you like to read it? Maybe it could help explain things better than I can." She patted her enormous purse.

I shook my head. "No, Sage. It's not that I don't want to understand, but . . . look. I still think of you as a girl. It's hard not to. And maybe we should just not talk about the other side of things for now."

Sage stood. I think she was slouching so I wouldn't seem so short. "I'd like that, Logan." She moved to hug me, then pulled back quickly. She held out her hand for me to shake.

What the hell. I gave her a quick squeeze.

There was one more thing I had to say. "Sage, listen. If you ever get desperate like before, just remember, you do have a friend in me. If you ever think about, um, hurting yourself, you'd talk to me or Tammi, right?"

I thought Sage was going to break down. "Logan, I've got a real friend. I haven't had that since elementary school. That makes all the difference in the world."

"I think I heard Rob pull up," I said, a little uncomfortable. We were almost having a moment.

Sage and I walked to the front yard. It wasn't Rob who'd arrived. It was my mom. Still dressed in her waitress uniform, she was walking to the house, exhausted from her early shift. Her tired face broke into a grin when she saw me walking with Sage.

"Why, hello there."

I felt like I did years ago, when I had first shyly introduced Brenda to my mom. I'd been so awkward, so terrified that Mom would flat-out ask if we were dating. I felt so nervous and proud, proving to my mother that her son was becoming a man. So why was I feeling that now? I was no more interested in Sage than I was in Tim.

"Mom, this is Sage."

Sage held out her large, soft hand. "Hello, Ms. Witherspoon."

"Nice to meet you, Sage. Would you like to come in and have a soda?"

Far down the road I could hear the squealing of tires and the blast of a horn.

"Thanks, but I think my ride's here."

Rob very nearly took out our mailbox, but Sage got in the car anyway. As soon as they peeled out, Mom winked at me.

"So tell me about your friend," she prodded as we went inside.

"That's all she is, Mom. A friend."

Mom removed her name tag and kicked off her shoes. "An awfully cute friend."

Two weeks ago, I would have violently disagreed. Instead, I tried to feel Mom out about Sage's sex. "You don't think she's kind of, you know, burly?"

Mom glared at me. "That's rude, Logan. She's a little tall, but she's very pretty. Don't be so judgmental."

"Yeah." I poured myself a soda. *Don't be judgmental.* Sage's family certainly judged her. I wasn't going to add to that. Her own parents didn't accept her. Society didn't accept her. It had almost driven her to suicide. But now she had me. I wouldn't judge her. Not anymore.

*chapter eighteen*

WINTER WAS OVER. The last of the snow was gone, turning half the roads in Boyer into muddy, impassable swamps. The county ambulance district stopped pulling burn victims out of meth labs and started scraping them off the highway again. The girls at my school, and the middle-aged women who dressed like teenagers, would break out the halter tops and Daisy Dukes before too long.

Now that football season was over, the track team enjoyed a few months of unrestricted use of the field. Coach Garrison had us running laps. Garrison also coached wrestling, softball, and JV basketball, so we didn't get much direction from him. "Run! Faster!"

The first track meet was in two weeks. Boyer would have its chance to square off against such mighty opponents as Moberly, Higbee, Centralia, Sturgeon, and a half-dozen other hick towns. The next few meets would be my last chance to compete. I felt foolish for thinking it, but I wanted to go out with an impressive record. Mom even said she'd come to most of my meets. Her manager had recently hired some new waitresses, and, as a senior employee, she finally was able to get a stable schedule. No more nights, and only two weekends a month.

Jack sprinted up beside me, moving easily. He sweated more than any human being I knew. Running near him was like passing through a car wash.

"Dude," he wheezed. "Three o'clock."

I looked over at the aluminum bleachers. Even from the other side of the field, it was impossible not to recognize the tallest "girl" in school. Though there was still a bite of cold in the March air, Sage was wearing shorts. Her long, long legs stretched down across two rows of bleachers.

I waved as I passed, and she smiled. She must have been there to watch me. Just like Brenda used to. It wasn't the same, of course, but it was kind of nice having a friend who'd sit out here in the chilly weather, just to see me run.

My next round, I made it a point to pass Jack and a couple of other guys. You know, just so Sage wouldn't be disappointed. But the round after that, I realized she was no longer watching me. She wasn't alone.

Phillip Myers. He was a junior, and that was about all I could tell you about him. He had spiky hair, had a wispy mustache, and had worn the same Members Only jacket since the fifth grade. He was sitting next to Sage, talking to her.

Sage was talking back. And laughing. I was watching them so intently I nearly missed my turn and ran into the fence.

The next go-round Sage and Phil were still chatting. What did I care? Why shouldn't Sage have other friends? I sure as hell wasn't jealous. It's not like I assumed I was the only guy in all of Boyer Sage would want to hang around with. But guys only started conversations with random girls for one reason. Sage needed to be careful.

On the following lap I tried to make myself not look in their direction, but failed. Phillip sat alone, staring at his feet. I glanced around, trying to locate Sage. I finally saw her trotting to the parking lot. Where was she going in such a hurry?

I nearly knocked Jack over in my rush to follow her. Through the gate, around the teachers' parking area, and right up to her truck.

She knew I was following her, or at least didn't show surprise when I collapsed at the driver's door. She had a grim look on her face, as if she'd just been unexpectedly insulted.

"Back off, Logan."

"Hey, I just wanted to see if you were okay." *What did Phillip say? Did he suspect the truth?*

She opened the door. "I'm serious, Logan. You smell like a jockstrap."

That would have been funny, except she still wasn't smiling. Finally, she rolled her eyes.

"Get in."

I sat, gasping for air, as Sage toyed with the radio. Though I tried to avoid looking at her legs, I couldn't help myself. They were long and shapeless, with freckles on the knees, large (though not huge) feet, and a couple of shaving nicks.

"Catch your breath, Logan, then leave me alone."

After what she'd put me through recently, I was starting to get pissed at this attitude. What had happened to the girl who'd said she needed my friendship more than anything?

"Just checking on you," I said, failing in my attempt not to sound pissy. "You ran off in a hurry."

She turned to me with a haughty smirk. "You know what that guy Phillip asked me to do? Right there? Right where anyone could hear him?"

I was afraid to ask. "What?"

"He asked me if I wanted to *go for a walk*."

My calf muscles were beginning to seize up from stopping so abruptly. I waited for Sage to finish, then realized there wasn't any more to her story.

"Go for a walk? That's all?"

She shook her head, disgusted with me for some reason. "Logan, do you know how many guys have asked me out since I came here?"

"Two?"

Her frown deepened. I think I was supposed to guess a much higher number.

"Yes, two. But this is a small school."

My sweat was soaking into the upholstery. "What's your point?"

"Nothing. Forget it," she huffed. Apparently, I was supposed to be clueing in to something.

"Sage . . ."

Sage placed her head on the steering wheel as if she was cuddling a pillow. "Logan, I just realized. I'm never going to have a date. Ever. In my entire life."

"What are you talking about?"

And then it hit me. She would never be able to date. Not me, not Phil, no one. She wasn't a woman. And she wasn't a man, either. Too masculine for a straight guy, far too feminine for a gay one. She was stuck between two worlds. I began to understand why she so desperately wanted that operation.

Sage roughly ran her fingers across her eyes, attempting to stop the tears before they started. "You showed me I can't lie to guys. But I can't very well say, 'By the way, I have male genitalia' on the first date, can I? Jesus, I'm screwed."

"C'mon, Sage. It's not that bad."

Sage reacted like I'd just told her she could make a fortune moving money out of Nigeria. "Not that bad? Logan, not everyone can be a monk like you, okay? I want to meet guys, just like any other girl, and I can't! I'm going to be alone."

I was utterly out of my depth. I tried to think of something to say to encourage her, but anything I'd say would just be empty words from someone who didn't really understand. No matter what kind of friend I was, no matter how supportive I acted, Sage's problems wouldn't go away. There was nothing I could do to help. Sage was doomed to walk a long, lonely road. Me shouting *Everything's going to be okay!* from the sidewalk wouldn't do her much good.

Sage turned the ignition key. The truck was already running, and it made that nasty grinding noise. I took my cue and left.

*chapter nineteen*

I STOOD on the football field next to Jack, flanked by the runners from Westran. Jack had placed in four events at our first track meet of the spring. I'd only managed to finish a close second in the 400-meter dash.

Coach Garrison looked down at his shoes as he addressed the crowd of dozens. "We'd like to thank everyone for coming out today. Our next meet will be on the twelfth, in Hallsville. Remember, Boyer T-shirts are still for sale at the ticket booth."

He tried to pass the mike to Principal Bloch, who just frowned and shook his head. I couldn't tell if Bloch was pissed because he had to come here on a Saturday, if he was disappointed that Jack and I were the only Boyer students who'd won anything, or if he was just being his usual unpleasant self.

As the Westran team high-fived their way to their bus, I

scanned the crowd for my mom. It took two seconds to find her.

"Logan, you were amazing," she bubbled as I joined her at the bleachers.

I shrugged like it was no big deal. Actually, I was really glad that Mom had come to the meet. I wished I had done better. Eighteen years old, and I still wanted to impress my mommy.

"Are you sure you didn't finish first in that last race? It looked awful close."

I wiped my forehead on my sleeve. "It was close, but he edged me out."

"You were robbed." I swiveled in time to see Sage returning from the snack bar. She sat down. I realized that the jacket on the bench next to my mother actually belonged to Sage. That meant she'd been sitting with my mom. Luckily, I was still winded, so my subsequent panic attack just looked like I was trying to catch my breath.

Mom smiled as Sage passed her a bottled water. Then Mom turned back to me. "Logan, do you need a ride home, or are you doing something with the team?"

It took me a stunned second to process her question. I was still trying to figure out why they had been sitting next to each other. "Uh, you go on ahead, Mom. I have to shower."

Mom hugged me, smiled again at Sage, and walked to the parking lot. As soon as she was in her car, I assaulted Sage with an angry stare.

"*She* asked *me* to sit with her," replied Sage, not the least bit defensive. "I couldn't really tell her no. It's not like I could lose myself in this crowd."

I could picture Mom trying to get to know her son's "friend." She had always peppered Brenda with questions whenever they were together. And now this new girl shows up to watch her son run. . . .

"What did you guys talk about?" I asked, not even pretending to be calm.

"I told her you were a tiger in the sack. And that we decided to name our first kid Durwood."

"Sage!"

She stared at her cuticles. "We just talked about the track team and school, nothing else."

"Sorry. Sorry." I shouldn't have worried. I knew Sage would have been on her best behavior. "Thanks for coming."

She flashed her braces. "You were pretty fast out there. I was sure you were going to beat that guy. Are you going to run in college?"

"Nah."

"I thought a guy like you might have an athletic scholarship." For a moment, Sage's eyes scoped out my body.

"No, just a poor-boy scholarship." The government was really coming through for me. If I could maintain a B average, school was almost paid for. "You?"

"Wealthy parents." We didn't look at each other for a second. We were both just a little ashamed of our families' financial statuses.

"Logan, about the other day . . ." She smiled awkwardly,

then closed her eyes with the air of someone about to give a rehearsed apology.

"It's okay, Sage."

"No, it's not. You were trying to make me feel better. I need to remind myself how special that is."

I looked down at the blacktop, a little embarrassed. I didn't realize a third person had joined us until it was too late to escape.

She was one of those middle-aged women who could probably pass for the older sister of a student. She had a round face dotted with brown freckles, a mouth permanently twisted into a smirk, and kinky rust-colored hair interlaced with strands of gray. Her resemblance to Tammi was striking.

Sage's mom folded her arms and looked down at me, even though I was much taller. Thankfully, she didn't wear the expression of rage that her husband had worn. Just the typical distrustful glare of the mother of a teen girl.

"Mom, this is my friend Logan."

"Hi, I'm Logan!" I shouted, desperately trying not to make an awful impression.

"Nice to meet you."

We stood there not saying anything. I was sweating through my already wet clothes. Sage broke the silence.

"Logan's a runner. You should have seen him out there."

"I'm a runner," I repeated.

"He's going to Mizzou next year."

"I'll be going to Mizzou." *Awk! Polly want a cracker!*

I slammed my foot down on the clutch and violently shifted my brain out of neutral.

Mrs. Hendricks was looking at me like I was special, but not in the way Sage thought. "Mizzou," she said, frowning. "Just like Sage."

"It's a great campus. My sister goes there, says she has the time of her life."

Her frown deepened, and I mentally kicked myself. She probably took that to mean there was a lot of drunken sex going on at the university.

Sage cut in. "I wouldn't know about the campus. I'm not allowed to visit," she said huffily.

Her mom turned toward her. "Sage, we've been over this. You're . . ." She paused for a second. "Too young to visit the college on your own."

Sage was eighteen. I didn't think her age had anything to do with it.

"C'mon, Mom," Sage whined. "I could go up there on a Saturday morning—"

Her mother held up a palm. "We'll discuss this at home." Her tone telegraphed the fact that there would be no discussion. Mrs. Hendricks nodded politely at me and took Sage's arm, leading her toward the family car.

So Sage couldn't even spend the day at Mizzou by herself. I wished there was something I could do for her. Help her get out of her parents' clutches for the weekend. It would be almost impossible to sneak her away for that long. As always, when faced with a situation that required underhanded, smarmy, double-dealing trickery, I asked myself the same question: *What would Laura do?*

Laura . . .

The perfect solution hit me.

"Hold on!" Sage and her mother turned back to me. I grinned, more confidently than I felt. "There's a program on campus, a freshman orientation, where Sage could spend the night with an upperclassman chaperone."

Sage looked wary; her mom, interested. I continued, the lies rushing easily through my teeth. "I'm surprised they haven't contacted you. Sage would stay with a Mizzou senior, have dinner in the dining hall, sleep in a dorm. She could tour the campus, meet some professors. Religious services Sunday morning, if she's interested." I was laying it on with a trowel.

Mrs. Hendricks rubbed her chin thoughtfully. Sage took a cautious step back until she was out of her mom's line of sight, then made violent slashing motions at her neck. I ignored her.

"And you say this is a university-sponsored program?" asked Sage's mother.

"Yep. I have the number at home. If you like, I can have them contact you."

She turned to her daughter. "What do you think?"

Sage had been spastically shaking her head, but stopped just in time to say, "It's something to think about." She was not enthused.

"Great," I said with a politician's grin. "I'll call them to-morrow."

Mrs. Hendricks smiled warmly at me. "It was very nice to meet you, Logan." She patted my shoulder. Sage glared at me until they reached their car.

I raced my bike back to the trailer, determined to get home before Sage did. The phone was ringing as I passed through the door, just like I expected.

"Hi, Sage," I answered before she spoke a word.

"Logan, I'm going to hurt you," she said evenly and with great seriousness.

"Why?" For once, I was only faking my ignorance.

"Do you really think I want to spend a weekend listening to the history of the campus with some twenty-two-year-old stranger breathing down my neck? I want to go there to meet people, not hear some lecture about safe sex and drinking responsibly!" She was bellowing, yet her voice was still unmistakably that of a girl.

"You really don't think much of me, do you?" I responded, trying to project my smarmy smile over the telephone line.

Sage paused. "What do you mean?"

"I mean you're going to be staying with the least responsible nonauthority figure this side of St. Louis. My sister, Laura."

There was a long silence. "Do you really think she'd let me stay with her?" asked Sage meekly.

"She'd be happy to help out any of my friends. Maybe not Jack. The point is, she's the most skilled liar I've ever met. Your parents will think you'll be bunking at a convent when she's through."

I waited for the laughter, but it didn't come. "Logan, you're my best friend. Thank you."

I was totally not used to being friends with a female, even a female like Sage. All this lovey-dovey sharing of feelings was giving me a complex. I mumbled goodbye and hung up.

Laura wouldn't be back at her dorm until the evening. I was sure she'd go along with my plan; my sister was always willing to bend the rules on principle, if nothing else. My only concern was that I'd opened my big mouth at Thanksgiving and admitted to liking Sage. I'd just have to tell Laura that it hadn't worked out and we were only friends.

Smiling, my mind drifted to the year ahead. Funny, I'd always pictured doing things at Mizzou with Jack and Laura. But I'd probably need frequent breaks from my future roommate, and Laura . . . well, she was my sister. She didn't need her little brother tagging along all the time.

But Sage was my friend. And we were both a little frightened about the future. For the first time since winter, I was completely happy that we'd be going to school together. Now that any chance for romance was gone, we could actually enjoy each other.

I stripped and jumped in the shower, but not before admiring my body in the mirror. When school started, I could be like a brother to Sage. I'd make sure no guys got too close to her, while she could build me up to the pretty coeds. It was a win-win situation. What could go wrong?

## chapter twenty

TIM CAREFULLY WIPED down his bookends with a rag. They looked as if he'd painstakingly carved them out of mahogany instead of smacked them together out of the cheap pine we worked with in the wood shop.

I studied my spice rack. It looked like something a fifth grader would make with his daddy's tools.

If my daddy had any tools, he'd taken them with him when he left. Tim's dad was a bank manager, but he'd still showed his son how to use a table saw and router. I could barely drive a nail.

Tim swabbed away a last blob of stain. "So, Dawn is on my case again."

Tim and Dawn had been dating for months. For a while, Jack and I had been worried that Dawn was actually a brain-eating alien in disguise. Tim, however, continued to survive, so we concluded that she actually really liked him.

"What is it this time?" I asked. The honeymoon was

over; the lovers were now sniping at each other over little things. Surprisingly, Tim's weight problem didn't seem to be an issue.

"My dog. She says he has a dumb name. Wants me to change it to Max or Rover or something stupid like that."

"You have to admit, Number Forty-Four Ninety-Three is an odd name for a dog."

"I keep telling you, that's what they called him in the animal shelter. He'll get confused if I change his name now."

I tried to force the back part of my spice rack into place. There was an ominous cracking noise. *Happy Mother's Day!*

"Well, looks like you're going to have to choose between your dog and your girlfriend."

Tim looked less serene than usual. "Yeah. Hey, Logan, can I ask you a serious question?"

"Sure."

Tim glanced around, making sure no one was listening in. Luckily, you can't really zone out in shop class, not if you care about your fingers, so no one was paying any attention to us.

Tim gnawed his knuckles. Maybe because he was nervous, maybe because this was the only class where he wasn't allowed to eat. Eventually, he spit out what was on his mind.

"How do you know when a girl is ready to . . . you know?"

*When your best friend tells you about it? Or when she explains that she was a boy until she was a teenager?*

"I dunno, Tim. You'll know." I wiped some sawdust

off the bench. Tim wouldn't be asking unless he thought the time was right. I was happy for him and completely jealous.

Tim grabbed my arm. "C'mon," he stage-whispered over the sound of the band saw. "I've never done this before. I've got protection, we've got places we could go, but what if I try and she freaks out?"

It killed me that not only was I an eighteen-year-old virgin, but that Tim and Jack assumed I'd been doing it with Brenda since I was fifteen.

"Tim, if she's not ready, she'll tell you. She's a girl; she's used to guys trying to get into her pants. Just take it slow and check your teeth first."

Tim nodded, mulling over my deep advice. The bell rang, and we cleaned up our work area while Mr. Adams hollered at us. I had shop sixth hour. Only American literature and track practice separated me from a lazy afternoon.

"Logan." Tim stopped short, halfway down the industrial arts hall. "Look."

I could see the familiar, statuesque figure of Sage, milling around with the shorter students in the commons area. But what had grabbed Tim's eye was who she was talking to.

Brenda. They were standing in front of the pathetic Boyer trophy case chatting. Brenda had a sort of intense look on her face. She kept adjusting her glasses, something I knew she did when she was uncomfortable. Sage looked calm, though not as relaxed as usual.

This was bad. Seeing the two of them shooting the breeze was like seeing your parole officer having a beer with your drug connection. Had Sage started the conversation, trying to size up the girl who'd dumped me? Or had Brenda been curious about this new girl who spent so much time with her ex? Were they just exchanging pleasantries, or were they sharing secrets? Girls seemed to break out their innermost feelings and fears shortly after being introduced. Guys only did that when they'd been in combat together or were cell mates.

"No good can come of this," I whispered to Tim, though we were well out of hearing range.

"Why? You keep telling us Sage isn't your girlfriend." Tim and Jack no longer asked me if Sage and I were dating. I'd told them we were just friends so often it was starting to sound like a mantra.

"But Brenda knows she's my friend. So why does she want to talk to Sage?"

Tim cocked his head at me. Maybe he was remembering how I'd slobbered over Sage one month, then acted like she'd never existed the next.

I was still staring at the girls. Sage laughed, patted Brenda on the arm, and walked off.

"What was that all about?" I pondered out loud. "It's not like Brenda tries to talk to you or Jack, right?"

"Well, maybe they were . . ."

"*Right?*"

Tim sighed. "No, Logan. So do you think Brenda's going in for a little backstabbing? Spilling those intimate little secrets that she swore she'd never tell?"

I watched as Brenda hurried to her next class.

"I don't know. But I'm going to find out."

*   *   *

I picked at my Big Mac, wondering if it had actually been stepped on or if it just looked that way. I'd invited Sage out to McDonald's to discuss the upcoming trip to Columbia (yes, Boyer has a McDonald's. We're not barbarians). Sage had paid for both our meals. Then she'd fluttered her eyes at the dude behind the counter and asked for some Happy Meal toys. He'd passed her a handful with a wink and a smile. I wondered what would happen if Sage didn't have to restrict herself around boys. There'd probably be two dozen guys lined up behind me. Or in front of me.

"Logan, your sister should win an Oscar! By the time she got off the phone with my mom, Laura had her convinced we'd be doing nothing but visiting the library and going to church. Mom doesn't have a clue she's your sister." Sage paused for a bite of her salad. "I'm so looking forward to next weekend. It's going to be a blast."

"Well, Laura's an expert at tricking parents. She used to sneak out with her old boyfriend when my mom worked the late shift. Never got caught." The plan to trick Sage's parents had gone incredibly smoothly. Laura told me she'd make sure Sage had a good time. I don't think she bought my story that I no longer wanted to date Sage, but that was just as well. I didn't want Laura trying to introduce Sage to any guys.

"So, what do you think we'll do with your sister? I mean, I do want to see the campus, but I'd like to explore the town, too."

I was busy picking yellow pickles off my burger and almost missed what she said.

"*We'll* do? Sage, I'm not going with you." Sage and I had bonded recently, but spending the night away from home, with only my libertine sister watching us . . . that was a bit much.

Sage held her plastic fork suspended halfway to her mouth. "Not going? But I thought . . . I mean, she's your sister. I just assumed you were coming, too." Her lower lip was quivering just a bit.

I squirmed. How could I explain to Sage that, even after my promises of friendship, I still wanted to keep a wall between us? I wanted her to know that I cared about her like any friend, but I didn't want to sleep in the same room with her. I could picture Laura volunteering to sleep somewhere else, leaving Sage and me to spend the night alone in the dorm room. To me, Sage was like someone's wife, a nun, a first cousin. I'd never make a pass at her, but spending the night together still felt wrong.

"Sage, you and Laura will have plenty of fun. Just a night out for the girls." My words were cardboard; the excuse, obvious.

Sage jabbed angrily at her lettuce. "I've never even met your sister. Why won't you come with me? You don't have a work schedule to keep. Your mom will let you stay with Laura. Please come." Sage's eyes were wide with fear.

"C'mon, you don't want me along."

"Of course I do! I'm sure your sister's nice, but I'm not going up there without you. I'm sorry, I should have mentioned this earlier, but I just assumed you'd be coming. What's the problem?"

I toyed with one of the toys and didn't answer. Sage pushed her food away.

"Oh. It's *that*." There was no question as to what "that" was.

"No, Sage."

"Don't bother, Logan. I guess I'll always be 'one of those' to you." Her voice caught; she was suppressing a sob.

"That's not it! Please don't think that!" I glanced about to make sure we weren't being overheard.

"What is it, then?" Her body was shaking.

"It's . . . it's nothing."

Sage laid her face in her hands. "Tell your sister I'm sorry, but I can't come."

God, not the crying. Anything but that. "Okay, okay, I'll come! I'll call Laura and ask her to find me a place to sleep." It wouldn't be that bad, spending Saturday night in Columbia. Might actually be kind of fun.

Sage's head shot up, a wide grin on her lips. "Great!" She began shoving food back in her mouth. There was no trace of tears on her face, and I got the feeling I'd just been bamboozled. It scared me. What else could Sage get me to agree to? I decided to change the subject.

"Sage, um, earlier today I saw you and Brenda talking." It was a forced segue. *Hey, boss, I see you're deciding on the promotions for next year.*

Sage immediately started smirking. "Yes. We were." She grinned. There was a piece of lettuce caught in her braces.

"About what?" I prodded, tossing around a little Hamburglar action figure.

"This and that," she said, being deliberately vague. I waved my fingers, encouraging her to elaborate.

"She wanted to know where I bought my earrings. We talked about clothes for a while."

I pounded on Hamburglar until his little head popped off. "Forgive me for being suspicious, but why would Brenda want to go up and talk to you?"

"Because she's a little jealous."

"Right."

"I don't mean *jealous*, jealous. It's just that she's so used to you liking her, she's having a hard time accepting that you're moving on."

I nodded, smiling. "That makes no goddamn sense."

"Allow me to demonstrate." She picked up some of the McDonaldland toys. "Let's say you're Grimace, here."

"Why do I have to be Grimace?"

"Fine, you can be Ronald McDonald. And Brenda is Grimace." She began bouncing the purple figure up and down. "Hi, I'm Brenda," she said in an insulting, whining voice. "Logan, I'm sick of how great you treat me. It's over."

Sage then jiggled Ronald and spoke in a mocking baritone. "Brenda, please don't go! I love the way you treat me like garbage and ignore me! Let's not kiss and make up!"

She picked up Brenda's figurine. "Sorry, Logan, I just don't want to date a handsome, funny guy. Ta-ta!" She tossed Grimace aside and picked up the headless Hamburglar.

"Hi, I'm Sage. I'm prettier and nicer than Brenda. Will you be my friend?"

I was biting my knuckle to keep from laughing. Sage continued, talking in a parody of my voice.

"I dunno, Sage. I'm not sure I like it when girls treat me like a human being. But let's go see a movie."

Sage retrieved Grimace and took on the parody of Brenda's voice. "Hey, that's my doormat there! What right do you have to tell him what a great guy he is?"

She returned to her own voice. "Hey, too late for you, toots! I mean, sure, Logan can be whiny and self-centered, but I think he's special, so back off!" She picked up Grimace and shoved him headfirst into her salad dressing container. She then switched to my voice.

"Oh, thank you, Sage. I'm so lucky to have a friend as wonderful and sexy as you! Even though I spaz the hell out every time I realize how beautiful you are."

I grabbed Hamburglar and imitated Sage's voice. "Thanks, Logan! Maybe if I didn't constantly need to be told that I'm pretty, things might be easier."

Sage glared at me from across the table, then continued to make Ronald talk like me. "I'm Logan and I think I'm the only one who's ever been dumped!"

"I'm Sage and I'm a big drama queen!"

"I'm Logan and I'm the only person who ever lived in a trailer!"

"I'm Sage and I'm afraid to go to Columbia by myself!"

We were shouting so loud that customers were staring.

*"I'm Logan and I don't know a good thing when I see it!"*

*"I'm Sage, and I don't realize how special I am!"*

We both grabbed for each other's toy at the same time, then fake-slapped each other's hands. Our table exploded in a flurry of plastic and protein. When the mess settled, we were glaring at each other, our fingers intertwined in a moment of hostile endearment. Then, with a burst of forced laugher, we let go. Neither of us made eye contact as we picked up our mess.

"Logan?" Sage said after a minute. "Um, when Brenda and I were talking earlier . . . I didn't say that you and I were dating. But I didn't tell her we weren't, either. She probably thinks there's something going on. I'm sorry, I just kind of wanted to rub her face in it. Let her know that you were gone forever."

A few weeks earlier, I would have insisted that Sage call Brenda right then and tell her that there was nothing, nothing going on between us. Now I simply shrugged and squished Grimace farther into the pool of ranch dressing.

"Who cares what Brenda thinks? C'mon." I stood. "I have to go call Laura and tell her I'm coming to Columbia, too."

We didn't speak as we walked to the parking lot. As I got on my bike and rode off, I could tell that Sage was watching me go. I failed in my determination not to look back, and I very nearly rode into a light pole.

## chapter twenty-one

T IM OBEDIENTLY WASHED himself in the algae-filled shower stall, as per the Columbia Civic Center rules. I waited in the locker room. Though Tim was wearing his swim trunks, I pointedly looked in the opposite direction.

It was the annual honor roll field trip. Bigger districts awarded high-performing students with tickets to Cardinals games or Six Flags. At Boyer, anyone who maintained a B average all year got to spend a Thursday afternoon at the huge indoor pool in Columbia.

The water turned off and Tim walked with me to the pool area, his man-boobs quaking as he moved. He kind of looked like Buddha, only without the all-knowing expression (and with a visible ass crack).

Columbia had a population of about eighty thousand not counting the college students, so the pool was enormous. It boasted a two-story water slide, a Jacuzzi, a high dive, and two sissy dives. The building was already packed with screaming preschoolers, veiny senior citizens, and half a dozen developmentally disabled adults.

I don't know why I come to these things. I didn't care for swimming, and none of the female honor rollers looked very impressive in their swimsuits. Brenda always qualified to come, but she never did. She didn't feel comfortable swimming. She was the only girl I ever knew whose bathing suit had sleeves.

Tim waddled to the high dive and made a fairly graceful plunge. I scoped out the girls from my school. Chubby, wobbly Cindy. Tall, gawky Vanessa. Chestless Carla. *Hey, who's that?*

She was sitting on the edge of the pool with her back to me. She didn't look familiar, at least from behind. This girl was talking to Carla; probably a friend of hers who'd already graduated. *Well, maybe I should go introduce myself.*

I approached cautiously, keeping an eye out for any gross physical deformities. The strange girl stood up to medium-range scrutiny. She was wearing a bikini top and swim skirt, though she wasn't exactly skinny. Still, her curves were nice. Her hair was totally crammed into a swim cap. Her skin was freckled; it looked as if her shoulders had been dusted with cinnamon.

So far, so good. Of course, I still hadn't seen her face. I decided to hop in the water next to her. If she was cute (or even average-looking), I'd say hi. If she was ugly, I'd just swim on.

I subtly checked myself for obvious wood, then splashed

in. When I looked the girl in the face, I almost became the first person to drown in the shallow end of the Columbia pool.

The girl, the person standing there in a bikini top, was Sage.

That wasn't even the jarring part. Something made me forget to swim when I hit the water. Something made me forget to hold my breath when I went under.

Actually, two somethings.

"Logan? Are you okay?" Sage bent over me with concern.

I coughed violently, trying to ignore the area below her neck. "Fine, fine, good to see you, didn't know you'd be here!"

"Yeah, my grades—"

"Great! Well, I'm going to go see Tim!" I dog paddled off, trying to think of a logical explanation for what I'd seen.

Sage had breasts.

Now, from the age of about eleven, every straight guy cannot stop thinking about boobs. Dirty magazines, porno movies, swimsuit catalogs, women's health pamphlets . . . We drool over whatever we can get our hands on. A lucky few get their hands on the real thing.

Sage had the real thing.

I bobbed by the rope that separated us from the deep end and stared at her. She was all the way in the water, though it only came up to her navel. The bunchy swim skirt completely obscured her crotch. Her tits, however, were almost on display.

That whole story about her being a boy was a lie! That

was the only explanation. All this time, I'd assumed she stuffed her bra, that her real chest was as flat as mine, and now this! That was a woman's body.

Then I remembered my confrontation with her dad. He had flat-out said Sage was male. But how?

Around me people swam, shouted "Marco Polo," and attempted to feel each other up underwater. I just gazed at Sage. Could they be fake, press-on boobs? She wouldn't dare swim with those on. They must be real. That bikini left little to the imagination, and besides, her headlights were on.

Maybe she had implants. But her parents never would have allowed that. I thought about asking her to talk in private, but there was nowhere we could go where she'd feel safe discussing this.

I floated in six feet of water, rotating to follow Sage like a navigational buoy. They jiggled like the real thing. She had love handles, but not the paunchy gut of a guy. When you didn't take her height into consideration, she was well proportioned.

Tim attempted to get me to join in a game of water volleyball, but I ignored him. Cindy, the class president, tried to talk to me, but I blew her off. All I could think of was Sage's sudden womanhood.

I didn't approach her. The temptation to ask would have been too great. I saw her look in my direction several times, but she never came near. Finally, when she'd joined the other girls in the locker room, I started to leave the pool. It was then I realized I was sporting an erection, and I had to stare at Tim until it went away.

Tim played it cool until we had dried off, dressed, and

climbed into his car. Then he hauled off and jabbed me in the ribs.

"Ouch! Christ, Tim, what did you do that for?" Tim wasn't one for displays of anger. He'd usually debilitate an opponent with sarcasm.

"To knock some damn tact into you, Logan. Jesus."

"What?" I couldn't face him. I knew what he was talking about.

"Sage! If you'd glued your face to her cleavage, you'd have been less obvious. Lots of people noticed."

I tried to pass it off as normal horniness. "C'mon, you've never sneaked a peek?" *At a male friend's breasts?*

"Yes! Sneaked a peek! You were drooling over her like she was a garlic steak, cooked medium rare, with creamed spinach on the side. . . ."

"Yeah . . ."

"And some of those little potatoes, you know the kind, with butter and sour cream. . . ."

"Tim!"

"Sorry. Look, buddy, there's no shame in looking. And I'm glad you've gotten over Brenda. But you know better than to gawk like that." He started the car and pulled out of the lot.

"Yeah." I couldn't explain that I hadn't been staring out of lust, but out of shock.

"One more thing. I know you freak out whenever we mention it, but why not just admit you like Sage?"

"Because I don't!" I growled.

"Well, I'm driving, so you can't hit me for saying this. You're full of shit, Logan."

I tried to ignore Tim. I rolled down the window, but it was too cold on my wet hair, so I rolled it back up.

"I don't like Sage." Why did I sound like I was saying *I don't have a drinking problem?*

"What's the big deal, Logan? Are you still hoping it's going to work out with Brenda? It's not."

"I know that." I wasn't lying, either. In fact, I'd been kind of relieved when Brenda hadn't shown up today. I didn't want to talk to her.

"Then what? Embarrassed that Sage is so much taller than you? Get over yourself."

"Tim, I'm going to say this, and then we're going to drop it. Forever. Sage and I are friends, and nothing more. I guess when I saw her body today, I was kind of . . . surprised, but nothing's changed."

We were silent for the half-hour drive back to Boyer. I waited until Tim's dust trail had disappeared before grabbing my bike and speeding off to Sage's house.

Since Sage and I had become friends again, I used her condition as an excuse not to think of her as a real girl. Every time I noticed her smile, her legs, or her hair, I'd remind myself what was under her clothes. I'd mentally constructed a torso that would shame Bigfoot: covered with hair from neck to navel, muscular and scarred, brawny and macho. True, I'd actually seen Sage's lower back and shoulders before, but I didn't let that affect the picture in my head. I'd tell myself over and over that under those wild dresses and loud shirts lay the masculine, male body of a man, and that it was pure sickness to imagine Sage any other way.

I'd certainly never imagined a cute, plump belly; a smooth, freckled back; and a chest that . . . oh, sweet Lord. In an instant, Sage had become the girl . . . the *woman* . . . she'd been to me when we first met. Her actual body was even more impressive than I would have pictured when we went to the movies.

Sage had a woman's chest. It was perverse! Unnatural! It wasn't even possible!

*And we were supposed to go off to Columbia together this weekend!*

I didn't even slow down when I turned onto Sage's street, and I almost completely lost control of my bike. I had to talk to Sage. She had a couple of things to explain.

*chapter twenty-two*

THE LIVING ROOM LIGHT WAS on, but there were no vehicles in Sage's driveway. Hopefully, that meant her parents were gone. I parked my bike, then stood on the front porch. What was I going to say? *Hey, I couldn't help noticing . . .*

Tammi answered my knock. She stood with her arms folded, like the doorman at some trendy club.

"Sage is in the shower."

"Ah. Well, tell her I stopped by." Obviously, I didn't meet the dress code. I walked back among the many lawn gnomes. Just before I mounted my bike, Tammi called me back.

"Why don't you wait inside, Logan?" There was a friendliness in her voice I'd never heard before. Cautiously, I entered the house.

I figured I'd be waiting in the living room, but Tammi escorted me to Sage's room.

"I'll tell her you're here." There was a definite welcome in her voice. I wondered what had brought on this change.

"Your parents are gone, right?" I asked nervously.

"You think I'd invite you in if they were here?"

I could see Tammi knock on the bathroom door, then pass inside. It blew my mind. For the first ten or so years of Tammi's life, Sage had been her brother. Now Tammi felt comfortable going into the bathroom while Sage was showering. Had she really accepted her new sister so completely?

I sat on Sage's bed. Tammi quickly stuck her head through the doorway.

"She'll be done in a second." She ducked out again. I heard the door to her room slam, and then a radio came on. Apparently, Tammi wasn't going to chaperone today.

Sage's room was as chaotic as her personality. It was in a state of total disorder, but not dirty. In one corner, a sewing machine stood stacked with dozens of half-finished outfits. Rows of books were piled along one wall, while a large bookcase was crammed to overflowing with rocks, fossils, and dried flowers. The desk was buried under a pile of fashion magazines, photographs, and an almost obsolete computer.

Tammi's boy-band music drowned out any other sounds in the house, so I refrained from snooping too much. It was tempting to look and see which Internet sites Sage had bookmarked, but I contented myself with examining the things on her desk.

A purple leather-bound book caught my eye. *Journal.* Sage kept a diary? I wondered what she wrote in there. I wondered if she ever mentioned me.

"Hey, Logan."

I turned. Sage was closing the door behind her. She wore a bulky bathrobe and a towel over her hair.

"Hi, Sage. Here, I'll leave while you change."

Sage sat down in front of a makeup table. "Why bother? You saw practically everything at the pool. Did you come to take pictures?" I couldn't tell if she was being sarcastic or was actually angry.

"Very funny." I awkwardly crouched on the end of her bed. I hadn't been that obvious, had I?

Sage removed the towel from her head and began brushing her wet hair. "You almost drowned back there. I never knew I had such an amazing figure."

"Neither did I, Sage."

She paused midbrush and swiveled in her chair. "You really had no idea?" She seemed legitimately surprised that I didn't know.

"How is this possible? You said yourself, you're technically . . . not a girl. But you have . . . you have . . ."

"Thirty-six B breasts. Thanks for noticing." She winked.

I remembered seeing her from behind at the pool, when I didn't recognize her. I'd thought she looked so beautiful, all wet in that bikini top. I had liked what I saw. And Sage knew it. I mentally begged her not to mention it. Didn't she realize I wasn't supposed to look at another boy that way?

"Sage, how did you . . . um . . . develop like that?"

Sage played with her brush. Then she pulled a small pill bottle out of a drawer of her makeup table and set it on the desk next to me. "I take synthetic estrogen. Hormones, Logan." There was shame in her voice, like she was admitting to having some kind of fungus.

I flopped backward on the bed. This was too much. "Like medicine? You actually grew those things?"

Sage sat down next to me. "I started when I was fourteen. It took a few years, but I'm happy with the results. But why are you so surprised? You had to have noticed before." She was leaning back, and I could see the ghost of her curves against her robe.

"I always thought you just wore a padded bra or something." Men didn't have breasts, not in my experience.

"You never wondered why I don't have a beard? You never noticed how soft my skin is?" She held her arm out to me as if she wanted me to feel her softness. I jumped up off the bed and began to pace.

"Of course I noticed, but I just thought you were girly. I guess I never knew you could change someone's body like that." I thought back to the pool. Pills could turn a guy into a chick?

Sage's oversized robe had slipped slightly, revealing her bare shoulder. "Only if you start before puberty's over. That's another reason I transitioned early. If *you* started taking hormones now, you wouldn't get nearly the results. Your breasts would stay small and pointy, and you wouldn't lose your facial hair. Your, ah, *other parts* wouldn't wither up as much, either."

I got a full-on case of the shudders. I certainly didn't like thinking about what hormones could do to me! Especially that last bit.

I picked up the pill bottle but didn't look too closely. "So you just go up to the pharmacy and order this stuff?"

"Ha! I wish. It's a catch-twenty-two situation for trans-gendered people. Hormones have to be prescribed by a psychiatrist, and most therapists won't let you start until you're in your midtwenties. By then they won't do you nearly as much good." Sage crossed her legs, revealing her bare, hairless calves.

I tried to read the label on the bottle, but it made no sense. "So how did you get these?"

"I order them from Mexico. My grandfather left me a few thousand dollars, and my parents were foolish enough to put it in an account with my name on it. It was supposed to go toward a car for me, but instead . . . Every month I have to buy an international money order, spend a bunch more on postage, and worry like hell that it won't go through."

"Your parents let you do this?" I figured Sage's father would cut off the medicine the second he found out.

"They don't know."

I stared at her skeptically, and she frowned.

"They know. But they won't talk about it. They don't want to deal with it. Mom knows I'm never going to go back to being a guy, and my dad . . . he'd never bring it up. He still tells me I'll end up going back to being a boy. I'm not sure if he's trying to be cruel or he's just deluding himself." She snatched the bottle of hormones and put it back in her vanity.

That night in the garage, when her father was yelling at me . . . all he had talked about was how Sage made him feel and how ashamed *he* was of her. Did it ever occur to him that Sage might be feeling ashamed? That she needed her dad to be proud of her, just like any other teenage girl? I wanted to tell Sage that her father was wrong. But not right then. I was still sorting out my own emotions.

"Sage, you're full of surprises. I'm sorry I wigged out at the pool." I got up to leave. "I just never realized that under your clothes, you were so . . ."

She stood, looking at me intently. "So what?"

"Um . . ." Ah, hell, there was no denying it. "So womanly." I said it with a grin, letting her know there was nothing sexual about my comment. I turned and placed my hand on the knob.

"Logan?"

I looked back. Sage was standing near her bed. The bottom of her bathrobe had fallen open, revealing that she was wearing a thick pair of gym shorts. Slowly, her hand crept up to the robe's belt and began to undo it.

"Sage, don't." I did not want to see her body again. I did not want to see her smooth belly or her freckled shoulders or her round, perfect chest. I knew I'd never be able to forget what I'd seen.

Her hand didn't stop. The knot fell apart. Her robe began to open. Slowly. I had plenty of time to leave if I wanted. Why was she tormenting me like this?

Her robe collapsed onto the bed. And there she stood, in nothing but shorts. Every detail of Sage's damp body was revealed.

This was the first time I'd ever seen an actual pair, in real life. Brenda, who was not as well endowed, never let me this close.

*I should leave. I should say something. I should close my eyes. I shouldn't just stand here. I really shouldn't be walking toward her.*

Sage stood silently, her hands held nervously at her side. What was she thinking?

*Do you still doubt I'm a woman, Logan?*

*Do you like what you see?*

*Would you like to do more?*

I was close enough now to see individual freckles. Close enough to smell Sage's shampoo, to feel the moisture radiating from her skin.

My hands raised and gently touched her hips. She was right, her skin *was* soft. Her body quaked. Our eyes locked. Sage was smiling a terrified smile. There I stood, holding a topless woman. I could feel her stomach expand with each breath.

She took my right hand in both of hers. Her fingers wrapped around my wrist. Gently, she guided me upward. Sage wanted to be touched. She wanted me to touch her. Hip, belly, ribs . . .

Just before my fingertips made contact, I broke away. No explanation. I was out the door and on my bike within seconds. I didn't stop moving until I had locked myself in the bathroom at home.

*Sage . . . oh, oh, Sage.*

Picturing Sage standing topless and damp in her room, I unzipped my pants.

## chapter twenty-three

OUR BATHROOM WAS only slightly larger than an outhouse. This had been especially rough when Laura lived at home and all three of us had to share.

I lay on the moldy bath mat, crammed between the toilet and the shower. I'd been there for a couple of hours, just sprawled out, staring at the dead bulb above the mirror. The phone rang a couple of times, but I didn't answer.

Well, I'd blown it. Totally, absolutely blown it. Months of trying to convince myself that Sage was my buddy, that I didn't have the tiniest speck of a sliver of a fraction of an interest in her . . . and now *this*. I had touched her soft, soft—dear God, it was *so* soft—skin. And if that wasn't enough, I'd pleasured myself just thinking about her. It was a little late to be pretending my feelings for Sage were pure brotherly concern.

The worst part wasn't what I'd just done. It was what

I'd almost done. Rushing out of Sage's house took a lot of willpower. What if she'd grabbed my arm? Or kissed me? What if she'd said, *Logan, please don't go?* That might have been enough. My defenses would have crumbled, all thoughts of the future vanished. Just me, Sage, and that body lotion I'd gotten her for Christmas.

And what then? After the smoke cleared, I couldn't just pretend that Sage didn't have a cock and balls . . . could I? Of course not. It disgusted me too much. And if her family ever found out, we'd both be sunk. Her father seemed like the sort of vengeful son of a bitch who'd tell my mom everything, out of pure spite.

I huddled in the bathroom corner, wrapping the filthy bath mat around my shoulders like a cape. I wondered what Sage was doing. Maybe primping in front of her mirror, smirking about how she'd almost landed me and planning her next move. More likely, she was hiding in her room, as confused and scared as I was.

I needed to talk to her, tell her my fears, beg her never to put me in a position like that again. I just didn't have the self-control. But not now. Things were too fresh.

"Logan, honey, are you here?" Mom's voice rang through the trailer.

"Just a second." I stood and checked myself in the mirror. I looked like someone you'd see urinating in an alley while talking to himself. I removed my cape, washed my face, and zipped my pants.

What Sage and I needed right now was distance. Just a week or so with no contact, followed by a promise never to be alone like that again. That was the only way our friendship could survive.

There was just one problem. We were planning on spending the weekend in Columbia together.

The next day was Friday. I was supposed to drive to the university on Saturday with Sage and spend the night. And now I couldn't allow that to happen. After the incident in her room, there was no way we could be alone together for that long. Sage obviously was willing to do just about anything with me. I had to avoid being in that position again.

I tried to call Laura to cancel, but there was no answer. I left a message for her to call me. I couldn't bring myself to phone Sage. Not so soon after seeing the effects of her Mexican medication.

That day at school, I avoided her. I even ran laps after the last bell until I was sure she'd left. We couldn't talk about what had happened when people could overhear. Besides, it would be easier for me to cancel on Sage if I didn't have to look her in the face.

Friday evening, I still hadn't called her. It was nearly seven. If I didn't pick up the phone soon, she'd show up at the trailer the next day, all packed and ready to go.

Mom was home that night and wanted to spend the evening with me. I couldn't really tell her no. In a few months, I'd be off at Mizzou and might not see her for weeks at a time. The idea frightened me a bit. In Columbia, there'd be no one to do my laundry, fix me breakfast, worry when I was out late, or give me a hug before classes.

Mom was setting up the Scrabble board as I stared at

the phone trying to get up the courage to call Sage. We only had the one phone, in the living room. Mom never deliberately listened in on my calls, but the trailer was small. This was one conversation I didn't want her accidentally-on-purpose overhearing.

I was still trying to think of a polite way to ask Mom to step out for a minute, when the phone rang. Mom answered it. Then she smiled.

"It's Sage," she teased, like I was fourteen and this was the first time a girl had ever called me. I took the receiver.

Mom stood up and walked to the front door. "I forgot to get something out of the car." The screen slammed after her. Obviously, she realized I wanted a little privacy.

"Sage?" My voice cracked.

"Hi, Logan."

"Hi." So far, so good.

The line might have gone dead; neither of us spoke. There was so much for both of us to say.

*Sage, I don't think we should see each other for a while. I still find you attractive, and I can't deal with that.*

Maybe Sage was thinking along the same lines. Finally, she broke the silence.

"So, Logan, am I still going to Mizzou with you tomorrow?" Her voice got higher throughout the sentence and ended with a squeak.

All I had to do was say no. She'd understand. After we'd both had time to calm down, we could take a day trip or something. Saying no would have been so easy.

"Of course, Sage. You're my ride." *Wait, wrong line!*

Sage giggled. "Okay. Just making sure. See you tomorrow around noon." She hung up without saying goodbye.

I stared at the phone until the recorded message told me to hang up and dial. What had I just agreed to do? Why?

*Because you wanted to. Because you want to see Laura and visit the campus and hang out with Sage. You're both nervous about going away to school, and you'll have fun exploring Mizzou together.*

Which is exactly why I should have canceled the trip. If Sage had been nothing more than a girl with a pretty face and a great rack, I could have forgotten about her. But she was also my friend. Which meant I didn't want to avoid her when I should.

I had to be Iceman this weekend. Mr. Cool. Sage and I would talk on the drive to Columbia. I'd ask her, for the sake of our friendship, not to come on to me again. She'd do that for me, I was sure. When we got to campus, I'd stay with Laura's friends. Hang out with the girls, but not be too chummy with Sage. My sister would just think she was a classmate of mine I'd asked out once. By Sunday afternoon, Sage would be back to being just another transgendered girl who I'd shared secrets and saliva with.

Mom came back into the trailer, pausing to make sure I was off the phone.

"Everything okay?"

I sat down in front of the Scrabble board. "Yeah, she just wanted to make sure we were still on for tomorrow."

"Hmm." Mom obviously had reservations about me leaving town with Sage. I'd considered not telling her who my ride was, but that would involve a lot of lying and getting either Jack or Tim to pretend to be going with me. In the end, I just emphasized that I'd be sleeping in another room.

I looked down at my letters. S, Q, P, P, T, B, and the blank. I shuffled my tiles, still thinking of Sage. She was beautiful and my friend, and obviously nuts about me. If the world made sense, this afternoon would have been the greatest experience of my life. Instead, it was just confusing and scary. Why couldn't Sage just be a normal girl?

She probably was asking herself that same question.

## chapter twenty-four

I CRAMMED the clothes I needed for the weekend in a canvas Houston Oilers bag I found in the shed. It had probably belonged to my father. Every so often, I'd come across something Mom hadn't thrown away: a soldering iron, some fishing tackle, a catcher's mitt.

*Dad, if you were still here, would I be such a romantic screwup? Maybe you of all people could have convinced me to get over Brenda sooner. Then I never would have known Sage. At least, not like I do now.*

Then again, the only advice Dad would probably give was to run away when things got too difficult.

Sage was picking me up shortly. Mom was in the kitchen, busy packing me a lunch. Apparently, there was no food in Columbia.

"Logan, are you sure you have enough money? You guys might want to go out, and things are a lot more expensive than in Boyer."

"I'm fine, Mom." I had forty bucks, the last of my snow-shoveling cash. I hoped Laura didn't want to go anywhere too fancy.

"How about a jacket? I know it's warm, but the weatherman says—"

"I'll be fine, Mom." I think if I'd been going on an expedition to the Sahara, she'd want me to take a jacket.

Mom joined me on the sofa. "Be sure and see how Laura's doing. She won't take any money from me, and I worry she's doing okay."

"I'm sure she's good." Actually, Laura had told me that her job paid really well. Barring unexpected expenses, she was planning on sending money home next semester.

Mom started to get up, then sat down. She picked up a gossip magazine and nervously flipped through it.

"Is something wrong, Mom?"

She frowned. "Logan, you'll be spending the weekend with Sage."

I manned the defenses. "We've been over this! Sage will be staying with Laura, and I'll be with some friends of hers." I prayed that Laura really had found me a bed in another dorm. It would be difficult to explain why I was sleeping in the hall, otherwise.

Mom cocked a knowing eyebrow. "I was young once, too, you know." She held up a hand to stop my protests. "Let me finish. You keep telling me Sage is just a friend, though I think you should give her a second look. My point is, if you should find yourselves—"

"Please don't say it!" God, not the sex talk. Where the hell was Sage?

Mom plowed on. "Logan, just in case. You're old enough now that I can't stop you. But please, promise me you'll take precautions. Will you do that?"

My thoughts briefly blinked to an image of Sage opening her robe. Too humiliated to speak, I just nodded.

"I'm not trying to embarrass you, sweetie. But you're about to go off on a great adventure this fall. If Sage ended up pregnant, that would be the end of that."

I wanted to protest that there was no way I was going to sleep with Sage, but I kept my mouth shut. If I argued too much, Mom might start to wonder just why I wasn't attracted to her.

"Mom, you have nothing to worry about." If Sage got pregnant, I'd be on the lookout for three wise men from the East.

There was a shy knock at the door. Sage stuck her head in.

"Hello?"

"Come in!" Mom was already standing to invite her in, to fix her a snack, to grill her about what we'd be doing this weekend. No way.

I grabbed my bag, and with a quick peck on Mom's cheek, I was gone. I didn't realize until later that I'd forgotten the lunch she'd made me.

I didn't want to give Sage a chance to ask to use the bathroom, so I nearly broke my best sprinting time dashing to her car. It was the family sedan this time. I guess her parents didn't want her taking the cranky truck out of town.

I'd thrown my bag in the back by the time Sage folded herself into the driver's seat. She was wearing jeans and a

T-shirt. Her hair was tied up in a scarf, and she wore sunglasses. I think this was the most conservatively I'd seen her dressed. For a moment, I remembered that there was no padding under her top; it was all Sage. Then I realized I was staring.

Sage smiled at me. Was she going to bring up what had happened in her bedroom or wait for me to say something? Could we just laugh it off as a mistake, or did we need to have a long, serious talk? And maybe she didn't even think what we'd done was wrong! For all I knew, she was planning on getting me alone this weekend and showing me just how much of a woman she was.

This was stupid. I shouldn't have come. I waited for her to make some mention of what we'd done. How I'd touched her. How I'd almost done more.

Silence. After a while, she instructed me to pick out a CD for us to listen to. Her window was rolled down. She had one elbow on the door, the other arm casually on the wheel. A few strands of hair tickled her forehead from under her headscarf. She looked like a confident, attractive girl, off to conquer a new town. A girl who was going to arrive at college and *own* it. And who didn't even care that she'd reduced her only friend to a miserable pile of jelly.

I jammed a random CD into the slot and stared out the window.

Sage drove maddeningly slow. I remembered how she'd mentioned her fear of getting a speeding ticket. The half-hour drive to Columbia was going to take nearly twice that. After fifteen minutes of silence, she finally spoke.

"We don't have to do this. I can take you back home if you want."

I knew I should say yes, but I kept my mouth shut. When I didn't answer, she spoke again.

"Logan, remember the night you met my dad?"

I snorted. "Vividly." Why was she bringing that up?

She removed her sunglasses. With her wide, sad eyes, she looked much less confident. "When we got to my house and he was standing there, I expected you to bolt. I wouldn't have blamed you at all. But you stayed and let him yell at you, even though you were still uncomfortable around me. That was the nicest, bravest thing anyone has ever done for me." Judging by her tone alone, you'd think I'd slayed a dragon or two.

"That night, I promised myself that I'd never do anything to hurt a friendship that special. You don't know how great it was to finally be able to talk to someone about everything in my life. But the other day, when I saw you checking me out at the pool . . . I think I let us both down." She massaged the bridge of her nose, then gripped the steering wheel with both hands.

"Sage, it's not like that."

"Logan, you're my best friend. I need that more than anything else. And trying to take advantage of you the other day, I almost ruined it. Can we just forget about that? Are we still cool?" She was breathing hard, and her steering had become slightly erratic.

"Yeah, we're cool," I said bluntly. There. We'd talked and put it behind us. Things could go back to "normal."

Only I didn't want to drop it. My best friend had allowed

me to see her bare body and now was apologizing to *me*. I couldn't let her sit there feeling ashamed of her beautiful, though highly inappropriate, gesture. But how could I put my feelings into words when I couldn't even define them? There was only one thing I could say.

"Sage?"

"Yes?"

I waited till she turned and looked at me. Then I winked. "Wow."

She rapidly looked back at the windshield, her eyes wide, blushing under her freckles. I rolled down my window and leaned back in my seat.

Everything was going to be okay. We'd experimented but backed off before we crossed the line. We could now go off to college as friends, instead of whatever horrible, awkward relationship we almost had.

As I half dozed for the rest of the trip, my thoughts floated back to Sage's room. She'd never be a real woman to me. But damn, seeing her without her robe . . . that had been a definite wow moment.

If parking was bad downtown, it was awful on campus. The lot Laura had directed me to was full, and every other space had ominous warning signs about towing and impounding. Eventually, we parked on the roof of a parking garage about three blocks from Laura's dorm.

I grabbed my bag from the backseat. I was going to take Sage's, but she had already hefted her two suitcases with no effort. We started down the stairs to street level.

"So, tell me about your sister, Logan."

"Well, she's a year older than me, though sometimes it seems like twenty."

Sage laughed. "C'mon. I talked to her on the phone. She didn't seem old or boring at all."

"It's not that." I paused to tie my shoe. "When Dad left . . . I was about four. Anyway, things were kind of rough. Mom was working double shifts, and then when she was home, she had two little kids to take care of. Not a lot of time to read bedtime stories or play catch." I stood up, remembering.

"At any rate, Laura really mothered me. Told me stories, played with me, made sure I did my homework. She helped me stay out of trouble, at least until high school."

We'd exited the garage and were trekking across a parking lot. I could tell we were on a college campus just by the bumper stickers: YOU CAN'T HUG YOUR CHILDREN WITH NUCLEAR ARMS. U.S. OUT OF _____. FLIP THE BIRD (a dig at the Kansas University Jayhawks).

I continued my story. "Things got a little better in the past few years, moneywise. But Laura still ran our household. Trailerhold. She made sure the bills got paid, went grocery shopping, took care of things. When she left . . . well, here Mom and I are, and we don't have a lot to say to each other. It's not that we're distant, it's just that . . . I dunno, we've just been living separate lives for so long. And I worry about what she's going to do with herself when I leave." Would Mom suffer from empty trailer syndrome? Would she finally start taking time for herself? Would she—I could hardly imagine it—go on dates?

Sage rumpled my hair. "Believe it or not, I know where

you're coming from. The whole time I was homeschooled, Tammi really stood up for me. When I first started to transition—" She suddenly stopped talking and walking. "Sorry."

"Sage, it's okay to talk about that." Previously, Sage's gender issues were the last thing I wanted to discuss. But maybe if she told me about her life as a boy, it would help remind me she wasn't totally a girl.

Sage glanced around for eavesdroppers, and then we sat on a bench. "When I finally told everyone that I was a girl inside . . . there was talk of having me institutionalized."

I had been staring at the observatory on top of the physics building, but her comment jolted me back to attention. "Like, the nuthouse?"

"Yeah. Mom and Dad didn't know how to deal with me and decided I needed to be sent away for a cure. I'm not sure if they thought that was the best thing for me or if they were just that humiliated. But Tammi threw a fit. I mean, screaming, hollering, kicking the walls. She refused to let them send me away. Eleven years old. She knew what an embarrassment I'd be to the family, but she didn't care."

Sage seemed to be collapsing into herself. Knowing better, I draped an arm around her back. She laid her head on my shoulder. Well, technically, due to our height difference, my head was on her shoulder.

"So Tammi kept me out of the asylum. I spent four years almost never leaving our house, getting taught by my mother. Mom's ashamed of what I'm doing, but she tries to make me happy. And you know how Dad feels.

"Tammi . . . she looked out for me. Before I was allowed to wear women's clothes full-time, she'd buy me clothes and hide them in her closet. She'd help me with my makeup and tell me I was pretty. She was the only one who knew when I started on hormones. Now that I'm a full-time girl, she spies on me. She doesn't want me to do anything reckless. That's why she wouldn't let us be alone at the park that one time."

I smiled, remembering. It all made sense now.

Sage continued. "Tammi never once said I was being weird or strange. Sometimes that was the only reason I knew I could become a real woman. If it wasn't for her, I'd have probably given up and stayed a guy."

Gingerly, I untangled myself from Sage. "You'd have been miserable that way."

"I'd be dead."

I remembered Sage's attempt at suicide. We needed to change the subject. I'd brought Sage here to show her how much fun she could have away from home, not to remind her of her difficult life choices.

Looking down at my watch, I realized I wasn't wearing it. "I think Laura's expecting us."

Sage led the way even though neither of us really knew where we were going. As we passed a group of male pedestrians, one of them turned to watch her pass. I don't think it was her height he was noticing.

# chapter twenty-five

SAGE AND I WANDERED around for about twenty minutes looking for Gillett Hall. Finally, we realized it was actually part of a larger complex, a group of white brick towers that surrounded a central dining hall.

Laura lived on the first floor. As soon as we left the lobby, the low *thunk, thunk* of someone's stereo assaulted us from an upper story. The corridor was empty, but each door gave a glimpse of the residents inside: film posters, more anti-Kansas bumper stickers, fliers for peace marches, little whiteboards for leaving messages.

I knew more about these strangers than I did about some of my neighbors in Boyer. I'd be moving into a dorm in the fall. What would I hang on my door?

Sage strutted down the hall, showing her usual self-assuredness. She'd lived in a big town before, but I felt like I'd just come from the farm. The students here would have me pegged as a hick right from the start. When two girls carrying tennis rackets passed us and smiled, it was like I was wearing a rope belt and no shoes. Could I really fit in at Mizzou?

I'd visited Laura here a couple of times, but always with Mom, and we always met downtown. I located my sister's room. The only decoration was a photocopied poster for an unfamiliar band. It might have been her roommate's.

The door flew open at my knock. Laura stood there grinning at me for a moment. Once again, I was struck by what a woman she'd become. When she'd left home, she'd been a tomboyish teenager. A girl who used to beat me at basketball and had broken Mark Jefferson's nose when he tried to feel her up. Now Laura was almost twenty and looked like someone you'd see working at a bank or modeling formal clothes. If I hadn't known her, I would have guessed her to be twenty-two or -three, a business major or pre-law, the sort of person who'd work a sixty-hour week and then shut down the bars every Saturday night. Had college done this to her, or was it simply being away from Boyer that had allowed her to grow up?

"Logan!" She embraced me. "I'm so glad you're here. We're going to have so much fun this weekend."

"Laura, this is Sage."

They shook hands, and Laura directed Sage where to put her bags. As Sage was unloading, Laura turned and gave me a conspiratorial wink. Great. Well, at least my sister didn't suspect Sage's secret.

The dorm room was obsessively neat, much more orderly than Laura's bedroom at home. I wondered what would inspire people to clean when they didn't have to. Must be a girl thing.

"Sage, you can take my roommate's bed," said Laura.

"Are you sure?" asked Sage. "Won't she mind?"

"Ebony's out of town for the weekend. She said it was okay."

I glanced at a family photo on Ebony's desk. Laura's roommate had very dark skin, very white teeth, and a very pretty face. I'd have to visit again when she was there and Sage wasn't.

Sage asked if she could go freshen up, and Laura directed her to the public bathroom down the hall. As soon as the door closed, Laura socked me in the arm.

"So this is the girl you like! She's cute, Logan."

I rubbed my shoulder, cursing myself for telling Laura about Sage at Thanksgiving. "We're not dating," I said, hoping Sage wouldn't return before I could try to explain things.

I could tell Laura wasn't buying it. "Uh-huh. Well, if you and your 'friend' want to be alone tonight, I can sleep somewhere else." She was grinning, proud to help her little brother do something naughty.

Time to nip this in the bud. I'd learned that saying I didn't like Sage only made people want to know why. I chose my next words carefully.

"Laura, you were right. Sage has some real problems at home. We're not going to get together. I brought her here because she needed to get away from her house for a while. Now, where am I sleeping tonight?"

For a moment, Laura looked disappointed and a little

concerned. "I just assumed you'd crash here on the floor. I have a sleeping bag."

Nope. Even with Laura in the room, I wasn't about to spend the night with Sage.

"I thought you said I could stay with your friends."

Laura opened her mouth to ask a question, but stopped. "Well, a couple of guys invited you to bunk with them, but I didn't know if you'd be comfortable."

Was I that obviously ill at ease? It's not like I was ten, spending the night away from home for the first time. Laura didn't need to protect me.

"I'll stay with them. That way you won't have to see me scratching myself."

Laura laughed. "That would be a nice change of pace. Their names are Brian and Paul, room one-oh-five. Just knock; they'll know who you are."

I marched down the corridor, determined not to embarrass myself in front of Laura's friends. I hoped they wouldn't ask me about drinking or women. I didn't exactly have an amazing track record with either.

Apparently this was a coed floor. Door #105 was slathered with heavy metal stickers and video game ads, along with a cryptic, hand-lettered sign: THERE'S NO PROB WITH "BOB." I could hear what sounded like machine-gun fire within. I knocked.

"C'mon in!"

The only light in the dorm came from a TV tuned to the Cartoon Network and from a computer screen. The shades were drawn and I couldn't make out anything. A damp, musty odor emanated from within. I was reminded of Devil's Icebox, a local cave.

"Hello?"

"Dude, you Logan?" As my eyes adjusted, I could see someone seated at the computer. The light from the computer game made his face look unhealthy, pallid. His hair was longish, and he was unshaven. He didn't have enough facial hair to grow a full beard, so odd tufts of whiskers sprouted randomly on his cheeks.

"That's me."

He paused the game but didn't get up. "I'm Brian. That's Paul." He gestured to a bed. What I had assumed was a pile of laundry was actually a man, asleep on his side. He was either black or Middle Eastern; I couldn't tell in the dark.

"Just throw your bag anywhere," instructed Brian. I stepped inside, disconcerted by the crunching noises that accompanied my every step. This room was possibly the filthiest place I'd ever been. Clothes, empty food containers, books, and computer equipment littered everything. I realized, to my horror, I'd be sleeping on the floor. So this was why Laura had tried to get me to stay with her. And now I couldn't back out. Maybe I'd just sleep in the lobby.

I balanced my bag on top of a big box fan, the only bare surface I could find. "I'm going back to see Laura. I'm not sure what time I'll be in tonight."

Brian had already gone back to his game. "Don't worry. I'll be up late."

"Yeah, but if you go out, give Laura a call."

"We won't go out."

As I returned to my sister's room, I decided that, just possibly, I would not be the most socially inept person on campus.

When I entered the dorm, Sage was trying on one of Laura's jackets. It was far too small.

Sage handed it back to Laura. "It's hard to find clothes in my size."

"We should go to the Wardrobe tomorrow, Sage," said my sister. "It's a used clothing store, I bet you could find some neat stuff there."

"Oh, I'd like that!"

"And maybe after we could sit and watch paint dry!" I countered. I didn't like the idea of Sage changing in a public dressing room. I also didn't like the idea of spending Sunday shopping for women's clothes.

Laura waved at me dismissively. "There's a bunch of music stores and stuff downtown. You won't be bored."

Eventually, I convinced the girls to grab some supper. Laura took us to the dorm's dining hall, which offered a wider menu than any establishment in Boyer. As we ate, Laura filled Sage in on the best clothing stores, stylists, and coffee shops in town. Laura had grown up in Boyer, but she was as cool as any girl from St. Louis.

It was obvious Sage was making friends with my sister. When she enrolled next semester, they'd probably get together. They'd become close. Laura could introduce her to people, and the three of us could hang out. Laura would probably keep hoping Sage and I would hook up, but she'd stop when I started dating someone else. My sister, I realized, had the potential to be a better friend to Sage than I was. Sage needed another girl to talk shop with.

Laura was talking about the various dorms on campus. "So have you got your housing assignment yet?" she asked me.

"Yeah," I answered. "Jack and I are going to be at Graham Hall."

My sister grimaced. "I have a friend who lives there. Vintage forties steam heat. How about you, Sage? Do you know who you'll room with?"

"No," she said with a shrug. "I'll probably just pay extra for a single."

"Don't do that!" objected Laura. "That's, like, a thousand dollars extra a semester."

Sage winced. "That much?"

"Having a roommate isn't as bad as you think, Sage. Ebony's like a sister to me. I know some girls who will need a roommate next year. I can help you find someone nice."

Sage smiled as I frowned. Sage wouldn't be allowed to move in with a girl. She'd eventually have to turn down Laura's offer. I wished she didn't have to put up with so much bullshit.

Laura brushed her hair while Sage sat at a makeup table putting on eyeliner. We were going to a frat party in a couple of hours. I lay on Laura's bed, tossing a tennis ball at the ceiling, bored out of my skull. The girls weren't ignoring me on purpose. It's just that when the conversation revolved around shoes and makeup, I couldn't add much. I smiled inside, thinking of how my sister was discussing fashion and hairstyles with a boy.

Sage was filling Laura in about her family. "So my sister's dating this guy from school, Rob."

"Jennifer's brother," I reminded Laura. "Redheaded guy."

Sage began to rouge her cheeks. "Rob's a nice guy, but I just worry. I mean, Tammi's my sister. I want to look out for her."

"You always want to look out for your little sister . . . or brother." Laura winked at me. "You don't think anyone's good enough for them."

Sage had been applying lipstick, but paused. Her eyes met mine in the reflection of the mirror. "Well, a special guy deserves a special girl." Sage's image smirked at me. I fumbled the tennis ball, which banked off Laura's desk and bonked her in the face.

"Watch it, Logan." She hurled it back at me, narrowly missing my groin. Hopefully, that distracted Laura from Sage's odd comment. What did she mean by *special girl*?

Sage finished coloring her lips. She puckered, then bit a tissue, leaving a bright red ring. "Well, are we ready to go?"

Laura grabbed her purse. "Let's do it. Maybe I can introduce you to someone tonight."

That got my hopes up. "Cute sorority chick?"

Laura laughed. "I was talking to Sage."

I stood up and took a good look at my friend. Her makeup skills, I realized, had improved since I'd first met her. And the way she was dressed: a long denim skirt and dark sweater. She wasn't wearing one of her wild outfits. The demure clothes emphasized her femininity, her long legs, her chest, her face. And she was about to go to a party with a bunch of drunk college guys. Every one of them would notice the tall, regal stranger. She'd drink, and Laura, if she truly believed I wasn't interested, would introduce Sage to other guys.

I was going to have to watch out for Sage. Make sure none of the frat rats got too close. Make sure she didn't drink too much or say anything compromising.

At the door, Sage stopped and adjusted my collar. She smiled at me, and I got a whiff of her perfume. As we left the building, I promised myself I wouldn't let her out of my sight the whole evening. You know, for her own safety.

## chapter twenty-six

SPRING WAS HERE. It was nearly seven at night, and the lights along Rollins Street were just coming on. I stared at my feet as we trudged toward Greek Town. In front of me, Laura and Sage laughed like a couple of sisters.

I viewed this evening with the mixed feelings Sage was so expert in bringing out. On the one hand, for the first time in my life, I could totally cut loose. No mom waiting up for me, no cops showing up to run us off, nowhere I was supposed to be in the morning. It would be good practice for next year. Could university girls be interested in a guy from a town that only ever made the news during tornado season?

On the other hand, Sage was here. And after what we'd almost done the other night, it would be kind of cruel to hit on other girls right in front of her. I'd be trying to get strange women to give me what Sage would happily give. And with Sage's forced dating ban, maybe we should just stick together. Not like a date. But we'd come here together, so it would be rude of me to wander off.

I walked a little faster and caught up with the girls. Sage looked at me warmly and slowed down. Laura was busy talking and didn't notice.

"Are you okay?" Sage asked.

"Yeah. You?"

Sage smoothed her sweater. "Nervous. Is it dumb for me to do this?"

She deserved an honest answer. "You look great. I'll be there with you if you need anything."

Sage bit her lip. "Logan, I couldn't do this without you. Thank you so much for everything."

We gripped hands for a moment, trying to dispel the fear in each other's faces. Laura, who realized we'd fallen behind, turned just in time to see me holding Sage's hand and gazing up into her eyes. We quickly separated.

Approaching Greek Town was like riding up to an encampment of angry Indians. I could hear their war cries long before I saw them. Solitary screams, laughter, and music broke through the still evening. As we passed by the Commons, I began to see the frat boys. They all wore expensive clothes and baseball caps with Greek letters stitched onto them. Several of them stared at Laura and Sage as we passed.

Fraternity houses lined the streets, bigger than anything in Boyer except maybe the electronics factory. The houses were beautiful: white columns, brick fronts, trimmed hedges.

We turned a corner, and Laura led us to a smaller, more

compact frat house. Inside, we could hear the voices and music of the party.

Laura danced up the steps. Sage and I paused on the sidewalk for a moment. Impulsively, I wrapped my hand around her upper arm and squeezed. Not a possessive gesture, and certainly not a romantic one. I just wanted her to know I was there with her, ready to help if she got scared. Sage returned my smile and we entered the building.

I had expected a fraternity house to be somewhat scuzzy, but the Kappa house was at least as nice as a midgrade motel. Thirty or so students milled around in the cigarette haze, drinking out of plastic cups. Everyone was completely at ease.

"Laura!"

The guy looked like something out of an ascent of man exhibit. He was short and swarthy and had one eyebrow that covered most of his jutting forehead. He didn't slouch, but it seemed like he'd be more natural dragging his enormous knuckles over the stained carpet. He looked at Laura, exposing his crooked teeth in a hungry smile.

"Hey, Laura!"

"Hi, Mike!"

And then they were kissing. I think Laura only meant to give him a hello kiss, but Mike smashed his face into hers, making growling noises and grabbing her butt. I wasn't aware I was lunging at him until Sage grabbed my arm.

Laura pulled away with a laugh. "Mike, this is Sage, and my brother, Logan."

Mike's smile froze, then shattered. He stared at me with raw panic, then extended his hand.

"Pleased to meet you, Logan."

We shook. I tried to play the hand-crushing game, but he quickly yielded.

Laura didn't realize I was about to throw down with this guy. "C'mon, Sage, there's some people I want you to meet. Mike, why don't you get Logan a drink and introduce him around."

Laura took Sage by the hand and pulled her toward a group of laughing girls. She glanced at me over her shoulder, but I had something else to do at the moment. Mike and I stared at each other for a couple of seconds. I did not smile.

"So, Logan. You're coming here next year?"

"Yes." I folded my arms and leaned toward him, demonstrating that I was the taller one. I fought an impulse to beat my chest.

Mike nodded rapidly. "Nice, nice. Got your housing assignment yet?"

"Yes."

"Did you ever consider going Greek?"

"No."

Mike stood there, trying to make eye contact and failing. When someone waved at him from across the room, he took off like a shot. I'd kick his ass later.

It took me a moment to locate Sage through the haze of smoke. She was standing with Laura and two other girls. I couldn't make out what Sage was saying, but when she bent and gestured at her shoes, I realized they were speaking Clothes, the universal female language. My friend seemed quite fluent. Since I only spoke conversational Clothes, I decided not to join them.

I was thirsty, and tradition dictated that I have a beer. The keg stood in a large common area, surrounded by a bunch of smokers. I grabbed a cup and tried to fill it, but nothing came out.

"Dude, you gotta pump it. Here." A skinny guy in a backward cap filled me up.

"Thanks." I was never much of a drinker and couldn't identify the brand of almost orange beer in my cup. I chugged it.

"Dude, you with the Deltas?"

"No."

"Tau Omega?"

I swilled the rest of the beer. "I'm still in high school. I won't be here till next year." I waited for him to blow me off.

Frat man emptied his cup, then refilled us both. "You ought to pledge with us next year. Kappa kicks fucking ass!" Around the room, guys raised their cups and whooped in agreement.

Huh. He actually wanted me to join his frat. I felt like much less of a hick.

"I'm Logan."

"Dalton." We smacked fists. "So, is that tall chick your girlfriend?"

Down the corridor, I could just make out Sage's back. She was talking to someone, but I couldn't tell who.

"She's just a friend." I downed my drink.

"Whoa, Logan," said Dalton. "Take it easy. Beer before liquor, never sicker."

I filled my cup again but just held it. The two beers I'd slammed suddenly hit me, and I felt less steady. I made my way back to the main room.

Whoever was in charge of the sound system must have been worried that people in Omaha couldn't hear the music. I could feel the sonic waves echoing off my lungs. I couldn't locate Sage in the hazy crowd, and she was not usually hard to pick out of a group.

Laura emerged from the shadows, grabbing my arm. "Hey, Logan!" she hollered.

"Have you seen Sage?"

She either didn't hear or was ignoring the question. "Come over here. I want you to meet someone."

She dragged me over to a couch held together with plywood and duct tape. A couple of girls sat there sipping mixed drinks. Laura propelled me to an empty cushion.

My sister leaned toward the nearest girl, one of the few female guests in jeans and a T-shirt. "Erin, this is my brother, Logan. Logan, Erin."

Erin was short, even sitting down. Her brown hair was long and almost impossibly straight. She had such dark eyes that I couldn't see her pupils. She wasn't wearing any makeup, though that accentuated her naturally pretty face.

"Hi, Erin."

Laura took a drink from someone else's cup. "Logan's

coming here next year. He's quite the track star. I'll be right back."

Erin scooted toward me, I guess so I could hear her over the noise. "Laura's told me a lot about you."

Normally, your sister is the last person you want to describe you, but this whole situation had setup written all over it. I glanced around, but still couldn't locate Sage. What the heck, she could take care of herself for a few minutes.

"So, Erin, are you a freshman?"

Erin, I learned from our screaming yet intimate conversation, was a psychology major from the Kansas City suburbs. She knew Laura from work. She didn't usually go to frat parties, but my sister had asked her to come.

I popped open a beer from a cooler near the couch. It must have been about eighty degrees in the building. Erin's hair was damp with sweat. Over the next six-pack, we exchanged bellowed life stories as the Greeks around us danced, smoked, and made out.

When the stereo began pounding out "Y.M.C.A.," the crowd joined in, slurring the chorus and doing the dance. Conversation was impossible. Erin, whose face grew cuter with every beer, smiled shyly at me. Someone collapsed at the other end of the sofa, shoving us together. We didn't attempt to separate.

Just as I was raising my arm to drape over her shoulders, a loud squeal of electronic feedback split the air. I looked up to see a man in a Kappa sweater standing on sort of a dais, talking half into a microphone.

He hollered incoherently for several minutes, but the

audience cheered anyway. Eventually, someone turned down the stereo, cutting off the screech from the speakers.

". . . third annual Tex-ASS hold 'em contest!"

The frat boys lifted their drinks and howled like wolves on crack.

"What's he talking about?" asked Erin. "Poker?"

"Nah," said a man who was busy holding up a doorway with both arms. "They get chicks to try to hold up cups of beers with their knockers. It's hilarious."

By golly, he was right. Already, a girl in a low-cut sweater was supporting a plastic cup, using only what God had given her. The MC poured a bottle of Heineken into the container until it overcame her assets and spilled down her front. She giggled, her face somehow expressing *Oh my gosh, I just spilled beer all over my enormous chest! How wacky!*

"C'mon, who's next?"

Erin had a look of intense distaste on her face. I tried to look equally disgusted as the next two contestants competed shirtless, in just their bras. I noticed a girl who looked suspiciously like Laura walking toward the stage. She glanced in my direction and quickly ducked into the kitchen. I'd pretend I hadn't seen that.

"Logan, let's go for a walk." Erin was standing, trying to take me by the arm.

A walk. Away from this noise and smoke. A stroll through Greek Town in the cool night air, a chance to clear my head. Me and Erin, alone under the streetlights. I got up.

We were almost to the door when I heard a commotion over the many other commotions in the building. Two guys had grabbed a girl by the arms and were dragging her toward the stage while another one pushed her from behind. She was protesting and trying to twist loose, a look of fear on her face.

It was Sage.

Without a word to Erin, I dashed through the room. My experience with the hurdles paid off; I was at Sage's side in seconds. I'd been prepared to threaten her kidnappers and fight all three of them if I had to. But right before I reached them, they all let go of Sage and ducked off in different directions. Apparently, I'd looked frightening.

Sage grabbed my wrist with a look of profound thanks. Her makeup was smeared and her hair messy, but she seemed okay. I led her to a quieter part of the house to make sure she really was all right.

"Logan . . ." Sage suddenly stopped, and I realized we were not alone. Erin had followed me. She seemed unsure if I was a hero who'd rescued a woman in distress or a jerk who was ditching her for someone else.

Luckily, my awkward explanation was cut off by the appearance of Dalton. He was now wearing a giant foam #1 hand on his head. The stench of alcohol in the air informed me that he had forgotten his *beer before liquor* advice.

"Logan!" he sang, and embraced me. Booze had turned me from a complete stranger into his brother. He hugged me to the point of awkwardness, then jerked away.

"C'mon, we need more players." He gesticulated wildly to another room. Sage immediately followed. With an apologetic look to Erin, I followed Sage. Erin walked after me. I could feel her angry stare at the back of my neck.

We arrived in some sort of a dining area, where six other people sat around a table (seven, if you count the guy facedown in the onion dip). Various bottles covered the tabletop.

The four of us took our seats. The girl at the head of the table began reading from a pile of cards.

"Player number three, pass an ice cube to another player, using only your lips."

Another participant slurped a cube from his glass and popped it into the mouth of the girl sitting on his lap.

Ah, a drunken party game. There was a board and spinner, but I think everyone was beyond such details.

"Player number four, chug your drink while humming 'The Star-Spangled Banner.' "

My brain felt like it had been massaged with Elmer's glue. I found a mostly full bottle of cola and poured drinks for myself and the two girls. Being a gentleman, I took the cup with the cigarette ashes.

We'd sit here for a few rounds. A nice, silly game, and a safe place to leave Sage when Erin and I took our walk. Erin, in fact, didn't look like she was enjoying herself at all, so we'd have to go fairly soon.

"Player number five, kiss another player on the lips."

I turned to see who would be doing the kissing. Just to the left of the guy who'd drunk to the national anthem sat . . . Sage.

Everyone was staring at her. She didn't look panicked, but she didn't look comfortable, either. Several guys at the table were trying to catch her eye.

Sage smiled a naughty smile and kissed me rapidly on

the cheek. As the game master picked up another card, Dalton objected.

"On the lips. C'mon!"

In order to avoid further argument and humiliation, I leaned in to give a quick kiss to the air in front of her face, figuring no one would know the difference. Sage zigged when she should have zagged, unfortunately, and our front teeth cracked painfully against each other.

Erin stood up, annoyed, and looked at me intently. That was my cue. Exit Logan, stage left. I guess I hesitated too long, because she turned and stormed out. Sage stared at me, then gestured after Erin with her head. I could follow her if I wanted to.

But I didn't. The thought of chasing after a girl I barely knew, apologizing for something I wasn't sure of, and walking off to a nonspecific location suddenly seemed like a dull task. It was easier just to stay here with my new friends and act silly with Sage. Sage was comfortable, familiar. At the moment, that's all I wanted.

"Player number six"—Dalton pointed his finger hat at me—"do your best belly dancer impression."

I groaned and attempted to stand. Sage cracked a smile. Something told me this would be a night I'd remember for a long time, whether I wanted to or not.

# chapter twenty-seven

THE PARTY BROKE UP around four in the morning out of sheer inertia. Bleary-eyed Greeks halfheartedly attempted to remember where they'd left their jackets, keys, and girlfriends. A tearful sorority chick screamed, "Don't talk to me!" to her boyfriend, who was passed out in another room. A man in a football jacket stumbled across someone's attempt at a beer can pyramid.

Dalton had become horizontally drunk by the time we'd finished the game. I helped one of his frat brothers drag him to his room and deposit him, fully clothed, on his bed. When I returned downstairs, I found Sage waiting at the front door. Her hair was brushed, her makeup more or less in place, her jacket hung neatly over her arm. She was mostly sober; I think she'd been nursing the same rum and Coke since we'd all gone to the backyard to watch two drunks attempt to fistfight.

I'd been less discriminating. While I hadn't pounded

back the shots like Dalton, there'd been a beer in my hand throughout the evening. Several beers. I had no idea where my sweater was, I suffered from temporary hearing loss, and I had the strongest desire to drink a gallon of ice-cold water.

"You ready to go, Logan?" Sage was smirking at me. I ran my fingers through my hair to make sure I didn't still have that bra on my head.

"Yeah. No. We have to wait for Laura." I hadn't seen my sister for several hours.

Sage danced from foot to foot. "I'm sure she's fine. C'mon, it's late."

"We need her to let us back in the dorm. Laura?" I called to the nearly empty front hall. "Hey, Laura?"

Sage opened her purse and pulled out a plastic card. "Laura gave me her ID. It'll get us back into the building."

"Why do you have it? How's she supposed to get back in?"

And then it hit me. Laura didn't need her ID because she'd be spending the night *somewhere else*.

I began to quake. "Mike's a dead man."

Sage placed a gentle hand on my shoulder. "Your sister's a grown-up, Logan. She likes this guy."

"Will she like him when his jaw's wired shut?" I looked around for a weapon. There was a paddle embossed with the fraternity's logo hanging on a wall. It was no Louisville Slugger, but it would have to do.

Sage leaned down until we were eye to eye. "Do you want your sister to be happy? Or do you want her to be some kind of nun so she can live up to this Polly Pure image you have of her?"

"That second one!"

"Logan . . ."

I deflated. Sage was right. "C'mon, let's go," I whined. Laura and I would have a long talk later.

The night air was almost cold. I shivered in my short-sleeved shirt. Sage and I said goodbye to the man loudly vomiting into the bushes and trotted toward Laura's dorm.

We didn't say anything for a while. The sidewalk seemed to wiggle and jerk suddenly, and I lost my footing more than once. Sage giggled at my staggering.

"Logan," she said as we approached the dorm. "Thanks. Back at the party, when those guys had me. It could have been bad."

I grew about a foot. "If I hadn't stopped them, someone else would have." I gave a modest laugh.

"Well, I was afraid I was going to have to deck one," said Sage, not ironically. "Or show off my chest."

"Hey, only I'm allowed to see that!" I replied without thinking at all. Sage made no response. She simply swiped Laura's ID at the entrance to the dorm as I blushed.

The lobby was totally deserted, a buzzing exit sign making the only noise.

"I guess this is where I say good night." I felt exhausted, and the prospect of sleeping in the garbage on Brian's floor did not relax me.

Sage pouted. "Not just yet, Logan. Come back to Laura's room and have a soda with me."

I ducked into a communal restroom and washed my face, wishing I hadn't left my toothbrush in Brian's dorm. When I returned to Laura's room, the door was locked. Sage opened it when I knocked.

In the short time I was gone, Sage had removed her makeup and changed into an enormous T-shirt that came down to her knees. She had her hair bunched into a ponytail that emerged from the top of her head, like an eighties pop star. She handed me a bottle of cola.

"Meeting me at the door with a drink in hand," I lamely quipped. "Nice."

"Do you want a real drink? Laura has some wine coolers in her fridge."

The thought of more alcohol, even girly alcohol, twisted my stomach. I chugged the soda in under a minute, and Sage passed me another. I felt much less light-headed.

Sage sat down on Ebony's bed. Though there were two empty chairs in the room, I half collapsed next to her. The overhead light was off, and the only illumination came from Laura's desk lamp and the glow of the parking lot lights through the window. We sat there, side by side, leaning against the wall, not looking at each other, not speaking, our bodies just barely touching.

"Logan, why didn't you leave with that girl?" Sage asked out of nowhere.

I shrugged. "I didn't want to leave you there."

She frowned. "I'm sorry. You didn't have to do that."

I repeated myself. "I didn't *want* to leave you." It was the truth. I'd enjoyed playing that dumb drinking game with Sage more than I would have enjoyed groping for kisses with Erin.

Sage squirmed and readjusted her position. We were now leaning against each other. I laid my hand on hers, which was lying on her bare thigh.

I knew it was time to leave. I knew I should creep on over to Brian and Paul's dorm room, and try to sleep as they played video games all night. But for some reason, just sitting in the dark with Sage, half drunk and completely exhausted, felt more pleasant.

I almost dozed off. I probably would have if Sage hadn't spoken.

"I think I can do it, Logan."

"Do what?" I mumbled. Sage's hand was no longer in mine. My fingers rested on her leg.

"Go to college. I mean, go as . . ." She trailed off.

I woke up a bit. "You're doing great. You're going to have the time of your life. We're going to have the time of our life. Lifes. Lives."

A strand of Sage's hair tickled my nose. It smelled like shampoo, but in a good way. I was sure I smelled like the smoking lounge at a brewery.

Sage whispered in my ear. "I feel brave when I'm with you."

I didn't know why, but that comment really touched me. It was just such a sweet thing to say. I took my hand from Sage's leg and placed it on her cheek. I savored her big sad eyes, her countless freckles, her quivering lips, her exploring tongue . . .

We were kissing. Deeply. Very deeply. I was kissing Sage, and I was not nearly drunk or sleepy enough to excuse it.

Sage's kisses were eager, like she had to get in as much lip time as possible. She probably expected me to jolt away at any second. But my only reference point was Brenda. Meanwhile, I was still lacerating my tongue on Sage's braces.

It would be so easy to leave. No explanations. Neither of us would bring it up again. Just a couple of friends who'd enjoyed a moment of forbidden passion. Something we could treasure.

But I didn't want just a moment. After half a year of knowing Sage, I could finally admit I wanted *her*. I wanted this beautiful, strange, wonderful woman. I didn't want some friend of my sister's. I didn't want to go on awkward dates. My best friend was a beautiful girl! What was wrong with that?

*Plenty. Logan, she's a—*

*I DON'T CARE!* I kissed Sage harder to drown out the voice. I wrapped my arms around her waist. We kneeled awkwardly, facing each other on the bed, holding hands across our laps.

I didn't care. I didn't want to care. Sage was so wonderful. I could worry about everything else later. Right now, I was making out with a special, special girl.

*I'll be just fine.* I mentally repeated the drunk driver's mantra as I lowered my arms. When my hand cupped Sage's rear, she let out a long, almost painful groan and leaned back. When she looked at me, there were tears in her eyes.

"Logan, I'm so sorry."

Was she apologizing for kissing me? Or for what we were about to do? It didn't matter. I grasped the hem of her shirt and began to lift.

"Turn off the light, please," she said shyly.

I couldn't reach the lamp from the bed. I nearly went sprawling over the sheets when I got up, and then I couldn't find the lamp's switch. I pounded it with my fist until the bulb's filament broke and the light from outside was all that shone.

When I turned back around, Sage was sitting on the bed wearing nothing but a pair of shorts. She was looking down at the floor, her hands pressed between her knees. I'd never been so turned on in all my life. I thought, for a strange moment, of Brenda. I was suddenly glad that we'd never made love.

I removed my shirt and sat next to Sage. She smiled at me. When I tried to kiss her, she fell backward onto the bed, her body on display. She was mine, if I wanted her. I touched her skin.

"Logan?"

"Yes, Sage?" God, why were we talking now?

"Please be gentle. It's my first time."

I kissed her. But not on the mouth. "Mine too."

We didn't speak again for another two hours.

## chapter twenty-eight

I AWOKE to the sound of gunfire and screaming. My head throbbed, and I felt like I was covered with bugs. I couldn't get my bearings. I wasn't at home, but I wasn't in Laura's room, either. I was facedown on a floor somewhere.

It felt like I'd been sleeping for hours, but darkness surrounded me. I focused on a square of light. A computer screen. Brian, who sat in the same position as when I'd last seen him, and his roommate, Paul, were playing a shoot-'em-up computer game.

I smothered my face into the gym bag I was using as a pillow, trying to drown out the noise. A desperate thirst attacked my throat, and I had to pee something terrible. Still, I attempted to get another half hour of sleep. Only when I noticed the ant-covered pizza crusts under the bed next to me did I decide to get up.

"Hey, sleepyhead," said Brian, not looking at me.

"Urgh." My cheek was sticky with drool.

"You look like hell. Want some coffee?"

The coffeepot was half full, but was so dirty it looked like it was overflowing. I shook my head, attempting to get the room to stop revolving, grabbed my bag, and stumbled to the bathroom.

I think I blacked out at the sink. Apparently, I brushed my teeth and washed my face while sound asleep. I came to in the dank public shower stall, struggling to remove my clothes.

The water was ice cold, but I didn't turn it to warm. I stood there in the torrent with my mouth open until the buzzing in my head grew faint. Finally, as I distractedly soaped, I let myself remember what had happened the night before.

Sage. Me. Naked. Well, I was naked. Sage had never removed her shorts. Things had started slowly. Touching. Kissing. More touching (Sage, I discovered, was amazingly ticklish in certain areas). Then—I turned the water even colder, remembering—the sweat, the touch of her mouth, the prick of her nails, the noise of the bed as it scooted across the floor.

Lying there afterward, absolutely spent. Sage burying her face in my chest and crying for ten minutes, then laughing. Snuggling with her, face to face, half awake, running my hand over her soft back. Then, just as the sun started slanting through the window, throwing on my clothes, kissing Sage, and staggering off to Brian's room.

There were no excuses this time. There was no deception. No being caught up in the moment. Even the alcohol had pretty much worn off. Everything we did, I wanted.

Just remembering it in the shower allowed me to carry my towel without using my hands. We had crossed a line that could never be uncrossed. Sage and I had done something that could never be undone.

We were two great friends who had suddenly become a whole lot more. Two young people with their entire lives ahead of them. And just one little complication. One teeny, little, microscopic, enormous, universe-sized complication.

Last night, when the world consisted of the two of us, nothing else mattered. But in the harsh light of Sunday morning, I could think of a million reasons to worry.

Sage's father, with his huge knuckles and garage filled with lawn mower blades. He'd crucify me if he found out what we'd done. And what if someone else discovered Sage's past? Locker rooms, bureaucratic screwups, confiding in the wrong person . . . a lot could go wrong in four years of college. If Sage's world came crashing down, would I be willing to stand beside her?

Of course, all of this was just sidestepping the big issue. The night before had been wonderful. But there were certain things Sage couldn't do, parts she did not have. She'd said it might be years after college before she could afford the surgery. How long could I date a girl who didn't have a vagina?

*Well, I dated Brenda for three years, hee hee.*

Sage had kept her shorts on. But if she ever got careless one day and I actually *saw it* . . . that would be an image I could never forget. It would turn me off so much that I'd never be close to her again.

Someone in the bathroom let out an enormous fart, and

I tried to get a grip. Turning the water to hot, I continued to lather.

In spite of everything, my worries in the morning didn't compare to the beauty of the previous night. And not just after we got back to the dorm. The party. The drive. Hanging out with my sister. And even before that: Seeing Sage in her bikini. Going to the movies. Exchanging Christmas presents. In fact, since the night we didn't see the comedian, I'd enjoyed every moment I spent with Sage. Every moment. That was too rare, too special to toss away.

I shampooed with gusto. We didn't have to plot out our entire lives right then. That was the mistake I'd made with Brenda. Sage and I had months, years even, to figure things out.

I toweled off and dressed. Even half hungover and bleary eyed, my reflection was kind of handsome. As I walked back to Laura's room, I remembered the MU blanket Sage had made for me. I wished I had kept it.

I found Laura sitting at her desk, already showered and dressed like she was about to host a high tea for the Princess of Wales. I had used the clothes I was wearing as a pillow, and it still felt like there was a garbage truck revving in my skull. Sage was not in the room.

"Where's Sage?" I asked, pulling a bottle of water from the minifridge and collapsing on Laura's bed. On Ebony's side of the room, the bed was made and Sage's belongings were neatly packed. There was no sign of what we'd done.

"I should ask you that," she replied coyly. "I just saw Brian, and he said you didn't show up until after six this morning."

"Hey, look who's talking!" I barked. "What's up with you and this Mike guy?"

She smiled. "I guess you could call him my boyfriend."

"I'd like to call him something else." *You're my sister, not some kind of . . . woman!*

Laura shoved my feet off her sheets. "You'd really like him, Logan. He's a physics major. We met at a basketball game last semester."

I narrowed my eyes and she socked me in the arm. "Hey, Logan, I made an effort to like your girlfriend. I even stayed at Mike's so you two could have some privacy."

"She's not my . . . ," I started to object from pure force of habit. But after last night . . . "I mean, well . . ." What was I supposed to say?

Laura just laughed. "I knew it! She was drooling over you all last night. I kind of figured even you weren't that blind."

I looked over at the empty bed, remembering what Sage and I had done only a few hours before. "Do you really not know where she is?"

"She left a note. She had to go meet with her academic advisor, but she'll be back soon."

I rubbed my eyes, picking at the mucus the shower hadn't removed. So what would I do when Sage came back? Nod politely? Give her a big hug? Smile secretly?

No point in playing it cool, not after the night before. I'd give her a little kiss, let her know I wasn't ashamed or regretful. We could talk a little on the way home, when we had some privacy.

When Sage returned five minutes later, all I ended up

doing was staring. She was wearing a sundress, a yellow strapless outfit that left her arms and shoulders uncovered. Details of the previous night returned. The skin that I'd touched, the places I'd kissed, the soft hands, the warm mouth . . .

We kissed. Right there in front of my sister, and not the friendly little peck I was planning. Laura giggled at us and mussed my hair when we disengaged.

Sage blushed a little from the attention. Unlike me, she didn't look like she'd slept in a cat box.

"Can I buy you ladies some breakfast?"

Sage allowed me to take her arm as we left the dorm.

It was actually a lot later than I thought, so we grabbed lunch at a Ninth Street bar called the Heidelberg. It was a beautiful day, so Laura took us on an insider's tour of downtown. We ducked in and out of various head shops, bookstores, used clothing places, and coffee bars. Laura gave us advice on hangouts, organizations, and meal plans. She told me there were good jobs with campus security, if I didn't mind directing traffic at MU Tigers games.

I barely paid attention. For the first time since Brenda, I was unashamedly holding hands with a girl.

Sage was not her usual brash self. She barely talked all afternoon. I wondered if she was as confused and scared and happy as I was. We never unlocked hands. Sometimes Sage gripped my fingers so tight it almost hurt.

We returned to campus and cut across the quad. I recalled the night we were here a few months before, when

Sage and I had cleared the air and I'd promised I'd be her friend. It had seemed like such a big deal at the time, being willing to hang out with someone like Sage. And now she'd given me a back rub while we were both almost naked.

Laura was lecturing about the life-sized statue of Thomas Jefferson and didn't notice when I stopped walking. Sage stopped short. I placed my hands on her cheeks and kissed her again. She returned my kisses and then some.

My sister had to clear her throat several times before we stopped making out. But hell, she was dating someone, too. I magnanimously decided I wouldn't break Mike's nose the next time I saw him.

The sun began to hang low in the sky, and Sage reminded me that we had to get back. As I walked through campus, one arm around my girlfriend's waist, the other clutching a bag of her clothing purchases, I felt almost serene.

Sage and I were going to have difficulties. I knew that. Maybe it wouldn't work out. But other couples had overcome obstacles. Men and women of different races, different religions, different social classes. Of course, the problem with Sage wasn't our differences, but what we had in common.

We'd just have to talk, when the time was right. It didn't have to be soon. We could take a couple of weeks to get our thoughts in order, and maybe squeeze in some alone time again. And again and again.

While Sage gathered up her stuff from Laura's room, I

ducked into Brian's room to say goodbye. The window was open, and he was sitting at his desk reading. He smiled when he saw me.

"Taking off, Logan?"

"Yeah. It was nice to meet you." We shook hands. In the light, he didn't look half as scary.

"You too. Hey, you ever play paintball?"

I shook my head.

"Well, if you're interested, we've got a team. Look us up in the fall. It's a lot of fun."

I found Laura standing outside her dorm room. She was pacing like she had to pee or something. When she saw me, she glanced over her shoulder.

"Logan!" Her voice cracked; she was agitated.

"What's wrong?"

She looked back down the hall again and shook her head. "Nothing. It was really good to see you. Come back soon."

"Hey, we'll be back in August. Maybe we'll double date." I was trying to be accepting of Mike.

Laura suddenly looked glum.

"Are you sure you're okay? Did Mike do something to you?" *'Cause I can break his head if you want me to.*

"Huh? Oh, no. It's just . . ." She turned suddenly and noticed Sage coming toward us. Laura took a breath and pasted on a smile. "It's nothing important. I'll call you tonight."

I tried to get her to talk, but she was too busy helping Sage with her bags. I was probably imagining things.

Sage tried to thank Laura for her hospitality, but my sister hurried us down the hall. She hugged me in front of her building, then quickly dashed inside.

"Is she okay?" asked Sage.

"Something's on her mind. Probably that asshole Mike upset her. We'll talk later."

"Be nice, Logan. Your sister likes him, which means he's probably a nice guy."

I grabbed one of Sage's bags. She linked her arm in mine, and we walked back to the parking garage.

When we reached her car, she wordlessly allowed me to load her bags. That was my job now. Just like opening the car door or pulling out her chair at a restaurant or remembering our anniversary. There was no point in pretending otherwise.

That night at the movies had been our first date. New Year's was our first fight, and Tim's birthday was our first making up. The past week had been my first attempt at second base. And last night . . .

I'd been Sage's boyfriend for months now. I'd only just realized it.

# chapter twenty-nine

SAGE HAD CHANGED out of her dress and was now wearing jeans and a Mizzou sweater she'd bought earlier. As she climbed into the car and fished through her purse for her keys, I stared at her, thinking about the previous night. That powerful yet soft and smooth back. That ticklish belly. Those strong, freckled arms with the gentle, gentle hands. A dopey grin spread across my face.

Sage noticed my smile and flashed me her braces in return. It was all I could do not to lean over and kiss her.

And then I remembered there was no reason not to.

We made out in the hot parking garage for nearly ten minutes. It wasn't nearly as passionate as the night before. We found a nice, steady pace and just kissed, something we should have been doing for months now. This felt so natural.

Of course, I wasn't so starry eyed that I truly believed everything was going to be perfect. Sage was a girl who could never use a public locker room or go skinny-dipping. I couldn't invite her parents over for a summer barbecue to meet my mom. And just registering for school . . . how would Sage work out her housing arrangements, her transcripts, her friggin' library card, when every document with her name on it said *male*?

As much as I cared about Sage, her sex intruded on every moment. It was like trying to enjoy Thanksgiving dinner with a toothache. And the closer we became, the greater the risk of hurt for both of us.

These dismal thoughts distracted me from what I was doing. I ended up just kind of slobbering on Sage's lips like Tim devouring an ear of corn. Sage soon realized my mind was elsewhere and pulled away. She draped her arms over my shoulders and looked at me sadly for a moment. I expected her to tell me we could go back to being friends if I wanted, but she just laid her head on my shoulder. I stroked her hair. After what we'd done in Laura's room, she wasn't going to offer me an easy out, and I wasn't going to take it.

Eventually, Sage sat up. Without looking at me, she started the car and executed the complicated back-up to get out of the garage.

It shouldn't be like this. We'd both lost our virginity the night before. We should be bubbly and excited, not glum. When we got on the highway, I put my hand on Sage's knee and began to squeeze. Gradually, like the turning of a knob, Sage's smile broke through. For the rest of the drive, I busied myself by rubbing her neck, tickling her ribs, kissing her cheek, and other perilous, driver-distracting caresses.

When we pulled into my driveway, Sage leaned over to give me a kiss, then stopped to glance around. I put my arm around her neck and pulled her to me. We could make this work. I'd just have a serious talk with her later in the week. Decide where to go from here. I could tell her my fears. We had all summer to make plans, to figure out the future. And maybe repeat some of what we did in Laura's room. My mom worked a lot, and the no-girls-in-the-trailer rule was apparently not being enforced. And if Sage really did get a single dorm room, then that opened up many interesting options. Perhaps Jack would be the one living alone, at least most nights.

"See you tomorrow," she said, running her fingers through my hair, deliberately messing it up.

"Maybe you could come by after school. Mom will be at work." I didn't mean anything dirty by that. I just thought Sage might want to hang out, watch some TV, and kiss for a few hours. Totally innocent.

Sage shook her head. "We have to be careful, Logan. My parents have no idea who I was with this weekend, and my dad doesn't trust you." I must have looked depressed because she quickly continued. "Don't worry, we'll have lots of alone time this summer." She kissed my cheek and drove off, leaning on the horn until all I could see was her dust trail.

I tossed my bag on the living room floor and flopped onto the couch. It was nice out, and I really should have gone and badgered the neighbors about my lawn mowing. Instead, I smiled at the ceiling and remembered the previous night. I was no longer a virgin (kind of). I could finally live up to Tim's and Jack's opinions of me. And, I admitted, I could throw this in Brenda's face, just a little. Make sure she saw me holding hands with Sage at school the next day.

For half an hour, I fantasized about me, Sage, an empty dorm room, and a tub of Cool Whip. I stretched on the couch, half asleep in my stuffy trailer, dreaming about the future. When the phone rang, I almost didn't bother to answer it.

"Yes?" I accidentally pulled the entire telephone off the side table but was able to talk while lying down.

"Logan?" It was Laura.

"Hey! What's up?"

"Logan, is Mom home?" There was something in her voice I didn't like. I remembered how odd she'd acted when I left. What was wrong?

"Mom's at work." I sat up. "Laura, is everything okay?"

"Are you alone? Sage isn't there, is she?"

I was almost panicking now. "Talk to me, Laura."

There was a long pause. "Sit down, Logan. I have something to tell you."

I was already sitting. I braced myself. Did this have anything do to with Mike? She said he was a nice guy, but what if he had a darker side? Maybe they'd had a fight and broken up. Or something worse.

It *was* worse. But it wasn't about Laura.

"Logan, this morning Sage went to the bathroom to

change her clothes. I had an outfit I wanted her to try on, so I followed her in. She didn't notice me."

I nearly hung up the phone right then. I knew what was coming. Maybe if I didn't listen, maybe if I refused to talk to my sister, I wouldn't have to face this.

"Logan . . . ," she continued. There was a long, long silence. "She was in a shower stall undressing. And . . . are you still there?"

"Ugh."

"I don't know how to tell you this. I only just glimpsed her behind the curtain; it wasn't all the way closed. But I know what I saw. Logan . . ."

Ten thousand years passed before I could bring myself to say, "Yes?"

"Sage has a penis. She's really a boy, Logan."

I sat alone on a tombstone, waiting. Sage approached from the west. The setting sun cast her body into a silhouette and I could only make out her outline. It killed me how feminine she looked. Her curvy figure, her long, wavy hair . . . even her walk was womanly.

As soon as Laura had dropped the bomb, I'd hung up on her. She'd called right back, but I hadn't picked up. I'd have to deal with that disaster later. Instead, I'd phoned Sage. Tammi answered. I didn't ask for Sage, I just left a message to pass on: meet me at Arborville Road Cemetery as soon as possible.

The graveyard was the most abandoned place I could think of. Brenda and I used to go there to look at the stars.

More recently, it was where Sage and I had our nasty New Year's Day confrontation. The day I'd told her I wanted her out of my life forever and that I was sorry we'd ever met. Why hadn't I just left well enough alone?

Sage passed under the shadow of a gnarled oak, and I could see her features: her red lips, her braces, her many freckles. She had a big goofy grin on her face, and I wondered why. Then I remembered. She was in love.

As she got closer to me, her smile began to falter, then died. I must have had an unpleasant look on my face. She sat opposite me on the wooden rail fence.

"I guess you didn't call me out here because you wanted a repeat of last night."

I didn't meet her eyes. "Sage, Laura knows."

The sun touched the horizon. It would be dark soon. "About what?"

I glared at her. "What do you think?"

Sage worked at a splinter in the fence and didn't reply.

"She saw you in the bathroom! How could you let her find out?" My voice boomed above the crickets that were just beginning to sing. Everything had been so perfect the night before, and then Sage got careless and ruined everything. We almost had something beautiful. Now when I looked at Sage, I didn't see the girl I wanted to spend the next four years with. I saw the person who made me look like a fag in front of my sister.

She sighed. "I wear a rubber device to hide my . . . parts. It was killing me earlier. I had to take it off. I was in a shower stall; I thought I was alone."

266

The shadows grew longer. In the eastern sky, I could see a few stars.

"Well, you weren't." I winced at the thought of what my sister had seen. What Sage kept hidden in those panties.

Sage stood and faced me. "So what did you do?"

"I hung up on her. I don't know what the fuck I'm going to say when I talk to her again." My nightmares were coming true. The person I was closest to in the world now knew my darkest secret *the very next day*! This was worse than anything I'd feared.

Sage leaned nearer but didn't touch me. "Just tell her the truth."

It honestly hadn't occured to me that Sage would suggest that. She took my stunned silence for quiet listening. "Tell her that you already know and we're happy together."

I came very close to screaming. Instead, I only bellowed my reply. "Sage, have you lost your goddamned mind? I can't tell her that!" Did Sage think this was some kind of stupid game? That because of what we'd done, I wanted the world to know?

The last feeble light sank below the horizon. Sage's face was hidden in the gloom. "She'll understand. She's just worried that I'm deceiving you. If you let her know that my—condition—doesn't bother you, then it won't bother her, either. I can tell she's an understanding girl. She won't judge." She smiled weakly, then frowned when I didn't grin back.

Night fell. The only light source was the beacon on a

faraway cell phone tower and the yellowish glow from the electronics factory parking lot two miles distant.

"Sage." My voice was barely a hiss. "I can't tell my sister I was willingly kissing a guy. She'll think I'm queer."

"A *guy?*" My eyes were adjusting to the darkness. I could see Sage standing there, arms folded. "Last night, when we were naked in bed together, I was all woman. But now that things are rough, I'm a guy again."

"You know what I mean." I'd been an ignorant sap, thinking that wishing and hoping could make Sage into a real girl. She was physically a boy, and it was time we stopped pretending.

"No, Logan, I don't. You can't just sleep with me, then bail on me because you think you'll get a little embarrassed."

"I'd be a lot more than a little embarrassed!" But I'd brought this on myself, hadn't I? I was aware of the risks. I knew this could happen.

"And you think I wouldn't be? You think I wanted anyone to know about this? Your sister wanted to be my friend, and now she thinks I'm not honest with you." Sage's voice lowered. "Laura's a nice girl. And if you're happy, then she'll be happy. I promise that if you call her and tell her . . . no, you don't even have to tell her. Just ask her not to bring it up again. She'll get the message. She'll never mention it."

I stomped on the unkempt grass. Sage was right. Laura was just worried that I was being lied to. If she knew the truth, then she'd be satisfied. My sister was one of the most accepting people in the world. As long as I was happy, she'd treat Sage like a girl.

But I couldn't do it. I just couldn't admit to Laura that the sex of my girlfriend wasn't important. I couldn't live with the image of Laura alone in her dorm, thinking, *So my big macho brother really likes guys, huh? I never would have guessed.*

"I can't do that." It wasn't a refusal, but an admission of weakness.

The wind began to pick up. In the dim light, I could see Sage's hair whip around her face.

"So it's over?"

How I wished I had Tim's eloquence right then. I wanted to fall to the ground, to explain to Sage how I wished to God I could be her white knight, her prince. How I longed for the courage, the self-confidence, the backbone to tell Laura that I loved Sage and she never kept any secrets from me. But I couldn't do that, didn't she understand? I was only eighteen! She'd awoken feelings in me that I'd never thought I could experience, not in a million years, and now she expected me to tell the world. I needed beautiful, silvery words to show Sage that I *just wasn't strong enough* to do what she was asking. I wasn't brave enough. Wasn't man enough.

But that was all a bunch of words. What Sage needed right now was action. She'd trusted me with her heart and given me her body. And I was running away.

"It's over?" Sage repeated, yelling over the rising wind. "You sleep with me, then dump me the next day?"

I should have tried to make peace. Instead, I was

deliberately hurtful, attempting to dull my pain by foisting it onto her. "Hey, I'm not the one who pulled my dick out at Mizzou!"

"*Yes, you did.* I was there."

I hung my head, stung. Above us, clouds covered the stars.

"Logan, I know this isn't what you want. I know you think Laura won't understand, but she *will*." The begging in Sage's voice was distinct. "It hurts me that I can't be a real woman for you, but I'm trying. That's what you do when you care about someone. Can't you do it for me? Can't you sacrifice something for me?"

Sage attempted to touch my arm. I pulled away. If I allowed her to touch me, I wasn't sure I could stand up to her. In the distance, heat lightning silently flashed.

"So that's the way it is, Logan? I guess it's all a pervert like me deserves." She was being sarcastic. Even after everything, I didn't think she was a pervert. "But if we break up tonight, you'll regret it. You'll want me back, and you know what? You won't be able to have me. Because I'll be gone. You'll want me back, and then it'll be too late. And you'll just have to sit there and think about what a wonderful thing we had and how you threw it away!"

I turned and leaned on the fence, my back to Sage. After a couple of minutes, I heard her footsteps recede in the distance. As the first drops of warm spring rain began to fall, I stood there in the dark telling myself I'd done the right thing.

*I did the right thing.*

And maybe, a thousand miles away, my father was looking at a faded picture of a couple of toddlers, telling himself the same thing. And maybe in a month, or a year, or ten years, I'd open a tattered yearbook and say it again.

*I did the right thing.*

And maybe by then I'd believe it.

## chapter thirty

THEY SAY the waiting is the worst part. The dentist, surgery, telling a family member that your girlfriend is really a man . . . Once you're through with it, you wonder what you'd been so afraid of.

That wasn't my case. As I walked home in the drizzling rain, I wondered how I was going to straighten things out with Laura. We'd have to talk about this sooner or later. Or did we?

Laura was staying on campus for the summer. If I avoided talking to her until September and then showed up at Mizzou with no mention of Sage, she'd get the message. Realize that Sage and I had broken up. Believe that Sage was a liar and a drag queen who'd deliberately misled me. Turn Sage into the villain, blame everything on her. I'd look like the victim.

What choice did I have? I couldn't pretend like Laura's

information didn't bother me. *She's a guy? That explains the power tools in her makeup case.* My sister would never buy it.

I remembered what Sage had said. How I should just tell the truth. Let Laura know that I already knew. Not that I was happy about it, but that I was . . . accepting?

No way. My feelings for Sage were as jumbled and confused as the wiring job on Jack's car stereo. One moment, I saw myself standing next to her after college graduation, saw us kissing in our caps and gowns. The next, I felt confused, wondering how I could experience such strong emotions for someone with testicles. How could I explain to my sister, the person I loved most in the world, what I didn't even understand?

What if Laura thought I *liked* the fact that Sage was born a boy? What if she thought I was dating her because of her penis? My sister would think I was gay. She'd probably suspect that Sage was just a stepping stone and that the next person I dated would be a big strapping football player named Bruce. Laura would be accepting, all right. Way too accepting.

I'd just have to forget about Sage. It wouldn't have worked out anyway. Something would have gone wrong eventually. It would be insane for me to bike over to her house and beg her forgiveness. To call Laura and try to explain things. To forget about everyone else's opinion for once and only worry about my own feelings.

Sage would survive. I'd survive. We were better off apart. Painful and quick, just like ripping off a Band-Aid. Well, more like gouging a piece of shrapnel out of my stomach, pouring a bottle of gin into the wound, lighting it on fire, and sewing my guts up with a dirty bootlace. But the concept was the same.

Mom was cooking a hamburger casserole when I got back to the trailer.

"Where in the world were you?" she asked, more concerned than angry. "I saw your bag on the couch, but you must have gone out again before I got home."

"Went for a walk." I really did not feel like talking or sitting down to dinner.

"In the rain? You're soaked. Leave a note next time, Logan. So how's Laura doing?"

I wiped my feet and took off my jacket. "Fine." *She had sex with some guy last night.*

"And did you have fun?" Mom prodded.

"Yeah." *I had sex with a guy last night.*

"And did Sage enjoy herself?" The question was casual, but this was the one she really wanted answered. She was groping for hints about what was going on between us.

The funny thing was, before I'd talked to Laura, I would have happily admitted she was my girlfriend. I wouldn't have told Mom what had happened in the dorm, but I might have "accidentally" admitted Sage was more than a friend. Bragged a little, let my mom know I was finally over Brenda.

Thank God Laura had called before I said that. Now I didn't have to explain why Sage was about to disappear forever.

"Sage had fun. I didn't see her too much. Today she had to talk to her advisor and hung out with people she knew in town."

Mom sighed. She'd been hoping for more information. Complaining of a stomachache, I exited to my room, lay down on my bed, and stared at the ceiling until dawn.

The next morning, I went to school determined to show the world that I didn't have any feelings for Sage (again). I had to prove to all my friends that we were not romantically involved (for the second time).

Tim and Jack obviously knew that Sage and I were more than casual friends. The way we always hung out, and the couple of months of me refusing to talk to her . . . People only act like that when there's something going on.

Then again, maybe I was giving them too much credit. The last time Jack put two and two together was in first-grade math, while Tim . . . Tim had other things on his mind.

He nearly tackled me when I was parking my bike that morning. Even before he said a word, I knew what was up. His grin was so broad he could have swallowed an entire Big Mac in one bite (which I knew he could do from first-hand experience). He was literally jiggling with excitement, his belly and breasts rippling like the ocean in a windstorm.

"Logan, guess what?" I hadn't seen him this worked up since they'd built the Pizza Hut in Moberly. This could only mean one thing.

"You and Dawn," I answered with a wink.

Tim nodded forcefully. "We were at her house Saturday. You were right, Logan. Things just sort of fell into place."

"You dog." I was happy for him. I had begun to worry that he'd never meet anyone.

"I had to tell someone." He paused and looked over his shoulder as if Dawn might be listening in. "So how was Mizzou?"

"Great!" I said a little too emphatically. "I met this chick at a frat party. We went back to her place . . ." I left it hanging.

"You dog!" laughed Tim, slapping my palm. "Who was she?"

"Girl named Erin." I answered with the first name that came to mind. "Damn, she was amazing. I hope Laura's roommate doesn't find out what we did in her bed."

"I thought you went back to her place."

I'd been thinking of Sage, remembering our night together. God, had it only been a couple of days before? "I meant Laura's room."

The warning bell rang, and we entered the building.

All day long I dreaded running into Sage. At the same time, I deliberately tried to find her. Now that I had calmed down a little, I wanted to talk to her. Tell her about my fears, about why I couldn't explain things to my sister and how I just wasn't brave enough to have a relationship with her, no matter how much I wanted that.

Sage probably wouldn't even talk to me. But maybe at

college, after we both had a few months to regroup . . . I'd run into her somewhere. We'd awkwardly catch up on what we'd been doing. Maybe agree to have coffee sometime (mental note: start drinking coffee). Start getting together. We'd never date again, but was being friends so out of the question? Lots of people stayed close to their exes. Why couldn't that happen for us?

Because the other option was never seeing Sage again. Never hearing her laugh. Not being able to talk about classes or my family or the lack of heat in the dorms. I wouldn't be the one to comfort her when she got scared. She'd be alone. So would I. She was the best friend I'd ever had, the girl who I cared for on a much deeper level than what I'd felt for Brenda, and I was risking kicking her out of my life forever. Just to protect myself.

Sage and I didn't cross paths all day, and I began to wonder if she'd stayed home. I didn't see her until after school as I was talking to Jack in the commons.

"The way I see it," said Jack, halfheartedly pummeling the soda machine, "if I bring my computer and you get a minifridge, our dorm will be pretty set, at least to start off. We might start saving for a DVD player later."

Jack could not contain his excitement about our freshman year. Saturday, I would have been just as eager. Of course, that was when Sage was going to be part of my college experience. Now she'd be there, but I'd never talk to her. Never hang out with her. Never . . .

"Sage!" shouted Jack suddenly. "Hey, Sage!"

There she was, strolling through the commons. She was wearing the same black-and-white dress I'd seen her in on her first day at school. Apparently, I'd misjudged; she wasn't at home weeping over my picture. Of course, she looked like she was ready to punch out the first person who talked to her.

"Sage!" hollered Jack, oblivious to her furious expression. "Gimme a buck!"

She iced by, not looking at either of us. I stared at her as she stormed out the front door, trying not to think of the now familiar freckles just under the back of her dress.

I almost followed her. Honest to God, I did. I'd grab her by the shoulder, spin her around, and apologize. But just as I was getting into my sprinter's crouch, I froze. Jack was still standing there. And he'd wonder what I was apologizing about. And if he ever found out . . .

She was gone now. Out in the parking lot, out of my sight, out of my life. I was deluding myself thinking she'd ever want to be friends again. If I tried to talk to her on campus, she'd probably call security.

"What did I do now?" whined Jack. He was used to apologizing for offenses he didn't realize he'd committed, and he thought Sage's brush-off had been directed at him.

I shook my head. "It's not you, it's me. She's all bent out of shape for some reason." I rolled my eyes, trying to project a *who the hell knows what chicks are thinking?* expression.

Jack didn't smile. "I think I know why."

My guts rattled. "Why?"

Jack sat on a bench, then immediately began tapping his feet. I sat down next to him. "Tim told me you slept with some chick at Mizzou." There was no admiration in his voice.

"So?"

"So, that's kind of sticking it to Sage, isn't it? I know you don't like her, but she's all messed up over you. I can't say I blame you for chasing some tail, but that had to have been hard for her."

*Yes, hard for her. Almost as bad as if I'd slept with her, then told her the next night that I was embarrassed by her. But what kind of a jerk would do that?*

"Thanks, Captain Sensitive." I marched off. Jack didn't know how right he was. I'd hurt Sage, but much more deeply than anyone realized.

I thought of a poem from eighth-grade English. I couldn't remember the title, or the poet, or any of the words. The gist was that everyone wishes they could turn back time, but of course, no one can.

For once, I understood a poem. If I could just turn back time a couple of days, then all my problems would be solved. I could . . . What? Warn Sage to be careful in the shower stall? Or . . . go straight to Brian's room after the party?

It was stupid even to think about. That was all in the past. I didn't know what my future would hold. I just knew one person who wouldn't be in it.

I couldn't avoid talking to Laura forever. Eventually, I'd have to say something. But I tried my damnedest to put that off. Every day that week, either I had track practice or I mowed lawns. I was collecting quite a little bundle of cash. Since I didn't have a car to pay for, I'd have plenty of spending money for my first year of college.

Sage and I didn't talk. Tammi never looked in my direction at school (I think I was more afraid of talking to her than to Sage). They were going to let me get away with it. No confrontations, no revenge; I was gone. We were both free to live our own lives.

I knew things weren't irreparable. The night we'd broken up, Sage had been pretty self-righteous. But she had to know how difficult things were for me. And right now I was sure a sincere apology would win her back. She wasn't vengeful or cruel by nature, and she'd said several times that I was a lot more understanding than members of her own family. All I had to do was drop her a note asking to meet. Tell her I'd panicked and didn't want things to end. And we'd go right back to how things were before, until the next crisis came along and I went scampering off again.

Every day I delayed, Sage's feelings would grow colder. And eventually, I'd no longer be worth the trouble. Back in November, I would have taken Brenda back, even after she'd cheated. But now I knew I deserved better. Sage would ultimately come to the same conclusion.

Thursday afternoon, I was trying to get my lawn mower running. There was water in the gas line, and it didn't want to start. I didn't realize I had company until I saw my sister's shadow fall over me.

"Laura!" *Shit!* "What are you doing here?"

Laura looked grim. I'd never noticed before how much she resembled our mother. That same pinched-mouthed, steely-eyed expression Mom wore when she went off to spend another ten hours pouring coffee and burning her

wrists on hot plates. The fatalistic determination of someone who wished she could avoid something but couldn't.

"Is Mom here?"

I gave the mower another halfhearted yank. "She's
working."

"Can we talk?" she asked, gesturing at the trailer.

I tugged the cord again. "Fine."

"Logan . . . about what I said on the phone."

I stood and walked away a few paces. "Do we really
have to discuss that?"

"I didn't want to humiliate you . . ."

*Then why did you?* "What's done is done, Laura. Sage
lied to me, and you made me see that. Do me a favor and
let's not talk about this again." I was speaking in a monotone, reciting the required lines, bad-mouthing a girl who
desperately needed a friend. With that last sentence, I'd
closed the door on Sage forever. I'd made her responsible
for my lies. I'd placed the blame on a blameless girl, and
now she'd never come back.

Laura, of course, couldn't let things drop. She was a
woman, after all, and always wanted to discuss relation-
ships, even other people's.

"Logan, I know this is hard for you."

I nearly yanked the cord out of the mower. It violently
coughed.

"But I couldn't not tell you," she continued.

"Yeah. Look, just go, okay? It's over. I'll see you this
summer."

"Logan . . ." She stopped. Eventually, I turned and
faced her. "Logan, something occurred to me the night

after you visited. I thought that maybe . . . I dunno . . . maybe I was telling you something you already knew." She grinned apologetically, but her eyes were questioning.

So Sage had been right. My sister wasn't going to judge, wasn't going to ask questions, wasn't going to mock. All I had to do was say yes. I didn't even have to do that. All I had to do was nod and the conversation would be over. Forever. Laura would understand that Sage was what I wanted and leave it at that. And by telling Laura the truth, I'd prove to Sage I was as brave as she needed me to be.

But there are some things you can't do. Some things you can't admit, not to yourself, and especially not to your family. My next words were hateful, offended.

"How could I have known? You think I would have dated her . . . him . . . *it* . . . if I'd known?" The insults were forceful, yet forced.

Laura backed up a step but didn't blink. "It's just that if you already did know, and didn't have a problem with it . . ."

"Shut up!" I hadn't physically fought with Laura since I was six, but I considered holding her mouth shut with my hand just to get her to stop talking.

"Logan, if you wanted to keep dating Sage, I'd understand. I wouldn't tell anyone." She spoke rapidly, like she was afraid of losing her nerve.

I screamed so loud it came out as a squeak. "Why don't you mind your own fucking business?"

Laura was crying as she rushed back to her car. I grabbed the lawn mower by its body, and with an enraged scream, hurled it six feet across the yard.

## chapter thirty-one

THE NEXT FRIDAY, we had our last track meet of the year. We kicked ass. Those douches from Higbee didn't know what hit them. We won nearly every event. I finished first in three races and broke the school record for the 200-meter dash. Jack tied his personal best for the hurdles. Coach Garrison's praise still echoed in my ears: "Good job, men."

It was a night to celebrate. The whole team, along with girlfriends, buddies, and various other people with nothing better to do, took off to Boyer's number one exclusive nightspot: the abandoned quarry.

I'm not sure they'd ever actually excavated rock there. I think they dug it out in 1935, then let it fall apart so four generations of Boyer High School students would have a place to get drunk, shoot off fireworks, and have illicit sex. Just two miles outside of town, the quarry was almost completely isolated. If you didn't mind risking a broken leg or drowning in a flash flood, you could have a fun time there. Even the meth heads considered the area off-limits, and the police never showed up. Maybe the cops remembered what they'd done in the quarry when they were teens.

There must have been forty people there Friday night, and not all of them were from Boyer. Someone had set up a boom box on a rock, and the crashing music vibrated into the otherwise silent night. We'd attempted to build a bonfire out of damp wood, and a flickering, smoky blaze cut a few feet into the darkness. In the shadows, I could just make out people I knew. Drinking, laughing, dancing, and making out. Everyone was there with a date. Even Jack was having his face chewed on by a cute runner from Higbee.

I sat on the ground, nursed a beer, and tried to pretend I was having a great time. I mean, I was having a good time. Really. My good friends, the tang of victory, a case of Bud . . . what more could I ask for?

I remembered how Sage had watched me practice. If I hadn't dumped her, she would have come to the track meet. And afterward, maybe we could have sneaked off to the abandoned gravel pits and run a victory lap.

But it wasn't the celibacy that was really getting to me. I just wished Sage was with me. I wanted to be near her. Wrap my jacket around her when she got cold. Make fun of the other people together. Share that special closeness without saying anything.

I chugged my beer, trying to drive those thoughts from my head. Laura had all but asked me if I was gay. No matter how understanding she was, I could not let her think that. Even if we never discussed it again, Laura would consider me a secret homosexual for the rest of my life. And aside from Laura, someone else might find out. I couldn't go through life with that hanging over my head.

But my sister had been right, hadn't she? Laura had suspected I liked Sage, despite (or because of) her sex. But instead of doing the right thing, I'd shoved Sage right out of my life. The girl who'd helped me get over Brenda. The girl who'd helped make me a man. The girl who'd told me how much she needed my friendship, and how the future wouldn't be quite so scary with me there. The girl who'd, years ago, once tried to . . .

Why couldn't she just be a real girl? Our lives would be great. She was so close to the real thing. But close didn't count.

Jack staggered toward me, his eyes bleary, lipstick all over his neck. He bent over to grab a drink from the cooler.

"Logan! BHS kicks ass!" His head zoomed from side to side as if he was daring anyone to suggest that we did not, in fact, kick ass.

I grunted.

"Hey," said Jack, looking at me like he'd just noticed something. "How come you don't have a date? You should have called that Erin chick you told us about."

"Yeah." Once again, I was having imaginary sex.

"You know, Stacey's here alone. You should go . . ." His cell phone rang and cut him off.

"Hello? Who? Who? What? Hello? Huh? Who?" He paused, then thrust the phone at me. "It's for you."

*Me? Probably my mother.* I took Jack's phone and slunk

into the darkness so no one could hear me checking in at home.

"This is Logan."

The female voice on the other end was almost incoherent. It wasn't my mother. Reception was nearly nonexistent in the quarry, and I had to shout to make myself understood.

"I can't understand you! Slow down! Who is this?"

There was a gasp on the other end. "Is this Logan? Your mom gave me this number. I need your help."

It was Tammi. She sounded almost hysterical.

"Tammi? What's wrong?"

"Sage just came home. She locked herself in the bathroom." Her words came out in a rapid, almost gibbering stream. "She won't answer, and I can't open the door. I think something bad happened to her tonight. I . . . I'm scared. My parents went to the movies and turned off their cell phones. Rob's out of town, and I didn't know who else to call."

Tammi didn't say it, and I didn't mention it. Sage had tried to kill herself once before. Why wouldn't she come out of the bathroom? Did this have anything to do with our breakup?

"I'll be right there."

After sprinting all day, I wasn't exactly in any condition to bike all the way across Boyer, but I made it to Sage's house in less than ten minutes. Something wasn't right. The truck Sage drove was parked half in her yard, half in the street. And the headlights were on. I remembered from

New Year's how quickly the battery drained. Sage wouldn't have forgotten about that unless she was really upset.

Dumping my bike in the lawn, I pounded on the door. Tammi, hyperventilating and in tears, answered.

"She's been in there for an hour. I can't open the door!"

My hands got clammy. "She just locked herself in the bathroom?"

Tammi shook her head. "She snuck out earlier. I . . . I think she went to meet some guy. I thought you two might be making up, so I didn't try to stop her. But about an hour ago she came running in. I was in my room. When I came out, she bolted the bathroom door. And look!"

Tammi pointed to the linoleum by the front door. Little brown spots of blood dotted the floor.

*Shit.* I rushed to the bathroom.

"Sage! Sage, it's Logan! What's going on?"

There was no answer. Tammi began to cry again. I motioned her back, and with a solid kick, broke open the door.

Tammi screamed when she saw her sister, and for a horrible moment I thought Sage had slit her throat. She was hunched over the toilet, blood dripping from her face.

I rushed over to her to inspect the damage. The half-clotted blood covered her mouth and nose. She hadn't done this to herself.

"Tammi!" I ordered. "Go get an ice pack and some clean towels. Go!" She ran off in tears.

Sage hardly seemed conscious as I inspected the damage. Her nose was obviously broken. Her lip was split, and her right eye was swelling shut. Inside her mouth, I could see the stump of a broken tooth, the remains of her braces digging into her gums.

I nearly joined her at the toilet when I realized this couldn't have been an accident. Someone had worked her over.

"Sage? Who did this to you?" She moaned and shook her head. Blood splattered on my clothes.

Tammi stood in the doorway clutching a pile of towels, her freckles standing out darkly against her pale skin.

"Help me with her, Tammi. She needs to see a doctor." That was one thing I could do for her.

Sage didn't resist as we helped her to her feet.

"What happened to her, Logan?" asked Tammi. "A car accident?"

I wished I could hide the unpleasant truth. "Someone beat her up."

Tammi let out a yelp and almost stumbled, but she didn't let her sister fall. We helped her into the truck. I drove, and Tammi sat on the other side of Sage.

"Moberly Medical Center's about ten miles from here," I said as I pulled out of the subdivision.

Sage had been leaning back in the seat, pressing the ice pack to her nose. For the first time, she seemed aware of what was going on.

"No!" Her voice was nasal, yet even with her injuries, she made herself sound feminine.

"You're hurt, Sage. You need to see a doctor."

She shook her head. "Not Moberly."

"It's not that bad of a hospital."

"Logan."

I looked over at Tammi, and she was shaking her head at me. Of course. Moberly was a tiny hospital not far from Boyer. Sage couldn't hide her gender from the staff, and you never knew who might overhear.

"We'll go to Columbia, then," I said as we pulled onto the highway.

We drove in silence for a bit until Sage leaned over and spit blood onto the floorboard.

"Who did this to you?" asked Tammi.

Sage shrugged. "A guy."

"Who?" I asked. My knuckles were white on the steering wheel. Whoever he was, he would soon be known as the man with no teeth.

"I met him at that stupid frat party. He gave me his number, but I didn't call him because I thought I had a boyfriend." There were no accusations in her voice. Sage was just telling what had happened. "When you dumped me, I decided to get back at you. I thought . . . I thought that if you knew I went out with someone else, you'd be jealous."

Christ, what could I say? "Sage . . ."

She ignored me. "So he takes me out to dinner. Takes me for a drive. Tries to kiss me." Sage stopped and spit on the floor again.

"You told him, didn't you?" asked Tammi gently.

Sage nodded and then grimaced. "I thought that if I was honest at first, then he might understand. The second he realized what I was saying, he smacked my face into the window."

I wanted to turn up the radio. I wanted to tell Sage to

shut up. I didn't want to hear more about her beating. It was all my fault.

"I tried to get out of the car, and the son of a bitch followed me. He fucking tackled me, then really started pounding on me. I kept begging him to stop, but he just smiled and said he was going to fuck me up the ass. I acted like he knocked me out. That's when he left. Then I had to walk back to where I parked the truck."

Girlish sobs filled the cab. It was me. I was bawling. If I hadn't been such a macho fuck, Sage wouldn't have gotten hurt.

"Logan, watch the road!" yelled Tammi.

"Who was it?" I screamed. "I want his name!"

There was no answer.

"Who was it?"

"Logan," groaned Sage, "I'll never tell you. Because if you hurt him, then he'll know why. And then everyone in the world will know why he beat me up."

"But . . ."

Tammi frowned at me, and I shut up. We'd discuss this later.

University Hospital was part of the Mizzou medical school. I figured it was big enough that no one would recognize Sage. I parked in the tiny emergency lot, then helped Sage through the front doors.

"You register her," said Tammi. "I'm going to try to get ahold of Mom and Dad. Their movie should be over by now."

It was nearly midnight, but the waiting room wasn't as

empty as I'd hoped. An old man sat on a bench, either asleep or in a coma. A black family chatted noisily in a corner. It was impossible to tell which, if any of them, was the patient. Two EMTs wheeled a guy in a neck brace by on a gurney.

I guided Sage to the reception desk. A middle-aged woman with many decorative buttons on her uniform took our information.

"Name?"

"Sage Hendricks. H-E-N-D-R-I-C-K-S," she spelled through a mouthful of blood.

"Date of birth?"

"September fifteenth." The receptionist entered the information into her computer as if Sage was applying for a job.

"What year?"

"Excuse me," I interrupted. "This is the *emergency* room, right?"

"Sir, there are a lot of people ahead of you."

"Will you look at her? This isn't Jiffy Lube, lady! She's hurt!"

"Logan," whispered Sage. She looked at me through her swollen eye. "I'll be fine."

I seethed as they filled out the huge admission form, though I nearly lost it when she asked the reason for Sage's visit. We were told to go sit in the waiting area, but almost immediately an orderly arrived with a wheelchair. Sage touched my hand.

"Go tell Tammi."

"Sage, I'm sorry." My apology sounded so trite. That guy could have killed her, and all I could do was shrug my shoulders and say *my bad*.

The orderly wheeled her off. Sage glanced over her shoulder. I think she was about to say something, but when she opened her mouth, she winced in pain. Her chair vanished into the interior of the hospital.

I found Tammi pacing in front of the emergency room doors. Every few steps she'd get too close, and they'd automatically swish open.

"They've admitted her. Did you reach your parents?"

Tammi nodded. "They'll be here soon. Logan, why would someone do that to her?"

And that was the million-dollar question. Why would someone hurt Sage? She hadn't hurt that guy. She hadn't done anything to him but reveal a secret. Why was that such a big deal?

*Why is that such a big deal? Why is it always such a big deal? If I'd been able to get over it, to see Sage as she sees herself, none of this would have happened.*

Someone was standing next to me. It took me a moment to place the towering bald man who was hovering at my side.

"Mr. Hendricks!"

He punched me so hard I didn't feel it. My face actually went numb. I was literally airborne for one second; the crush of my skull on the concrete drove white spikes through my line of vision.

He loomed over me, a look of pure hate on his face. I couldn't move. For the first time in my life, I feared I was going to die. Sage's father was going to stomp me to death, right there in front of the hospital.

"It wasn't him!" Tammi was screaming, trying to block her father. "It wasn't him, Dad! He didn't . . ."

Mr. Hendricks grabbed me under the arms and yanked me to my feet. "Get out of here!" he shouted. "If I see you again, you're dead! Do you hear me, Logan? Dead!"

Bobbing and weaving, I stumbled across the parking lot, not paying attention to where I was going. I wanted to get away from Mr. Hendricks, but also, I just wanted to get away.

I found myself in an unfamiliar area, hospital offices on one side, an empty construction site on the other. I leaned against an orange-and-white barrel until my eyes began to focus.

*This was my fault. All of it. I put Sage in that hospital, the same as if I'd punched her in the face and left her bleeding on the side of the road.*

She'd been upset because of me. She'd wanted revenge because of me. I was even the one who'd taken her to that frat party. All of this happened because of my own stupid self.

Eighteen years old, and I'd already ruined someone's life. Sage might not recover from this, at least inside. And I had no idea how to make things right.

## chapter thirty-two

I WANDERED through the morass of parking garages and hospital office buildings. My skull hurt worse than the hangover from the other day. Every lot, every garage looked identical. When I passed a pickup truck with a tarp in the bed, I considered lying down for a quick nap.

Eventually, I noticed the Rollins Dining Hall. Behind that was Gillett, Laura's dormitory. The building was locked up for the night; you needed to swipe your student ID to enter. Luckily, a couple was bidding each other a slobbery good night on the stairs and buzzed me in so they could have a little privacy.

So what was I going to do, just stagger into Laura's room with a head injury and no ride home? I thought about banging on Brian's door. He'd probably still be up, but that might have been a bit much for a guy I hardly knew. I paused in front of Laura's dorm room, took a deep breath, and knocked. After about thirty seconds, an unfamiliar female voice mumbled, "Who's there?"

"It's Logan."

I heard someone get out of bed and walk to the peephole. "It's some guy. He looks drunk."

"Get out of here, or we'll call the police!" Laura blearily shouted.

"It's me, Logan!"

"Huh?" I heard Laura get up and pause in front of the door. "Logan!" She quickly threw the door open.

I didn't pause to say hello as I collapsed on Laura's bed.

"Logan! What's the matter?"

I opened one eye. Laura and her roommate, Ebony, were staring at me. Laura looked deeply concerned. Ebony looked like someone who'd been woken from a sound sleep by an incoherent stranger.

"Aspirin," I muttered. "Water."

Laura began rummaging through her medicine cabinet. Ebony approached me with a somewhat less contemptuous expression on her face.

"Sit up," she ordered. She then placed her thumbs on my cheek and stared me in the eye.

"She's a nursing student," explained Laura.

Ebony examined my eye, which had almost swollen shut.

"Get in a fight?" she asked, gently poking at my scalp.

I shrugged. Up close, Laura's roommate was even cuter than in her picture. Longish hair, chocolate skin, and dark, dark eyes.

"You've got a pretty big goose egg on the back of your head. How many fingers do you see?"

"Three."

Ebony waved a finger in front of my face, making sure my eyes could follow it.

"Your brother will live, Laura. But he needs to go to the hospital."

"I can't," I replied, swallowing the pills my sister offered me.

"Why not?"

"Because the guy who did this is there."

Laura was trying to help me to my feet. "Then we'll go to Boone Hospital, or the VA. C'mon."

I pulled away. "Laura, I just need to crash."

She sat down next to me. "Will you tell me what happened? What are you doing in Columbia, anyway?"

"Um . . ." Ebony sat on her bed, obviously wondering if she was going to get any sleep that night. She let out a long-suffering sigh and grabbed a robe.

"I think I'll go stay with Bethany. And you really should see a doctor, Logan."

When we were alone, Laura handed me a soda. "So are you going to talk to me?"

"I . . ." I suddenly noticed that Laura was wearing a T-shirt that read PHYSICISTS DO IT WITH FORCE. I remembered Mike's major, and my eyes narrowed.

"Logan, c'mon."

I took a swig of the soda and looked at my sister. Because I'd lied to Laura, Sage was flat on her back in a hospital bed, and I'd just had the shit knocked out of me by her father. I lacked the strength for more lies. I needed advice.

"Laura." I didn't look her in the eye. "You were right about Sage. And . . . I knew. She was honest with me from the start. I didn't like it, but . . . I dunno, I guess she got to be kind of special to me. I tried to tell myself it didn't matter. But when you found out, I was just so embarrassed. I broke up with her." There. I'd said it. There was no going back. I think I might have felt relieved at this confession had it not come exactly one day too late.

Laura didn't reply. When I looked up, her face was in her hands. "Logan, I'm so sorry. I should have minded my own business. I was just afraid she was lying to you, but I should have known she wouldn't do that. Why did I have to go and open my mouth?"

I gingerly placed my head on the pillow. "I was the one who fucked up. I made Sage into the bad person, and she was the one who told the truth."

Laura sniffled. "If you want to get back together with her, we can just pretend this never happened. I won't mention it again."

So Sage had been right. As long as I was okay, Laura was okay. But now it no longer mattered.

"It's not that simple, Laura." I briefly related how Sage had tried to get back at me and ended up in the hospital. I glossed over how her dad had used me as a punching bag.

"Oh, Logan, I'm so sorry. What kind of bastard would hit a girl? Even a girl like Sage?"

I thought back to New Year's and how I'd been a hair away from punching her myself. In this whole sorry episode, I'd done nothing right. I'd had a thousand opportunities to be selfless and understanding, but I'd always been small-minded and cruel. I'd yelled at Sage when I found out her true sex. I'd mocked her at the comedy club. Then I'd slept with her and then dumped her to avoid a minor humiliation. And now she was in the hospital.

Sage would have been so much better off if she'd never met me.

"Logan? Are you asleep?"

I kept my eyes closed. "I'm on my way."

"Can I do anything for you?"

Blackness surrounded me. "Call Mom. She doesn't know where I am. Tell her I went for a ride with Jack or something. And Laura?"

"Yes?"

"Thank you for being understanding. I wish I had your attitude."

I felt Laura kiss me on the forehead.

"Good night, little brother."

I heard her make a brief phone call. Then she turned off the lights and crawled into Ebony's bed.

## chapter thirty-three

"LOGAN, are you sure you don't want me to come in and talk to Mom?" My sister and I were dusting down the gravel road toward home. Laura had gotten me up early to drive me back to Boyer. I'd thought about trying to visit Sage before we left, but decided to wait. Especially if her father was still at the hospital.

"I'll be okay. Mom's working the breakfast shift, so she won't be home, anyway. You told her Jack and I went driving and ended up in Columbia, right?"

"Yeah, but you know she's going to assume the worst. Especially when she sees your face."

My eye wasn't black from Mr. Hendricks's punch, but my cheek was discolored enough to make Mom ask questions. I had a strange center-of-the-brain headache, and I wondered if maybe I should have followed Ebony's advice and seen a doctor.

I tried to smile. "I'll think of something. And thanks for everything."

Laura parked in front of the trailer. She kissed my cheek, causing me to wince, and drove off.

Mom's car was still in the driveway, but she sometimes carpooled with another waitress. I was glad she wouldn't be home. All I wanted to do was drink a gallon of water and sleep for twelve hours. Then I could face the world and decide what I could do for Sage.

Tammi must have told her parents what had really happened. After I got some sleep, I'd call the hospital and see if it was okay to visit.

But then what? If it hadn't been for my ego, Sage wouldn't even be there in the first place. I'd promised to always be there for her, and I wasn't. I'd promised to be her friend and help her when she got scared, and I ran off. I'd promised Tammi that I'd look out for Sage and protect her. So where was I when that psycho was punching her teeth out?

I was so preoccupied that when I found Mom sitting in the living room, I almost said hello and headed to my room.

She had moved her easy chair to the middle of the floor and was staring daggers at me. For all I knew, she might have been sitting there since Laura had called the previous evening.

"Mom!"

"Where were you all night?" She was calm. Too calm.

"I was in Columbia. Didn't Laura call you?"

Mom didn't get up or uncross her arms. She just stared. I wanted to get a drink and sit down, but I was frozen.

I stood there in the doorway, trying to think of something appropriate to say. *My transsexual girlfriend got gay-bashed* wasn't it.

"Jack and I went for a drive."

"You *went for a drive*." Though Jack and I had covered many miles together over the years, Mom made this sound like an absurd story. It was like I'd told her I'd been kidnapped by clowns.

"Yeah . . ."

She cut me off. "So why didn't you just drive home with Jack?"

In English class we read a story about this Eastern European guy who is tried, convicted, and executed, though he's never charged with any crime. At that moment, I could relate.

"He met this girl in Columbia and went back to her place." I tried to give a knowing laugh, but it came out as a nervous giggle. "You know, three's a crowd."

I could hear the clock ticking in the kitchen. After ten ticks, Mom spoke. "Laura said Jack had car trouble."

A blunder, but I could salvage the lie. "Well, yeah, that's what I told Laura."

Mom crossed her legs. "Is that the truth?"

She knew I was probably lying, but I couldn't back out now. "Yes."

"That's funny. Because I ran into Jack and his father at the gas station this morning. Jack said you got a strange phone call and just ran off. He wanted to know if you were okay."

*Stupid concerned friend.* "Um."

Mom didn't speak. I was caught. No use digging myself in deeper.

"Okay, I wasn't with Jack. A friend of mine had a personal crisis, and I had to go help her."

"Was it Sage?" Mom's anger dropped just a hair.

"Yes."

"What was she doing in Columbia?"

How could I put this? "I can't tell you. She's having some real problems, and I had to go talk to her."

Mom stood. "You've been acting funny since you two got back from Mizzou last week. Maybe I should call Sage's parents and find out what's going on." She took a step toward the phone.

"DON'T." Both Mom and I were stunned by the manly authority in my voice. Mom stopped walking.

"Sage is in trouble, but you have to trust me on this: talking to her parents would only make things worse. I don't know if she's going to be okay or not, but . . . it's none of your business. I didn't do anything wrong last night, I swear. I'm sorry I didn't call, but I really didn't have a chance."

Mom stared at me for a minute. "What happened to your face?"

That would be a little harder to explain. I considered telling her I ran into a door, but I'd sound like one of those terrified women on *COPS*.

"That happened later. Some guy took a swing at me. I probably had it coming."

Mom's anger returned. In her universe, there was no legitimate reason for someone to hit her son.

"Logan, I called in sick this morning. I could tell Laura was covering for you, and I didn't know what was really happening. Can't you see how scared this makes me?"

I touched her shoulder. She was trembling. "I wish I could tell you what's going on. You just have to believe what I say. This isn't about me."

"I've heard that lie one too many times." She pulled away.

I was almost indignant. "I've never lied to you!" Well, not about anything like this.

Mom shook her head. When she spoke again, her voice was hoarse. "Not from you, Logan. From your father. He used to get strange phone calls and stay out all night and come home looking like someone had beat him up."

She rarely talked about her ex-husband. "Mom, I'm not like Dad."

She faced me and gave a weak smile. "I know you're not, honey. You're a wonderful boy, and I have to accept the fact that you're almost a man now. Almost. But I worry."

"It's what moms do." It occurred to me that, for the first time in my life, I was on my own. Mom couldn't bail me out of this one. While I hadn't always turned to Mom when I was in trouble, it was nice to know I had the option. Now I was facing a huge crisis, and it was all down to me. Mom couldn't help me, and neither could Laura or anyone else.

Mom wasn't quite ready to end our conversation. "Answer one question. Sage . . . she's not pregnant, is she?" Mom braced herself, terrified I was going to say yes.

"No!" I chuckled at how obsessed Mom was over a disaster that could never happen.

Mom glared. "I don't see what's so funny, Logan."

I swallowed my grin. "Nothing, Mom."

Mom smiled at me, resigned. I think she realized there was no one she could call, no punishment she could hit me with, no advice she could give. Not this time. But she wanted to help, and that made me feel a little better.

Grabbing two sodas, I went to my bedroom to hide. I had to figure out how to get revenge on Sage's attacker, convince Sage that her life was not as fucked up as it must seem, and show her that I deserved one last, last chance to prove I was worthy to be her friend, if nothing else.

And I was drawing a complete blank. This was one of those situations where there were no answers, no easy (or difficult) solutions. The only thing I could do was wait and pray that when the next bad thing happened, it would be to me and not Sage.

All that Sunday, I mowed: fields of weeds as high as my kneecaps, petite little yards with grass as trim as a golf green, dusty vacant lots overgrown with the dead plants of last summer. Someone even paid me once.

I had to lose myself in the work. If I stopped, even to get a drink, I'd start to think. About Sage, lying there on a plastic hospital mattress with tubes and needles in her body. About how some son of a bitch had punched her until she couldn't stand up anymore and then left her on the side of the road like . . . I couldn't think of an appropriate simile. About how if I had any balls at all, I would have told my sister—the sister who thought the world of me and only wanted me to be happy—how special Sage was. But instead, I told lies.

The most frustrating thing was how helpless I felt. I longed to do something, anything, to help Sage. But I didn't know who had assaulted her, so I couldn't go stick his face in the mower blades. I was willing to tell anyone how much I cared for Sage—my Mom, Jack, Tim, whoever—but that was pointless. She probably hated me. The only straw I could grasp at was the hope that, after she'd recovered a bit, she'd need a friend. Even a false friend like me.

When I'd slaughtered every blade of grass in Boyer, when I'd used up every drop of gas in my can, when my hands were cramped into claws from holding down the safety bar on the mower, only then did I slink home. Though it was only eight o'clock, I crawled into bed, a grimy, grassy mess.

I almost skipped school that Monday, but a faint hope forced me to go. I sat in the commons that morning, knowing that Sage wasn't going to show up. But still . . . I pictured her barging in, all brash and angry, a tiny bandage on the bridge of her nose. How she'd listen to my heartfelt apology and punch me in the arm. Then this whole horrible episode would turn into a bad dream.

Sage didn't come to school. I didn't see Tammi, either. Right before the first bell rang, Jack passed by and swatted the back of my head.

"Wakey, wakey, Logan."

Jack was his usual manic self, and I wasn't exactly in the mood to talk to him. I started to walk to class. He followed.

"Where did you run off to after the party? When you got that call . . . Jesus, who gave you that shiner?"

I zombied my way to biology. "I went to Columbia. Some drunk tried to take my wallet. I wouldn't give it up."

Jack whistled, impressed. By lunchtime, he'd spread the story around school. I believe his exact words were *Logan beat off some guy in Columbia this weekend.* That probably left a lot of people wondering what exactly I did with my free time.

That night I had an almost physical relationship with the telephone as I sat waiting for someone to call with information about Sage. Laura called to check on me, but I ran her off the line. Luckily, Mom was working, so she didn't start to wonder again if I was using drugs.

I wanted to call Sage. I went so far as to look up the hospital number, but I couldn't do it. What if her father answered? What if she hung up on me? Or what if she wanted to talk to me just to tell me how badly I'd screwed up her life? Maybe her condition was worse than I'd suspected. Or they might have admitted her to the hospital as a boy. Jesus. The entire staff probably knew. They might even have taken away her hormones.

I ended up being too chickenshit to call. I swore if I didn't hear from her by the next afternoon, I'd contact the hospital, no excuses.

Tammi saved me the trouble. I found her after school

Tuesday, distractedly tossing some books into her locker. She looked like she'd just recovered from a long illness: pale, tired, and not totally there.

"Tammi?"

She blinked, then stared at me for a moment like she didn't remember who I was. Finally, she gave me a thin smile. That was a relief. At least she didn't hate me.

"C'mon, Logan." I followed her down the west hall and into the band/music/choir room. She shut the door behind us and sat on the edge of the risers. I sat opposite on the piano bench.

"Tammi, how's . . ."

"She's fine. No, no, she's not. But she'll recover." She spoke flatly.

"How bad . . ."

"*She'll recover*, Logan." That was the official statement. Tammi knew more, but I was no longer in Sage's inner circle.

"Did they . . ."

She shook her head. "Sage won't talk. Not to the police, not to Mom, not to me. Maybe it's for the best. Daddy would shoot the guy if he knew who it was."

I thumped the piano. "I'd like to get ahold of him myself."

Tammi rolled her eyes. In her mind, I was all talk. My threats were bluster and bravado, nothing more.

"Do you think I could visit Sage?"

"Are you sure you want to, Logan? Someone might find out." There was no inflection in her voice, but the dig was there. Had Sage told Tammi about my problems with Laura? Did Tammi know I'd slept with her sister?

"I want to see her."

Tammi stuck out her tiny jaw. "Well, she doesn't want to see you. She said if you asked, and she didn't think you would, to tell you to stay away. That you'll both be happier."

So that was it. Sage was at one of the lowest points in her life, and the last thing she wanted was to see me. Two weeks before, I'd been the one who understood, her best friend, the guy she could depend on. And now I was a coward, the boy who ran away when things got rough and abandoned her to the wolves. I laid my forehead on the keyboard.

"Logan?" I had nearly forgotten Tammi was still there. "Logan? Um . . . it's not that she doesn't want to see you. I mean, that's what she says, but I know her. She doesn't want you to see her. She looks bad. Plus, my father's not your number one fan. We both told him you didn't have anything to do with this, but you still should avoid him for now."

I hammered a chord with my fist. "I deserve it. This is my fault."

Tammi's voice took on an edge. "No one likes a martyr, Logan. You were a self-centered asshole, but you weren't the one who knocked the shit out of my sister." She paused. "I'm more to blame than you are."

"Huh?"

Tammi swiveled on the riser until her back was to me. "I dunno. It's just . . . Sage told me about her . . . girlish thoughts when I was about ten. But she was always feminine. I liked the idea of having a sister; she practically was one already. When she told me she was going to tell Mom and Dad, I said she should go for it. I was only eleven, but even then I knew they'd freak out. I should have warned her, told her to wait."

"But you were just trying to be supportive." *Wasn't she?*

"Maybe. Or maybe I just wanted to watch the fireworks. You know how it is with sisters. When the other one is getting her ass chewed, you look like an angel."

I shrugged. "That's just the way it is."

Tammi looked back at me for a second. "Logan, when things got rough—and believe me, things got *real* bad there for a while—I'd sometimes sit in my room, listening to them all scream at each other, and think, 'I'm the good one. I'm the one who doesn't cause problems. I'm the *normal* one.' You have a sister, right? Did she ever really screw up, and things suddenly got better for you?"

I traced the dust on the piano with my finger. "A few years ago, Laura's boyfriend got picked up for DUI. The cops drove her home in the middle of the night. She caught hell for that for a month. Yeah, I was the golden boy then. I hated to see her in trouble, but when I got a D in history, I didn't even get grounded."

Tammi was staring at the wall again. "That's what I mean. I never wanted Sage to get hurt. But at the same time, my parents wouldn't have let me date Rob if Sage had been a normal boy. It's like, 'At least Tammi likes boys. At least Tammi acts like she's supposed to. Maybe Tammi's only a freshman, but she's doing normal things.'"

Tammi snorted, then fished in her purse for a tissue.

"And now my big sister's hurt, and maybe if I'd thought about her instead of me, this wouldn't have happened. I should have told her to wait. I should have told her not to take those hormones. Maybe she'd still be safe."

I stood up and joined her on the risers. She didn't move away.

"Tammi, you remember how Sage once tried to hurt herself, right?"

She nodded.

"She wouldn't have done that if being a woman was something she could forget about. I think she needed you to tell her that she wasn't weird, that she didn't need to be ashamed. Sage always talked about you. She said you were the only one who understood her. You can't fake that. Stop blaming yourself. You were supportive when no one else was. Not even me. Especially not me."

Tammi turned to me with a desperate look on her face. "I should have protected her."

"You did. Hell, you didn't give us a moment alone together when we first met."

Tammi almost laughed. "I knew what you had in mind. I only let you two go out when she said you knew her secret."

We both smiled, then stopped. The image of Sage bleeding in the bathroom jumped into my head, and probably Tammi's as well. She stood up, not making eye contact.

"I'm telling everyone that Sage hurt her back in a car wreck, and that she'll be in traction for the rest of the school year. Please don't say otherwise."

"Right."

Tammi walked to the door, then stopped and turned. "Logan, I'll talk to her, see if maybe she'll give you a call. She's mad at you, but I think she's angrier at herself."

I thanked her and she left the room.

## chapter thirty-four

I LAY on our living room couch counting the cobwebs on the ceiling. My brain screamed for action. I should be doing something, something to make everything okay. But what? I needed someone to talk to.

When people are stuck in frightening and confusing situations, they don't want advice. They want someone to tell them what to do. To be ordered, commanded. I needed someone to march in and tell me what the next step was in such a way that I couldn't wimp out.

And I could talk to no one. Jack, Tim, even Brenda . . . they might be able to advise me, and at this point, I was desperate enough to tell them the truth. But I couldn't violate Sage's privacy like that.

The phone rang and I lunged for it. Maybe it was Tammi, or even Sage.

"Hello?"

"Logan?" said a gravely, unpleasant voice. Someone who I never expected to call me.

"Mr. Hendricks?"

There was a pause, and I hoped we'd been disconnected. Then: "Can you come over to our house now? I want to talk to you."

The last time we'd talked, he'd tried to break my face and said he'd kill me if he ever saw me again. How the hell did he expect me to answer?

"I'll be right there."


Sage's truck was parked in the driveway. Next to it stood my bike, where I'd abandoned it after taking her to the hospital. There was no sign of anyone.

Why had Sage's father asked me over? Maybe he'd told the cops I was the one who assaulted her and was luring me here to be arrested. Maybe bruising my face wasn't sufficient, and he'd decided he really wanted to work me over. Or maybe Sage had insisted he try and make peace with me.

Whatever the reason, it was dumb for me to be here. But this was my only connection with the weird girl who'd put me on a four-month emotional roller coaster. I had to find out how she was doing. I rang the bell.

"Come in," Mr. Hendricks growled from inside.

I almost bolted. It was my desire to see Sage again that forced me to open the door. There were almost no lights on in the house, just a dim glow from the kitchen. Fully expecting a crowbar to the head, I slunk through the dining room.

Sage's father sat at the table, a lone fluorescent light reflecting off his bald head. He was leaning on his elbows, his eyes on the table, a mostly full bottle of beer in front of him.

"Get a soda," he ordered. I was reminded of those police shows, where the cop offers the suspect a coffee before grilling him. Warily, I grabbed a generic lemon lime soda from the fridge and sat opposite him. He still hadn't looked up.

"Sir?"

Mr. Hendricks held up a palm, and I shut up. After a moment, he spoke.

"I guess I owe you an apology. Tammi said you drove Sage to the hospital that night. I was angry and over-reacted. Sorry."

The apology was sincere, but completely lacking. It was like he'd forgotten to feed my cat or had been brusque with me over the phone.

"It's okay," I said, mentally not forgiving him.

He took a sip of beer, or at least appeared to. The liquid level didn't really change. "Logan, you didn't tell me the truth about what was going on with you and Sage. Don't deny it." He wasn't accusing me of anything, just stating something he already knew.

Every time I'd lied recently, I'd only made things worse. I decided to tell the truth; it wasn't like Sage's father could hate me more than he already did.

"Mr. Hendricks, I wasn't lying when we talked that time. Sage and I weren't dating. All I wanted from Sage was friendship." I was careful to avoid feminine pronouns. "But after a couple of months, we . . ."

He held up his palm again. "I'm not interested. So you dated my son. Great. And now look what happens. You know whose fault this is?"

Ah, this is why he wanted me over. To blame me for Sage's beating. To have a face he could hate, a name he could curse. I wasn't about to deny it. Sage's father couldn't have a lower opinion of me than I did of myself.

"I guess I was . . ."

Mr. Hendricks banged the table with his fist, and I stopped. He looked up, and I was shocked to see his face. It was like he'd aged from forty to sixty since I'd last seen him. His eyes were bloodshot like he was drunk. Or had been crying.

"Logan, you didn't do this. I wish I could say this was all because of you, but it wasn't." He took a drink, a real one this time. "Four years ago, Sage told me he wanted to be a girl. I thought he'd gone nuts. We sent him to a psychiatrist. Fat lot of good that did. She kept telling Sage his feelings aren't wrong and he should go ahead and prance around in dresses if that makes him happy." His knuckles went white around the bottle's neck, like he was throttling Sage's understanding therapist.

"For the past four years, I've had to watch my only son dress like some drag queen. He shares clothes with Tammi, he does her makeup. Fuck, Logan, he takes drugs that made him grow tits. I never expected him to be a football player, but this!" He paused.

"At any rate, not a day went by that I didn't tell him what a mistake he was making, what a fool he was being, how ashamed his family was. Though I guess I was the only one who was really embarrassed. His mother and sister sure seem to accept things. I always hoped he'd stop. But when he first told us, when I first realized the problem wasn't going away, I told him . . ."

He suddenly froze and stared at me, like he'd forgotten I was there. He placed his face in one hand and massaged his eyes.

"I told him . . . I'd rather see him dead than acting like a girl."

If this was a made-for-TV movie, there would have been a loud musical score and a cut to commercial. Sage had never told me that. I knew her father disapproved, but telling her he wished she was dead . . . I didn't think that was possible for a parent. How could he look at his crazy, wonderful kid and be that ashamed?

Mr. Hendricks seemed to be waiting for me to say something. I had a couple of things I wanted to say, but reined in my temper. And I wasn't going to tell him that what he'd said was understandable, if that's what he wanted.

Eventually, Sage's father started talking again. Rapidly, like we didn't have much time.

"Logan, I didn't mean what I said. I swear to God, I didn't mean that. I just thought that if I showed Sage how much I hated what he was doing, he'd stop. Fathers have to do that sometimes. Be the bad guy to keep their kids in line. You know what that's like."

"I don't have a father."

Mr. Hendricks looked at me, and for the first time I think he saw something other than the kid who was corrupting his child. But the moment passed, and he continued his story.

"Sage wouldn't stop acting like a girl. It was like he had to spite me. Throw his lifestyle in my face. Show me that nothing would stop him. I'll tell you something, Logan. The day I said that horrible thing to Sage, he stopped loving me. But I never took it back. Never said I was sorry."

Maybe he was looking for absolution, maybe he was just finally admitting to himself that he hadn't done right. I wanted to rub his nose in it. Yell at him, lecture him on how if he'd just been more understanding, Sage wouldn't have tried to hurt herself and wouldn't have been so confused and scared. But I'd had enough of the blame game recently. I certainly wasn't the guy to point fingers.

"Sir? You feel guilty, Tammi feels guilty, I sure as hell feel guilty, and Sage probably does too. But we all know the SOB who beat Sage up is the real bad guy here, and I doubt we'll ever know who that was." Numbly, Mr. Hendricks nodded. I continued.

"I guess neither of us really knew how to handle someone like Sage. But she's the one who's hurting"—the *she* slipped out before I could stop myself—"and we need to worry about Sage."

"Yeah." He took another fake sip of his drink and was silent.

"So how is Sage doing?"

"Broken nose, a couple of cracked ribs."

*Ribs? Shit, what did that bastard do to her?* "Could I visit Sage tomorrow?"

Mr. Hendricks wouldn't look at me. He wasn't telling me something.

"Sir?"

"Sage . . . is no longer at University Hospital, Logan," he answered evasively.

I didn't want to ask the next question. "Where is she, then?"

"A private clinic," he mumbled into his hand.

I felt my stomach acid boil. Sage had told me her family had once discussed having her institutionalized.

"You mean a nuthouse? A psycho hospital?"

Mr. Hendricks nodded.

"She gets her ass kicked, and you have her *put away!* Just stick your family's embarrassing little secret in the loony bin! That's how you deal with this?" I wanted to grab my soda and throw it at him, but I wasn't feeling quite that brave. He didn't say anything.

"Answer me!"

Sage's father looked right at me, and I calmed down. His expression wasn't exactly friendly, but there was less hate there than before.

"Logan, after the attack, Sage said he was going to kill himself. He's tried to before. More than once."

"Jesus." I didn't know Sage had attempted suicide more than the one time she'd told me about.

"We can't bring him back home like that. We'd have to watch him every second, not let him go out. He wouldn't even be able to go to the bathroom by himself. His mother and I thought maybe the doctors could help him. Help us all. Deal with this so he won't feel that way."

I must have looked angry.

"I meant feel suicidal, Logan. I know the other thing won't change." He sounded defeated.

I stared at my can of soda, which still wasn't open. "Could I visit her?" The *her* wasn't an accident this time.

Mr. Hendricks handed me an envelope. "Directions, visiting hours. You could go tomorrow, if you like."

I stood up. We didn't shake hands, and I turned to go. As I opened the front door, Sage's father called to me from the kitchen.

"Tell her I'm sorry, Logan!" he shouted almost desperately. "Tell her I didn't mean it! Please . . . tell her I didn't mean it."

I barked some sort of affirmative and rode off on my bike. I pedaled blindly. Luckily, there's no traffic in Boyer, so I didn't wind up returning to the hospital as a patient.

We all hated ourselves. Me, Mr. Hendricks, Tammi, and, I was sure, Sage. The perverse thing was, none of us had really been all that greedy or self-absorbed. Sage's father, cruel as he was, only wanted his son back. Tammi just wanted a sister. I wanted a "normal" girlfriend. And Sage— all she wanted was to be herself.

I must have been doing fifteen miles an hour. I didn't bother to notice where I was or where I was headed.

Sage just wanted to be herself. To be something that half the people on the planet become when they're born. She just wanted a little acceptance, a little understanding. And because she had the gall to look in a mirror and say *I am a woman*, she'd been rejected by her father, denied a normal childhood, abandoned by a boy she thought cared for her, and had her bones broken and face smashed.

But now Sage had me. Not the wimpy *what will the neighbors think?* Logan. I was through worrying. Sage needed an ally. That was me. She needed a protector. I could do that. She no longer had to be alone. Starting the next day, I'd stand by her, no matter what happened, no matter who found out her secret. And if that painted me queer in the eyes of the world, then fuck the world. It had never done much for me, anyway.

When I visited Sage the next day, she'd see a man who would never let her down again. Someone who deserved to be called her friend.

*chapter thirty-five*

I'D NEVER SEEN a mental hospital in real life and didn't know what to expect. Some sort of grim stone fortress, where patients gibbered and drooled from behind bars? Or maybe an ultramodern facility with gleaming chrome fixtures and a plastic-faced staff who passed out pills to keep the inmates in a drugged stupor?

"Logan? Are you sure you can't talk to me about this?" Mom was driving me. I had asked to borrow the car, and she insisted on knowing where I was going. When she found out that I had to visit Sage in a mental facility, she didn't ask any questions. But she forced me to let her drive.

I continued to look out the window at the billboards along the highway as we approached Columbia. "I can't, Mom. I'm sorry."

While we drove in silence, I contemplated what I was going to say to Sage. I'd felt so brave the previous day, but as I got closer and closer to my actual meeting, my courage abandoned me. Why would Sage even want to see me again? I wasn't sure what the hospital rules were, but I assumed she had the right to refuse to see a visitor. And if she did want to talk to me, what would I say? How could I prove to her that my friendship was worth anything?

When Sage had first told me about her past, she needed me to be understanding. I was hateful. When she needed a friend, I turned into a lover. And when she needed a lover, I wanted nothing to do with her. How many times could I apologize? I sounded like one of those alcoholics who keep swearing that this time, they're really going to stay sober.

One thing was certain, though. I wasn't my father. Things were rough, but I was going to stick around. Maybe it would be months before Sage would forgive me. Maybe years. But we'd be going to the same college. I had lots of time to help her get her life back on track.

"Logan? We're here."

The clinic was a compact brick building of four stories. It had that healthy, generic look of most medical facilities. Looking at it from the outside, you'd believe that it was filled with proctologists' offices and blood labs. Only the security fence around the perimeter showed otherwise.

"Mom, could you wait in the car?"

She shook her head. "I'm going in with you. But I'll wait in the lobby, and you can take as long as you need."

I didn't have to take Mom with me. I could have borrowed Jack's car or had Laura bring me. But I don't think I could have handled it. Visiting a friend in a mental facility . . . it was too *adult*. It's not something you did in high school. I wanted my mom to be with me, for moral support, if nothing else.

The lobby was tiny and almost completely undecorated. I'd half expected to see guys in white coats dragging googly-eyed men in straitjackets through the door, but this was as bland as my dentist's office. I leaned through the receptionist's window.

"I'd like to visit"—I couldn't bring myself to say *a patient*—"someone."

She smiled. "Who would you like to see?"

"Sage Hendricks."

I had to fill out several forms. Mom flipped through a magazine and tried not to ask any questions. I'd never signed a *no hostage* waiver before; I wondered just what I was getting into.

"Mr. Witherspoon?" A tall, skinny guy with an enormous Adam's apple was standing in the doorway. He was dressed in scrubs. I shot a thin smile at Mom.

"Take as long as you need," she reminded me. I followed the aide.

In a tiny antechamber, he waved a metal detector over me and made me empty my pockets. He then lectured me that I was not to give anything to the patient, that I would be under observation during my entire visit, and that I could be asked to leave at any time.

I felt depressed. What sort of rules was Sage living under?

The aide gave me a visitor name tag. He punched in some numbers on a keypad, and we passed into the main building. It resembled a generic hospital. I couldn't see any of the patients, which is probably just as well. I would have stared.

This wasn't right. This was an asylum for insane people. I wanted to shout that Sage wasn't crazy, that her family had stuck her here, that all she needed was for people to be understanding. I kept my mouth shut. The time for me to be understanding had come and gone.

I was led to a door labeled CONFERENCE ROOM A, a bare room with a table, chairs, and a whiteboard. Inside, a plain woman of about fifty sat at a table reading a file. As I entered, she smiled and removed her reading glasses.

"Please, leave us." The aide shut the door behind him.

"I'm Dr. McGregor," she said, gesturing to an empty seat. "You can call me Sally, if you like."

I nodded and sat down. "Doctor."

She looked at me with such a friendly smile, I almost forgot she was holding Sage prisoner. I had to remind myself not to let my guard down.

"Logan—may I call you Logan?—I'm Sage's therapist. I've been working with her for the past few months."

"Months?"

"Yes. I'm helping her work through her gender identity issues. I'm not affiliated with this hospital."

I felt a little less hostile. Mr. Hendricks had said Sage's therapist was understanding.

"Sage doesn't belong here, Doctor." Someone had to say it.

Dr. McGregor frowned. "They're not planning on keeping her here. But she said she wanted to kill herself.

We can't ignore that. When people say something like that, especially at Sage's age, they usually mean it."

I thought back to my freshman year when some burnout senior had hanged himself in an abandoned barn. I wondered if he'd tried to warn anyone.

"Can I see her?"

"In a moment. I just wanted to talk with you for a few minutes."

My defenses went up again. Was she going to try to get me to talk about Sage? Reveal things she'd told me in private? Or . . . talk about what Sage and I had done?

"So talk."

The doctor toyed with her glasses. "Sage has told me a lot about you. She talks about you at every therapy session."

"What does she say?" I asked, eager for information and a little flattered that Sage discussed me with her therapist.

The doctor flipped through a file on the table. "I'm afraid that's confidential. Though she thinks highly of you. She still does. And that may be a problem."

I suddenly felt trapped. I'd heard how these psychiatrists can twist your words, make you say things you didn't mean, reveal things you didn't want to admit. She continued.

"Logan, when people visit here, they usually feel guilty. They think of a thousand things they did wrong, ways they feel they might have hurt the patient. They're often desperate to make things right."

I remembered telling Sage I couldn't see her again, then later driving her to the hospital, her face a bloody mess. I would have done a lot to undo that.

"What's your point?"

"My point is, please be careful what you say. When you see her, you'll be ready to promise the world, to say anything to make her happy. But don't. This"—she gestured to the empty walls—"isn't the real world. Things that happen in here aren't the same as on the outside. I guess what I'm trying to say is, be careful what you tell her. Don't make her any promises that you might not be able to keep. You'll end up hurting her."

The doctor was clearly warning me against trying to get back together with Sage. I'd been mulling over the same thing. I'd even considered asking her to take me back, hoping it would help her out of her depression. Or help me.

"What business is that of yours?" I asked, trying to remind the doctor that I wasn't her patient and didn't have to do what she said.

"It's my business because I care about her. Just like you do. Sage is hurting right now. Just go in there and listen. She needs an understanding friend right now more than anything."

I wouldn't admit it, but the doctor was right. I would have promised Sage whatever she asked to make her happy again, but when she left the hospital, nothing would be different.

"Are we through here?"

Dr. McGregor smiled and led me through another door. It was an airy room, painted light green, with bright, wire-mesh windows and many plastic plants. Games, puzzles, and books were stacked on various tables. Overhead, a TV watched us with a blank blue face.

Sage sat slumped on a couch staring at her hands. She was wearing sweatpants, a sweater, and slippers. Those might have been men's clothes, but it didn't matter; she still looked like a girl. An ID bracelet was strapped around her wrist. Her face was turned away.

"I'll let you two talk," said the doctor. "And remember . . ." She pointed to an overhead security camera, then left.

Sage didn't acknowledge me, just kind of sat there. Jesus, they hadn't drugged her, had they? I sat down on the same couch, a cushion away.

"Sage?"

She didn't look up. "You shouldn't have come, Logan."

"How could I not have come?" That sounded too defensive, like I was doing her a favor by being there.

Sage looked up at me, and I cringed before I could stop myself. My face had almost totally healed. Hers had gotten much worse. Her left eye, nose, and lip had all swollen together, melting the side of her face into some kind of grotesque clown mask. Her braces had been removed, and there was a gap where a tooth had been. What would that maniac have done if Sage hadn't pretended to be unconscious? That guy might have killed her.

"Pretty nasty, huh?" said Sage.

"You look fine."

"Liar." There was just a hint of a smile in that voice.

"You look terrible."

"That's better." I couldn't tell if she was grinning or if that was just the way her face had swelled.

"Sage, I . . ."

"Don't." There was something very final in the way she said that. "Don't apologize, don't say you're sorry, don't ask me what you can do. My family's been giving me that bullshit all week."

"But . . ."

She sighed. "Let me make it easier for you. You used me, and that makes you a prick. You wouldn't stand up for me, and that makes you a wimp. After everything you promised, you still thought of Logan first."

So much for her wanting to get back together. She turned and faced me again, and she really was smiling this time.

"But I don't hate you. I don't really like you, but I can't actually hate you, either."

"I didn't mean—"

She cut me off. "I swear, Logan, you give me a whiny apology, and I'll get you thrown out of here."

My thoughts regrouped. "How are they treating you?"

Sage rubbed her side. "It's kind of a weird place. They lobotomized some guy last week, and then this big Indian threw a sink through a window and escaped."

"I'm pretty sure that was a movie."

"Okay, the food stinks and everyone keeps wanting to talk about my feelings."

I tapped my fingers on the arm of the couch. There was a question I had to ask to put my mind at ease. "Sage, your father said you . . . threatened to hurt yourself. Did you mean that?"

Sage leaned her head back, grimaced in pain, then

slouched forward. "I'm not going to kill myself. I wouldn't hurt Tammi like that. Or my mom. Or you, I guess. But sometimes I do want to die."

"You're too wonderful to die." It slipped out before I could stop myself, and it was dangerously close to what the doctor had warned me about. But I kept talking. "Sage, I've never met anyone like you before. You're too bizarre, too tacky, too ridiculous for words." That didn't sound right. "I mean, I just really enjoy you. You're fun and loud and . . ."

Sage almost laughed. "I can see why you're not on the debate team. But thank you, Logan. You know, you always made me feel normal. I suppose we should have stayed friends. I guess I just wanted us to be more."

"That's what I wanted too." And then, when I got what I wanted, I ran away.

Sage seemed to straighten up. "I guess I'm not the first girl who got fucked over by some asshole." She looked at me with false contempt. "And I'm not the first girl who got her teeth knocked out by some psycho. When I decided I wanted to be a girl, I forgot that I'd be inheriting a whole new set of problems."

She sounded hopeful that she was going to put everything behind her.

"How long will you have to stay here?"

"Not long. Maybe two more weeks. My folks are working it out with the school so that I can make up my work and still graduate."

I'd been worried about that. "I'll visit you again. Every

day, if you want." Then I could spend the summer proving to her that I was worthy of her friendship. That if she gave me another chance, I wouldn't let her down.

Sage wouldn't meet my eye. "No, Logan. We won't ever see each other again."

She said it matter-of-factly, like she was dropping a class or something. I hoped she was joking.

"What?"

She turned until I was facing her back. "You heard me."

"Why? We'll be at Mizzou together. I know I've used up my asshole points, but don't tell me you don't want to be friends anymore! Is that what you really want?"

"Keep your voice down or they'll kick you out." Sage stared up at the blank TV screen for a moment, her hand gently touching her bruised cheek. "Logan, I'm not going to Mizzou. I'm going to take a year off and go to school . . . somewhere else."

"Somewhere else? What for?"

Sage just looked past me, running her tongue along her damaged smile.

I was ready to start climbing the walls like a resident. "Sage, if you want me out of your life, fine. Get a restraining order. I won't go within fifty feet of you. You don't have to talk to me again. But would it really be so horrifying to live in the same city as me? Mizzou's huge. We'd probably never run into each other."

I was yelling, hyperventilating. I waited for Dr. McGregor to come in, but she didn't.

"Are you through, Logan?"

I caught my breath. "Yeah."

"I don't want to go to Mizzou because I don't want you to see me as a man."

I blinked in confusion. "What the hell's that supposed to mean?"

And then it hit me.

"Sage? Jesus Christ, you're not thinking about . . . living as a guy, are you?" After all the fighting, the misery, the struggle to become a girl, she wasn't going to give that all up. She couldn't.

Sage pulled her knees up to her chin but still wouldn't look at me. "I can't do it, Logan. I could live with a father who hates me, and a society that treats me like a damn joke, and a body that's too tall and too muscular . . . but when that guy started pounding me, and calling me a fag, and kicking me in the crotch . . ." She stopped talking for a bit, then continued, almost whispering.

"I realized that I'm never going to be a woman. Even if I have the surgery, I'll be faking it. I'll always be a boy to my family, and I'll live the next sixty years wondering if my secret will get out. I just can't take it anymore. I tried and I failed, so I'm quitting. I wish we could stay friends, but after what we did together, we couldn't face each other man to man."

Had Sage had some kind of breakdown? "You've lost your mind!"

"That's what they tell me."

"You know what I mean. Sage, you're not a guy! You're a chick! Things are bad now, but in a few months . . ."

She swiveled slowly until we sat face to face. I flinched. I'd never seen anyone look so dejected, so beaten. "It's always been bad. I smiled for the world, but I've been dead on the inside. Ever since I first tried to be a girl, I've felt like I was drowning, like I had to swim with all my might *just to live, day to day*! I have to get out of the water, Logan. I'll go under for good, otherwise."

I stood up. This wasn't right. It had never occurred to me she'd do this. I somehow knew that if I said the wrong thing now, then I'd never see Sage again. "You think you'll be happy as a man?"

"I'm not happy now."

"You'll be miserable as a guy. You'd hate yourself. Is that what you want, to wake up twenty years from now and realize you pissed away your only chance at happiness?"

That struck a nerve. "I think you should leave, Logan."

I didn't budge. "Don't do it, Sage! You'll regret it. Can you really deny that you're a girl? Look me in the eye and say you're a man. Do it!"

"Dr. McGregor!" she called. The therapist must have been waiting right outside, because she burst in, along with a different guard.

"Sir, you need to leave." His tone left no room for argument.

I didn't have much time. "Sage, just think about this. Think about what we shared. Tell me that wasn't wonderful. I fucked it up, but tell me that you didn't enjoy it!"

Sage buried her face in her lap, sobbing quietly.

"Sir!" snapped the guard, not at all friendly.

"Don't let a couple of jerks ruin your life."

The guard grabbed my shoulder, but I pulled away. Big mistake. He had me in a half nelson almost instantly. I was being dragged to the door. Sage didn't look at me.

"Sage! Just think about it! Please!"

I was through the door. It slammed in my face. The guard let me loose.

I couldn't bear to stand there and be chastised by Dr. McGregor. I sprinted down the hall. Then, to my humiliation, the door to the lobby wouldn't open. I had to wait while the guard unlocked it.

Mom looked upset when she saw me bolt through the lobby and out the front door.

"You have to sign out!" the receptionist yelled after me. I jumped into the car. Mom joined me soon after.

"Logan?"

I wanted to tell her I was fine. I wanted to tell her to drive, that it was none of her business, to leave me alone. But I just started crying. I couldn't stop. Mom held me and stroked my hair, and I bawled harder than I had since elementary school. I cried so hard I felt like I'd puke. I cried until I was exhausted. It was only when I collapsed in a daze against the door that Mom drove off.

*chapter thirty-six*

## BERNAL C. HENDERSCHMITT

### 1890–1920

Remember friend as you pass by
You are now as once was I
Now I lie in a cold, cold bed
And so shall you, when you are dead

IF I KEPT HANGING OUT in this cemetery, they'd probably talk about having me put away. I wasn't sure what time it was, though the moon had traveled halfway across the sky. Mom hadn't said a word as we drove home, but I couldn't follow her back inside. I felt like I'd suffocate in that trailer. I had to be alone. I leaned against a tree and stared at Bernal's tombstone. Was he urging me to seize the day, or was he just pissy about being dead?

So Sage was going to change her sex. Again. Go back to being the boy she once was. The very thought hurt my soul. I couldn't describe it. I felt like Sage was on death row, like they were strapping her into the electric chair, and only I had the evidence to free her, but I didn't know what to do.

This was worse than Brenda cheating on me. Worse than when I found out Sage's secret. Worse than when Laura found out Sage's secret.

Why did it bother me so much? Maybe it was the thought that in a year, Sage would be a hulking, burly man, and that I'd have to live with the fact that I let a macho guy like that give me pleasure.

No, that wasn't it. For one thing, Sage would never be macho. She'd turn into a swishy guy, one who'd set off gay-dar alarms at fifty feet. Sage couldn't pull off the man thing. And then there were the hormones. I didn't know how they worked, but taking estrogen during puberty probably had some lasting effects.

I hated the idea that I'd never see Sage again. She was my buddy, my friend, the first girl to touch me naked. I didn't want her last mental image to be me screaming as the nuthouse staff dragged me away.

But I'd never expected to talk to Sage again after I dumped her. I'd been willing to pay that price. What had changed my mind?

Dew was forming on my pants. The mosquitoes were torturing me. Still, I could not make myself get up.

I was upset because I thought Sage was making a huge mistake. That's all there was to it. Sage made such a great girl. She'd told me herself, she was miserable as a boy. But now she felt she had to go back. Had to run away from all she'd accomplished. Because of one bully. One guy who hurt her. Sage, the girl Sage, was going to die. I couldn't bear the thought.

And there was nothing I could do to make everything right.

That week, I tried to convince myself that things really weren't black and hopeless. Sage had just suffered the worst week of her life. That's why she was so determined to give up everything she'd achieved. But people say things all the time they don't really mean. That was one lesson I learned from Brenda.

I decided not to contact Sage for a week or so. Let her do some thinking, talk things over with her doctor and her family. Then, after she'd had a while to reflect, I'd ask Tammi to tell Sage that I really wanted to see her again. I didn't think Sage would refuse me, not after everything that happened this semester.

I'd tell her if she didn't want to be friends, it would be my loss, not hers. But I had to make sure that she wasn't going to kill off the girl I'd almost allowed myself to love. Sage would see things my way. She had to.

I lasted six days before I broke down and called the hospital. To my surprise, whoever answered the phone informed me that Sage was no longer a patient there.

This was great news! She'd been released early! That

must mean her mental condition had improved. Maybe she'd even come back to school. I eagerly dialed her home number. Tammi answered.

"Tammi? The hospital said Sage isn't there anymore. Did she come home?"

The long pause told me I'd been too optimistic. "Logan, I need to talk to you in person. Can I come see you?"

I immediately went back to depressed mode. People never want to tell you news face to face unless it's bad. "Yeah, come on over."

Mom was in her bedroom. I knocked.

"Hey, Mom, feel like going for a drive?"

She smiled. We hadn't discussed things since the day at the hospital. Maybe she thought I was going to open up to her.

"Okay. Should we pack a snack?"

"Oh, um. I mean, do *you* feel like a drive? Sage's sister is coming over."

Mom opened her mouth, then paused. She hadn't asked me why Sage was in the hospital or what had gone on between us. Lord, did she ever want to. She never suspected the truth was worse than anything she'd imagined.

"Okay, Logan."

Mom grabbed her jacket and left the trailer. When I heard her car start, I went running out the door and leaned in through the car window. I had forgotten to tell her something.

"Mom, thanks. Thanks for everything. Thanks for working so hard. Thanks for believing in me. Thanks . . . just thanks." I was babbling.

Mom smiled, and I think she blinked away a tear. "I love you too, Logan." She drove off.

Half an hour later, Tammi rode up on a bike. Wordlessly, I led her into my home.

"This is a nice place, Logan." She sat down. "Are those your track trophies?"

"Tammi, c'mon." No small talk, not now.

She sighed. "Right. You want to know where Sage is."

"She's not at your house?"

Tammi looked at me with pity. "Logan, my family discussed things. And we all agreed that it would be best for Sage if she didn't live around here anymore."

Why couldn't Tammi just come out and answer me? "What do you mean?"

"Mom and Sage have moved to another city. Dad and I will join them when the school year's over."

I suddenly felt very alone. "Back to Joplin?"

"No, out of state. Dad worked out a transfer."

"Another state? Where she doesn't know anyone?"

Tammi shrugged. "She doesn't really know anyone here, except you."

I looked at Tammi in horror. "So she's leaving to get away from me?"

Sage's sister looked at me with surprising anger. "Logan, for once in your life, think about someone else. There's a psychopath in Columbia who tried to kill her. That's twenty minutes from here. Do you think she wants to risk seeing him again?"

I tore at my hair. In my mind, Sage's attacker was a faceless slasher movie monster. I hadn't really considered he was a real-life guy who Sage might run into again and again. I might have even seen him at that party, maybe even talked to him.

Tammi patted my knee. "Sage needs a fresh start. Mom's rented an apartment, but we'll buy a house as soon as we can sell our old one. . . ."

We were getting off topic. "Tammi, Sage told me . . . she didn't want to live as a woman anymore."

Tammi didn't answer for a long while, then nodded.

"She's not still going to do that, is she?"

"It's her decision. Sage thinks she'll be better off as a man."

For the first time in my life, I understood what a panic attack was. "You'll try to talk her out of it, won't you? You told her she's making a huge mistake, right?"

Tammi shook her head. "Sage has to do what she thinks is best."

I jumped up. "Listen to yourself! Sage tried to commit suicide because she thought she couldn't live as a woman."

Her sister didn't blink. "And someone tried to beat her to death because she did live as a woman."

"That won't happen again!"

Tammi folded her arms. "You don't know that. Look, Sage's life is her own—not mine, not yours. The best thing anyone can do is let her figure this out for herself. The rest of us have our own reasons for wanting Sage to be a girl or a boy. Especially you."

I was on the verge of hyperventilating. "Can I call her? Or write to her? Where did she move?"

Tammi stood. "She made me promise I wouldn't tell you. If Sage wants to hear from you, she has your address."

"She has a lot more than that." I lay facedown on the couch feeling utterly alone.

Tammi might have said something. I ignored her, and she left. When Mom returned, I pretended to be asleep.

I had absolutely failed Sage. I could have made her happy. She was so close. Close to being my best friend. Close to being my girlfriend. Close to being a girl.

But close didn't count.

## chapter thirty-seven

THE SCHOOL YEAR SPUTTERED to a close like the dying gasps of a car with no gas. We'd all been so excited about graduation, we didn't really stop to think what would happen next. For the first time in our lives, we wouldn't have to listen to teachers. For those of us going to college or the military, we wouldn't have to listen to our parents. The thought was terrifying.

I used to have this cat that would spend all day pounding against the screen door, desperately trying to escape. And whenever he did get out, he'd freeze on the porch, too terrified to move, until I came and got him. That was how I felt as the big day approached.

Sage was really and truly gone. Tammi never talked to me anymore. Sage had done it. Moved away. Forgotten about me.

I tried to be angry and cynical, tried to push her out of my mind forever. It was her life, her body, her mistakes to make. I had my own problems. But I had become disgustingly sentimental. Every time the phone rang, I dove for it. Every time I came home from school or mowing lawns, I half expected to find her sitting on the porch waiting for me. When the mail came, I always hoped for a letter from her. Just a little note, saying goodbye. We never had a goodbye. There were things I wanted to tell Sage. Things I wanted to hear her say.

I started a couple of letters to her, hoping that Tammi would forward them. I tore them up. What would have been the point?

In two weeks, I'd graduate. High school would be a memory. And what would I remember? Ten years from now, what would I think about when I thought of the past four years? Not my friends. Not running track. Not my love for Brenda or my hatred for Brenda. I'd think of Sage. It would always be about Sage. I wanted to see her again.

But Sage was either dying or dead, and a strange man would take her place forever.

It was a gray spring day, and the forecasters were calling for rain. Still, a couple hundred spectators braved the elements to sit in the football bleachers and watch the spectacle. A stage had been set up on the fifty-yard line, decked out with bunting in blue and white, the school colors. Principal Bloch, bursting out of his moth-eaten graduation gown, lurked at the back, ready to shove diplomas at us. The graduates, all forty-eight of us, sat shivering on folding chairs.

Gretchen Patrick, the valedictorian, was grinning at us

from the podium, talking to us as if we were athletes at the Special Olympics.

"In conclusion, Boyer graduates, remember that we have our whole lives ahead of us. Take a stand. Make a difference." *Spout a cliché.*

Mr. Bloch approached the podium and raised the microphone a foot or so. Even on a happy occasion like this, he looked like he was about to tell us we all had detention.

"Ladies and . . ." Whatever remarks he was about to make were cut off by a blaring recording of "Pomp and Circumstance." It was the best the music director could manage; half the marching band was graduating. The first row of students slouched toward the stage. I'd seen more excitement in the lunch line on pizza day.

"Benjy Anderson," announced Mrs. Day, the vice principal. Bloch thrust a diploma at him and shook his hand while a photographer snapped a picture.

So this was the end. Thirteen years of complaining about public school, and now it was over. It somehow didn't seem real. I felt like after the summer, I'd report for another year at BHS, along with Tim and Jack and my other friends. Maybe it would sink in later.

"Brenda Martin." She glided onto the stage, her cheap white nylon robe billowing behind her like a ball gown. It was kind of funny; the previous semester, this was the girl who'd made me want to bang my head against the wall in frustration and rage. Now she was just someone I knew. A pretty girl, no different from a hundred other pretty girls. Like some actress or model I'd once had a crush on.

"Jack Seversen." Jack came tearing across the stage

like Batman in a rented blue robe and white socks. He snatched his diploma (actually, it was an empty folder; we'd get the real ones in the mail) and waved at his family in the audience. Mr. Bloch had to yank him back by the shoulder so he could get his picture taken.

"Timothy Tokugowa." Tim lumbered onto the stage, to the cheers of his family and Dawn. If I wasn't mistaken, he'd lost some weight recently. There'd even been rumors that he and Dawn had been spotted in Rock Bridge State Park in Columbia, *hiking*.

"Logan Witherspoon." I took to the stage, and Bloch handed me one of the last diplomas. From the stands, Mom, Laura, my grandpa, and my uncle cheered. Tonight, before the Boyer graduation party, they'd take me out to dinner. I'd get a few hundred bucks in gifts. This summer would be the last time I would really live in the trailer. I'd come back to Boyer to visit and for vacations, but it wouldn't be my home. I really didn't have a home anymore.

The last student filed past the principal. Mrs. Day shuffled her notes.

"One Boyer student could not be with us today. Sage Hendricks."

A loud cheer in a tiny voice floated above the polite applause. I turned to see Tammi, sitting in the highest bleacher, cheering for the sister she no longer had. Her parents were not with her.

*Sage.* So she'd graduated. She'd only managed to spend four and a half months at Boyer. Less than half a year. But Christ, the mark she made.

I was aware that people were cheering, that I was being struck by falling graduation caps. As the grads got up to meet their families, I just sort of sat there, remembering. Her husky laugh. The way she'd shove me all the time. Her crazy clothes. Her soft hands and warm tongue. How, for one wonderful night, she'd been mine. No matter what she did with her life, no matter where she ended up, I was the first (and possibly only) guy who'd kissed her. She'd always remember that.

I just wish we could have shared some more memories. I just wish we could have said goodbye.

"Logan?" Mom was standing next to me. "Are you ready to go?"

I glanced back at the bleachers, but Tammi was gone. I stood.

"Let's do it," I said. "I'm starved."


Seniors in Columbia take an end-of-the-year trip to Chicago. Seniors in Moberly get a weekend in St. Louis. Seniors in Boyer are rewarded with a night locked in the gymnasium at Boyer Baptist Church, a deli tray from IGA, and the church's stereo system belching out preapproved music. Party on.

I stood in a corner drinking an overly syrupy fountain soda and watching my classmates mill around. Some were playing the carnival games set up by the PTA. Others stood clustered in groups talking to their friends. No one was dancing. Thirteen years of school with these people, and this was our last night together.

The booster club had taped our yearbook photos to a

large sheet of construction paper. We'd all written where we were headed the next year. There were few surprises. State and community colleges, the marines, the police academy, one adventurous fellow headed for California. Just four graduates planned to stay in Boyer. Only Sage's picture had no caption.

This was truly the end of the life I knew. Everyone but my mom was leaving town. Laura and I would only come back here to visit her.

"Hey, you."

I smiled and turned to the familiar voice. "Hi, Brenda."

My ex stood there looking regal and shy as always. She wasn't wearing her glasses. She must have finally gotten the contacts she always talked about.

Brenda glanced over at the poster. "Still going to Mizzou? I think you'll have fun there. It's a great school."

I shrugged. "And you?"

"Washington U."

I nodded. We stood there looking at the hardwood floor for a moment. She eventually broke the silence.

"Hey, let me give you my e-mail address." She scribbled something on a piece of paper. "You can tell me what you're up to."

My Boyer School District address had already been canceled. By the time I got around to getting a new one, I'd have already lost Brenda's. But it was a nice gesture.

"I'll do that." We both shifted from foot to foot. This was probably the last time we'd speak. Did we really have nothing left to say? "Guess I'll see you around."

"Yeah. Bye, Logan."

We didn't walk away, and within two seconds we were hugging.

"You take care of yourself, Brenda." I meant it, too.

"I'll miss you, Logan."

We squeezed each other tight, then walked off in opposite directions. I was glad we could end things like that. Although, I kind of wish we'd said goodbye at the end of the evening; now we had to avoid each other for the rest of the night.

I found Tim and Jack at the free-throw booth shooting hoops for cheap prizes.

When Jack saw me, he shouted, "Seniors! We're out of here!"

He was as loud as always, but there was something forced in his yelling. For four years, we'd bitched about high school. Now it was over. Forever.

The three of us walked away from the booth and leaned against a blank wall. No one spoke for a while.

"So when do you guys go off to Columbia?" asked Tim eventually.

"Late August. When do you leave?"

"Same." By a happy coincidence, both Tim and Dawn were going to Truman State up in Kirksville. Jack and I joked about how much money we'd spend on gas visiting each other. But the more I thought about this, the more I had my doubts. The three of us would have new friends, new jobs, new lives. We'd probably only get to see Tim once or twice a month.

And what about after college? None of us had the desire to return to Boyer. Laura had already given up on the town, and I was probably next. We'd all come back here for holidays until our parents moved or we got married and they came to visit us. My friendships with Tim and Jack would turn into Christmas cards and an occasional summer camping trip. A sad ending for guys who'd spent the past decade plus together.

Luckily, Dawn interrupted our melancholy thoughts by coming up and kissing Tim. As a non-Boyer student, she was absolutely not supposed to be at this party, but no one stopped her.

"Logan," said Dawn, "I just heard what happened to Sage."

My armpits grew cold. "To Sage?"

"That car wreck. Tim told me she injured her back. I'm surprised it wasn't in the papers."

I bit my lip, acting sad over news that was much less depressing than the truth. "It happened when she was visiting friends in Joplin."

"Poor girl! I wish I'd known about this sooner." She paused to glare at Tim, who hadn't kept her in the loop. "She must be bored. When would be a good time for me to visit? I could bring her some DVDs, or read to her."

"She's, uh, not taking visitors right now. But thanks for offering. I'll tell her you said hello."

"But she must be lonely," insisted Dawn. "Couldn't I just stop by her house and drop off—"

"Dawn," Tim interrupted, "let's go play bingo."

I watched them go, hand in hand. I really liked Dawn. She was sweet and was a good influence on Tim. For once, he was at a party and wasn't making love to the buffet table.

"Hey, Logan," said Jack, looking unusually serious. "You never did tell us what was going on with you and Sage."

"It's complicated."

Jack made a clucking sound with his tongue. "You know, Logan . . ." He didn't finish his thought; he just kind of randomly waved his hand. I'd known him long enough to translate the words guys never actually say to each other sober:

*You know, Logan, I'm your friend, and if you ever need to talk, I'm here for you. I want to help.*

"Thanks, man." We smacked fists and he left me alone.

I watched my few dozen former classmates eating popcorn, playing games, and acting like nothing had changed. But this was really it.

It was sad, but not depressing. It was time for us to move on. I'd be ready, if not for one enormous regret.

My regret was six feet tall, beautiful, and out of my life forever. And until I could say goodbye to her, until I could go to bed knowing that she was safe and happy, then I couldn't get on with my life.

How did I end up loving a person I'd driven away and would never see again?

## chapter thirty-eight

GRAHAM HALL WAS BUILT just after the Second World War. The tiny dorm room I'd be sharing with Jack consisted of a bunk bed, two desks, two closets, and one electrical outlet. According to Laura, some sociology students had proven that the average convict in a Missouri prison had more floor space than the average Mizzou student.

Mom hadn't been able to drive me to campus; as usual, she was working. I was happy to learn, however, that she'd requested fewer hours. With only herself living in the trailer now, expenses were down. She'd even talked about applying for a management job at the Moberly Wal-Mart, but I doubted she really would. She liked her routine too much.

I was folding clothes and hanging up posters. Jack sat on the top bunk kicking his feet. His bags still lay in a sloppy pile in the middle of the floor.

"Are you through, already? We've been here for, like, twenty hours and haven't met any girls." He jumped down from the bed and began to pace. I wondered if agreeing to live with the human Super Ball had been such a bright idea.

"Laura said she'd come by later."

I stopped to adjust the sputtering window AC. Through the upper pane, I had a narrow view of campus. I could easily see the University Hospital grounds. A dozen or so smokers in scrubs lingered not too far from my dorm. Orderlies and nurses, forced into exile by the hospital's strict tobacco-free policy.

It had been over five months since Tammi and I had driven Sage there to get her nose fixed and her ribs taped. That was the second-to-last time I'd seen her.

Jack was leaning over my shoulder. "C'mon, quit daydreaming. Let's go do something."

"You go ahead. I'll wait for Laura."

Jack took off, not even closing the door behind him. I lay on my bed for about twenty minutes after he left. I'd lied about Laura; she didn't get off from work for another couple of hours. Eventually, I stood, went to my desk, and pulled out an envelope.

I'd found it in our mailbox about a week ago. The postman hadn't delivered it; someone had placed it there. Even before I opened it and saw the familiar pink butterfly stationery, I knew it was from Sage.

Sitting down on my new chair, I reread the letter.

*Dear Logan,*

*I promised myself I would never write you, at least not this soon. My plan was to leave town and cut you out of my life forever. But I can't do that.*

Logan, I wonder if you realize how much you changed my life. Before I knew you, I was so unsure of myself. I thought I was a fraud, a fake woman, a transvestite.

But then you came along. And you gave me hope. You treated me like a girl. A real girl. You made me believe I could do this.

Hope is cruel, Logan. When you start hoping, you think you can do anything. You made me think that maybe this could all be easy. That the one thing I thought I would never have—love with someone who fully accepted me—might be possible. Even after you dumped me, I wasn't willing to give up. I had tasted what it felt like to be loved, and I wanted that feeling again. That was my mistake. Someone like me can't let their guard down, even for a moment. That's the cruel fact of it.

I wish I could join you at Mizzou. I wish I could still be your friend. Even when I was in the hospital, I kept having these crazy fantasies about going off to college with you. Going away on spring break to some beach, watching the sunset, holding hands with you in the waves. Even after everything that happened.

But it wouldn't have worked for us, would it? I would have been found out again, or you would have worried that I would be. Maybe, if I was found out, you'd stand by me this time. I'd like to think you would. But it's too much of a risk for both of us. I deserve someone who loves me the way I am. You

*deserve someone you can love without hesitation. We
both came so close. But almost perfect isn't the same
as perfect, is it?*

*Logan, over the past half year, I've gotten to know
you, probably better than you know yourself. And I'm
sure you're beating yourself up, thinking this is all
your fault. But sometimes bad things happen, and
there's no blame to be placed. You didn't always do
the right thing, but you* always tried.

*I wouldn't have lasted a month at that school if it
hadn't been for you. You were a friend when I didn't
have one. I don't think you realized it, but sometimes
the only reason I showed up in the morning was
because I knew you'd be there. And even after things
got rough, when no one would blame you for wanting
to avoid me forever, you were determined to be my
friend.*

*Maybe it was stupid for us to try to be more. Or
maybe luck was against us. But the day you asked me
to the movies was the first time in my life I felt things
were the way they were supposed to be. And nothing
can ever take that away.*

*I don't know what I'm going to do now. I told
everyone I was going back to being a boy, but I can't
bring myself to do it. I keep thinking that maybe,
somehow, somewhere, I could be happy. I don't know
where, or how, or when. But I keep taking my
hormones while I try to figure it out.*

*I'd like to keep writing to you and hear what*

*you're doing, but I can't. Please don't try to find me.*
*Whatever my next step is, I have to take it on my own.*
*And don't wait for me. I might never be back.*

*When you think of me, don't remember that last*
*time we saw each other. Remember that night at*
*Mizzou. Remember our friendship. Remember that*
*you helped me when I needed you.*

*Give my best to your sister and the gang. I'll think*
*of you often.*

*Goodbye,*
*Sage*

I reread the letter, then folded it and stuck it in my empty desk. I stared into space for what seemed like hours, thinking about what to do next.

I could track Sage down. Rob would know where Tammi had moved to. A guy like that wouldn't be a hard egg to crack. And then what? Show up at her new house one day, after she asked me not to? And tell her . . . what? To move back to Missouri? That was terrible advice in any circumstance. Tell her I still cared about her? Thanks to my mental hospital breakdown, she already knew that.

Alone in my dorm room, I suddenly felt trapped. So I decided to go outside and get some air. I hoped that would clear my head.

I locked up and cut across the small grassy area between Graham Hall and the parking lot. I sat on a concrete bench and wished that I was a smoker. This was my first day of college, and all I could think about was the woman who had made me angrier and happier than anyone else. If

354

I allowed myself to forget Sage, then I'd be no better than my father, bailing when things got rough. But if I sat around and waited for her to come back, it would be Brenda all over again.

The nasty truth was, I might never see Sage again. It was what she said she wanted. She deserved to be happy. And if happiness meant leaving the state, then so be it. Even if it meant cutting off all contact with me. Tammi was right; that was Sage's decision, not mine.

I thought back over the past year with her. The fighting, the talking, the kissing, the friendship.

Sage drove me crazy, but I didn't regret knowing her. She made me too happy. She once told me I made her feel beautiful, special, like she belonged. I'd never told her she did the same thing for me. I'd never forget her. It would be Sage, not Brenda, who I compared future girls to.

I chuckled. Any future relationship I had wouldn't be nearly as complicated as the one I'd had with Sage. And probably not as fun.

I'd never give up hoping for that letter with an out-of-state postmark, but it might never come. Sage knew how to reach me. In the meantime, we both had our lives to live.

Speaking of girls, over in the parking lot, a skinny chick was struggling to remove a packing crate from the back of a hatchback car. The box probably weighed more than she did. She'd lift one end, then collapse after a second or two. Wearily, I got up to help her.

Up close, the girl was almost scrawny, nothing but gristle and bone. She had thin blond hair that rose up too high on her forehead, no chin, and two big blue eyes that thanked me before I even offered to help.

"Thank you!" she gasped as I hefted the box. She attempted to hold half of it, but it was easier for me to carry it myself. When she closed the back of her car, I noticed it had Ohio plates.

"You live in Graham?" I asked.

"Yeah, first floor." As we walked to the dorm, she buzzed around me with the annoying persistence of someone who wants to help but can't. She held the door for me, then stood awkwardly in the doorway, not realizing I'd have to squeeze by her.

She repeated her thanks as she fumbled with her room's lock. "I'm from out of town. I didn't have anyone to ask."

I set the box on a bare bed. In fact, the entire right side of the room was empty.

My neighbor jingled her keys in an irritating manner. "I was assigned a roommate, but she joined a sorority."

"So you got a single. Good job."

"Yeah. I guess." She didn't look happy.

I nodded and started to leave.

"Wait!" she suddenly squeaked. I turned.

"Would you like a soda? It's warm, and all I have is diet Sprite and . . . and . . ."

Her eyes were almost ungodly huge. She was a thousand miles from home and didn't know anyone. And not every new student made friends as easily as Sage.

I smiled at her. "You hungry? Want to check out the dining hall?"

"Yes!" She threw up her hands, causing her keys to fly across the room. As she retrieved them, I laughed inside. I'd just gotten to college and had already made a friend. Cute in a lost-puppy kind of way, though I really wasn't interested in that end of things.

"I'm Logan," I told her as we left the building.

"I'm Chris."

Chris chattered the whole walk to the dining hall. She had a pleasant voice and was rather articulate once she calmed down. I was glad to get to know her. Her half-empty room might be a good place to hang out when I wanted to get away from Jack. She wasn't a girl who would turn heads, but that wasn't important. All we were doing was having lunch.

And what if it did turn into something more? If not with Chris, then the next Erin. I knew someday I'd start feeling lonely enough to date again.

There was no point in worrying about the next girl in my life right now. All I knew was that she would have a hard time measuring up to Sage.

This novel wouldn't have been possible without all the real-life Sages who were willing to share their personal tales with me. I was hurt by the stories of those whose parents rejected them even more harshly than Sage's father rejected her, and I was inspired by those who had their own Tammis and Logans to lean on. I have nothing but respect for those of you who must follow a difficult path.

So for any of you who are walking in Sage's shoes, what now? Where can you turn? While researching this novel, I found that the one common feeling among transgender teens was that of being completely alone. Well, you're not. There are others like you, and there are people out there who can help you make sense of your feelings and decide what to do next.

If you can't discuss your feelings with a parent, counselor, clergyperson, or family friend, I'd suggest contacting Parents and Friends of Lesbians and Gays (PFLAG). Go to www.community.pflag.org.netcommunity and check for a chapter in your area. PFLAG also provides a lot of information for gay, bisexual, and transgender people, as well as those who just have questions. Its Transgender Network (TNET) can help point you to a sympathetic counselor.

The Gender Public Advocacy Coalition is an American grassroots organization dedicated to helping transgender youth cope in school and in the community. You can find the coalition at www.gpac.org/youth. Antijen, at www.antijen.org, is another transgender youth site that offers some good, practical information and stories. The Transsexual Road Map is a nuts-and-bolts site that discusses transitioning and legal issues, and networking opportunities to families of transgender youth. It's at www.tsroadmap.com.

The Internet is full of great resources for transgender people. It's also full of creeps who would love to meet a sexually confused teenager and take advantage of him or her. Please remember, if you contact anyone online, NEVER GIVE YOUR REAL NAME OR HOME STATE. Things are not always as they seem. No matter how sincere someone sounds online, do not give them the benefit of the doubt.

Also, if you are concerned about privacy on Internet Explorer and use a Mac, click Tools, Delete Browsing History, and Delete History. On a PC, click Tools, Internet Options, General, Clear History, and Okay. (My boss still doesn't know that I spent most of my workday reading Wikipedia.)

If you find yourself trying to understand a transgender friend or family member, please keep an open mind. Imagine how hard it must be for them to come to terms with their gender identity. Sage's assault and suicide attempts were based on real-life incidents. The best thing you can do is listen. You may be the only one in the world they can turn to.

One final note: Sage's decision to take illegally obtained hormones—which can be extremely dangerous if used improperly—was ill-advised, and under no circumstances should anyone attempt this. To quote one of my sources, "Hormones are not womanhood in a bottle. They are medication and should only be prescribed by a physician." Misuse of synthetic hormones can lead to stroke and permanent liver damage. Never take medication that your doctor hasn't prescribed.

Thank you for reading this book.

ACKNOWLEDGMENTS

I would like to thank the many people who helped with this project: Thanks to Barri, Heidi, Margo, and Elaine, who helped me turn my incoherent scribblings into a readable book. Big thanks to my editor, Claudia Gabel, who took a risk on this unusual YA book. I'd like to thank the many real-life Sages who were willing to share their stories with me via the Internet. Big hugs to Andrew Schlafly; every time I had doubts about this project, your blog convinced me I was doing the right thing. Finally, I'd really like to thank my wife, Sandra, and my daughter, Sophie, whose love and support made all this possible.

**BRIAN KATCHER** is the author of *Playing with Matches*. He is a school librarian and lives in Missouri with his wife and daughter. You can visit him at www.briankatcher.com.